Praise for W.
Kathleen O'Neal Gear

"The Gears have done it again ... This crafty weaving of past and present is a wonderful journey of learning and adventure."

— *Romantic Times* on *The Visitant*

"This is the prehistoric epic at its finest, with a gripping plot, lots of action, well-developed characters, and a wealth of interesting and authentic historical fact."

— *Booklist* on *People of the Masks*

"A first-rate 'murder mystery, anthropological information on pre- European Native America, a slight dash of sex, and plenty of politics."

— *Booklist* on *People of the Mist*

"An exciting, skillfully crafted, and fast-paced story that also serves as an engrossing look at ancient culture."

— *Publishers Weekly* on *People of the Silence*

Where the Basilisk Dreams

Also by W. Michael Gear and Kathleen O'Neal Gear

Where the Basilisk Dreams
The Anasazi Mysteries Part Two

W. Michael Gear

Kathleen O'Neal Gear

WOLFPACK
PUBLISHING
— EST 2013 —

Where the Basilisk Dreams

Pottery House

Spindle
Whorl

NORTH

War Club
Village

The Great
Kiva

Talking
Stitch
Tseh

Casa
Rinconada

Scorpion
Village

Owl
House
Be 60

1

Dusty leaned back in his lawn chair and tipped his chin to the breeze that buffeted the tents. Early that morning, they'd pulled the green rain flies from the tents and attached them to posts to create four ramadas around the central fire pit. It felt much cooler beneath them. Blond hair fluttered around his deeply tanned face. His tie-dyed black-and-white shirt, and Army green shorts, clung to his body like wet snakeskin. The noon temperature sat at an ungodly 108 degrees Fahrenheit. He'd just called an end to work and told the crew to take their two-hour midday break. People had immediately headed for the shade.

Hail Walking Hawk napped in her red tent.

Maureen and Maggie sat to Dusty's left, hunched over a fold-out table that Maggie had brought them from the Park Service headquarters. The wood-veneer top was strewn with the bones of two females. One appeared to be an adolescent girl—Maureen said she was probably eleven or twelve—and the other was the woman Sylvia had excavated, about twenty-two years of age. A magnifying glass, microscope, calipers for measuring the width and breadth of skeletal materials, and a bottle of Lipton's unsweetened iced tea sat in front of Maureen. She'd braided her long hair and clipped it up in back, but damp black wisps fringed her forehead. At dawn, she'd appeared wearing a white T-shirt and tan shorts. Now, her shirt matched her shorts.

Maggie quietly watched Maureen pick up the magnifying glass and study the length of a femur, the large leg bone. As Maggie leaned forward, short black hair framed her round face, accenting her rich brown eyes. She wore Levi's cutoffs, black tennis shoes with white socks, and a cream-colored T-shirt.

Dusty gazed across the fire pit, between two tents, and down the length of the canyon to the west. The cliffs wavered like golden phantoms. Not a single cloud adorned the pale blue sky, which meant there was no relief in sight. Without an afternoon thundershower, the heat would remain high well into the evening.

Sylvia rummaged around in the ice chest to Dusty's right. "God. This heat is almost too much even for me."

Locks of soaked brown hair straggled from beneath the brim of her straw hat and glued themselves to her freckled cheeks. She looked like a skinny drowned rat. Her soaked khaki shorts, and brown tank top, had a spiderweb of muddy folds where her perspiration had mixed with the tan dirt. She dragged two cans of Coke from the chest and grabbed a plastic bag of snacks. As she handed one of the Cokes to Dusty, she said, "I feel like the Wicked Witch of the West: *I'm melting, melting.*"

"Let's not talk about witches, hmm?"

He glanced at the open tailgate of his Bronco. He'd carefully packed the *basilisco* out of sight, buried beneath neatly labeled brown paper sacks, soil specimen bags, and Ziplocs. Maggie and Mrs. Walking Hawk, of course, did not know he'd mapped and collected it—as he would have any other artifact.

Dusty popped the top and took a long drink of the cold sweet liquid. It went down like the nectar of the gods. "We'll see how the temperature is later this afternoon. If it hasn't dropped to below one hundred by three, we might just take the rest of the day off."

"Hallelujah," Sylvia said.

"Don't hallelujah yet. If we take the afternoon off, we'll go over to the headquarters, take showers, and refill the water jugs. After that, I want field notes updated and an inventory done on the collections to make sure the artifact bags match the field specimen log."

"Ugh," Sylvia said, and walked over to the ramada in front of her tent. She dropped into her lawn chair and set her bag on the ground. For several seconds, she held the cold Coke can to her forehead, then rubbed it over her sweaty neck, before finally opening it, and swallowing half the can in four gulps. "If I pass out, just leave me until dark."

"Well, if you feel it coming on, throw me the rest of your Coke. We're running low."

Sylvia clutched the can to her chest. "Dale is supposed to bring supplies tonight. Do you think we ought to call and tell him to bring two more cases of Coke and another six cases of beer?"

Maureen looked up, shook her head in disgust, and went back to rearranging her bones.

Dusty said, "Might not be a bad idea."

Sylvia tipped her can up, and finished her soda, then reached for the snacks. She dragged out her favorite meal: a package of flour tortillas, a bag of those awful little cheese-flavored fishes, and two strips of teriyaki jerky. She laid out a tortilla, filled it with cheezy fishes, rolled it up, and took a bite. In between crunches, she ripped off hunks of jerky and chewed.

Dusty made a face. "I can feel the rigor mortis settling into your blood vessels."

Around a crunchy mouthful, Sylvia said, "Don't you ever look at those 'food group' charts they plaster on the college dormitory walls? A perfectly balanced diet is white, yellow, and brown."

"You're supposed to *read* the posters, Sylvia, not scan the colors as you pass. Those white, yellow, and brown things are cheese, bread, and meat. Not polysorbate substitutes."

Sylvia took another bite. "You should talk. Your favorite meal is sour-cream-and-onion potato chips, washed down with brown bog scum."

"At least I get my vegetables."

A broad smile spread across Sylvia's face. She said, "God bless America."

Maureen scowled at the two of them. "Nero fiddling."

"Fiddling with what?" Sylvia asked with genuine interest. "Wasn't he like a king or something?"

Maureen went mute. She lifted a brow, and something akin to puzzled dismay crossed her face. "The American school system is certainly going to bring about the Second Coming. I'm sure God wants your history to end as much as everybody else does."

Dusty reached for the paper bag of snacks by Sylvia's chair and pulled out a big package of jalapeno crackers. "Hey," he said. "I didn't know you'd bought these."

"Yeah, I thought we needed more fiber in our diets."

"I love these." Dusty opened the bag and ate one of the green jalapeno-shaped crackers. "Umm-umm." He pulled out another one and held it up for Maureen to see. "What sort of god could destroy a people with this kind of cultural legacy?"

Maureen studied the cracker through slitted eyes. "The sort who realizes Canadians should inherit the earth."

Sylvia tore off another hunk of jerky. "You and cockroaches. You'd better start stocking up on Raid."

Dusty lowered an eyebrow. "If Canada's so great, how come Quebec wants to succeed? Not enough Tim Horton's?"

"I believe you mean *secede,* you moron. As in secession, to leave a political body." Maureen gave him a disgusted look.

"Yeah, well, if you ask me, those guys in Quebec just want to join the United States so they can unthaw."

"Unthaw?" Maureen lifted a pair of stainless steel calipers. "How does one 'unthaw?' Either you thaw, or you freeze. Or is this another example of the way Americans are exterminating the English language?"

Dusty dug out a handful of the spicy crackers and shoved them into his mouth. He washed them down with the last of his Coke, stood, and went- to sift through the ice chest. Around the collection of half-melted cubes and bottles, soggy pieces of labels swam. He grabbed a naked bottle of what looked like root beer and went sit down again. As he unscrewed the lid, he gestured to the skeletal remains. "So, tell me how those bones disprove my war and slavery theory?"

"I need to see the other skulls, first, Stewart. The ones that are partially exposed, and currently covered with black plastic, as well as the ones that are still under rocks."

He had been going very slowly with the Haze child burial, making sure that every curiously shaped pebble was documented, just in case it turned out to be an artifact under the microscope. "Tomorrow," he said. "I'll have the Haze child, and his mother, pulled. Sylvia can finish burial number three, too, I think."

"Yeah, boss," Sylvia said with a nod.

Maureen held up the chunk of bone she'd been studying and turned it over in her hands. "I can already tell you, though, that this was a very sick group of people."

Sylvia took a big bite of white and yellow, and slurred, "How do you know?"

Maureen placed two malformed pieces of bone together. "You may not recognize them, but you're looking at the eleventh and twelfth thoracic vertebrae. They've been eaten away by infection. For it to have so severely eroded the anterior bodies of these vertebrae, this poor girl must have had a huge paravertebral abscess. I'll bet the abscess cavity contained ten cubic centimeters of pus, enough to... What's the matter?"

Maureen squinted at Sylvia who had an enormous half-chewed mass of food in her cheeks. She looked like a wide-eyed, but well-fed, chipmunk.

Dusty leaned forward. "Okay, so she was filled up with pus. What caused it?"

"For a twelfth thoracic lesion? Rampant tuberculosis. This girl must have been in constant pain. Her back muscles would not have relaxed in any position. She would have suffered incapacitating spasms, and probably had difficulty standing, let alone walking. I'd even wager she had to support her upper body with her arms while sitting, or the pain of the collapsed vertebrae would have been unbearable. Just the pressure of the gigantic pus sack on the nerves—"

Sylvia made a disgusting deep-throated sound.

Dusty said, "I thought tuberculosis was a lung disease?"

"Pulmonary tuberculosis is. What we're seeing here is a case of advanced extrapulmonary tuberculosis, the type that affects the body outside of the lungs. Extrapulmonary tuberculosis infects the joints, eyes, lymph nodes, kidneys, intestines, even the larynx, and skin. When the tuberculosis bacteria enters the brain, it causes meningitis, meaning it attacks the meninges—the three membranes that cover the brain. As the membranes swell, the pressure inside the skull changes, producing violent headaches, often accompanied by vomiting and disorientation.

When I was in Iran several years ago, I dissected the brain of a tubercular victim with so many abscesses, it literally oozed in my hands."

Maureen propped her elbows on the card table and extended her fingers, as if Dusty could see them dripping.

Sylvia choked down her lunch and flopped back in her chair with a sour expression her freckled face. "God," she said. "No more yellow in my diet."

"Who's going to finish all your Coors?" Maggie asked.

"Not me. I don't drink anything that smells like a fire hydrant. I'd rather die," Dusty vowed and unscrewed the lid on his root beer.

Sylvia said, "I can't wait to see what Maureen finds when she dissects you. Or worse, doesn't find."

Dusty's blond brows lowered. "Don't you dare bring up Cortez again."

Sylvia grinned, but Maggie and Maureen gazed at him as if they hadn't the slightest idea what he was referring to.

When Maureen's right brow arched, Dusty rushed to say, "Let's get back to the bones. All right, tell me how this tuberculosis bacteria works? It's passed through sneezing and coughing, right?"

Maureen nodded. "Primarily, yes, though it can also be passed by contact with items touched by an infected person or even by drinking unpasteurized milk from a cow with tuberculosis."

"How long is a person contagious?"

"An untreated person can be contagious, off and on, for his entire life. I've seen cases of long-latent tuberculosis suddenly flare up, particularly in older people, and cause epidemics in third world countries."

Dusty crossed his legs and propped his root beer on his knee, wondering how the Anasazi would have interpreted the disease. He remembered hearing an elderly Zuni woman talk about an illness that had carried away a number of her people during the 1940s: *Their blood turned to water and came out their mouths mixed with white spots. Some of them took a long time to die. We could do nothing for them. Witches caused it. They*

*buried bad medicine bundles around the village. When-
ever anybody stepped on one of these bundles, they got
the sickness and died."*

Maureen said, "The tubercular lesions aren't the
only interesting thing about these bones though." She
picked up the battered skull of the young woman.
Dusty could count at least three cranial depression fractures, dents, on the right side of her head. "Did southwestern peoples practice cannibalism?"

Dusty glanced up sharply. The issue was hotly
debated in the southwest. "Tim White, Christy Turner,
and I say 'yes,' but there are a lot of people who want to
slit our throats for that. Why do you ask?"

Maureen picked up her magnifying glass and
studied the top of the skull. "There are unusual cut
marks on this skull, and several of the long bones."

Sylvia wiped her hands on her dirty shorts and
reached for the bag of jalapeno crackers. "Are you sure
they aren't marks left by animal teeth? Mice? Wolves?"

"I'm sure. These are long, straight cuts. Rodents
make parallel marks from the incisors that look like
gouges under the microscope. The canines and
carnasials...uh, wolf fangs, leave irregular shallow
grooves. These cuts look like deep v's, as though
someone carved through the muscles, to the bone, and
sliced the meat off in long strips. Only sharpened stone
tools make this kind of incision."

Sylvia peered seriously at the skull. "Like
butchering something?"

"Yes."

"Or..." Dusty left the word hanging for affect. He
consciously didn't glance toward his truck, and *el
basilisco.* "It could be witchcraft."

Sylvia, mimicking his exact tone of voice, countered, "Or...it could be an upset daddy using stone cutlery to carve his point into mommy's head."

Maggie met Dusty's gaze. She didn't say anything for a few seconds, then began, "I remember a strange story I heard when I was little. Witches from Tesuque pueblo went to Nambe. They spent a few days there, making evil dolls that would cause people to cough. They stuffed chili seeds, dirt, and rags into the dolls and placed them around the village. Then they turned themselves into cats and dogs and escaped up the arroyo that runs through Nambe."

"What happened to the witches?" Sylvia asked.

The lines around Maggie's eyes tightened. "They were caught and tortured until they vowed they would stop their witchery, but I think they all died from the torture."

Dusty nodded. "I remember that story. By 1910 the leaders of Nambe had executed so many witches the village population had dropped by half."

"The way I heard it, it was a real reign of terror," Maggie agreed.

Maureen turned the skull in her hands. "I don't understand. Why would you think these long cuts might be witchcraft?"

Dusty leaned forward, his eyes on the skull. "Corpse powder."

Sylvia suddenly whispered, "God! Of course!"

A look of revulsion tensed Maggie's face. She pushed her chair away from the table.

"Corpse powder?" Maureen frowned. "What is that?"

Dusty took a long drink of root beer and wiped his

mouth on his shirt sleeve. "Don't you read Tony Hillerman? You know, Jim Chee and Leaphorn?"

At Maureen's blank look, Sylvia said, "Wow, the only anthropologist in the world who's illiterate."

"Right," Maureen agreed dryly, "so, enlighten the benighted heathen from the north, okay?"

Dusty took a moment to bask in her scowl. "Some southwestern tribes believe that at death the good soul leaves for the afterlife, and all that is left in the body is evil. Witches harvest this evil by stealing corpses and reducing the flesh and bones to a fine powder, which they sprinkle on their enemies. Supposedly corpse powder can drive a person crazy or even kill him."

Maureen's hand crept up to clasp the silver crucifix at her throat. She casually rotated the clasp around to the back of her neck, as though the action had nothing to do with the discussion, but when she dropped her hand to the table again, she drummed her fingers uneasily.

Maggie stared at Maureen. "Maybe I should wake my aunt. She might be able to tell us more. She—"

"No," Dusty said gently. "Let her sleep. I think this heat has been harder on her than anyone. We can ask her later tonight."

Maggie nodded. "Yes, you're right. She didn't sleep well last night, either. She woke me in the middle of the night to ask me if I heard the ghosts walking around the tents."

Dusty straightened when he saw Maureen's face suddenly go pale.

"What?" Dusty asked.

Maureen looked up. "Hmm?"

"Don't 'hmm' me. What's wrong?"

A gust of wind shuddered the tents. Maureen turned away until it passed. When she turned back, her eyes had narrowed as if against some hidden strain. "Oh, nothing, really. It's just that I had the strangest dream last night."

"What dream?"

"Well, it—it was odd." She put the skull down and folded her arms tightly across her chest. "It began with the sound of a baby crying. Then frantic steps ran past my tent. Soft steps, like sandals in sand, and a man and woman shouted at each other. I couldn't understand their language, but I knew they were upset and frightened. I thought it had to do with the child." She looked at Maggie. "Isn't that strange, that your Aunt would hear steps in the night and that I would dream..."

Maggie's brown eyes fixed on Maureen. "Aunt Hail told me you were a Soul Flyer."

"*Me?*" Maureen smiled in genuine amusement and pointed at herself. "Sorry, Maggie, this time, you've got the wrong person."

Maggie tilted her head as though debating whether or not to say something else. It piqued Dusty's curiosity.

"Is that all your aunt said?" he asked.

Maggie ran her fingers around the base of the adolescent girl's skull. She answered, "Yes," but the way she said it meant "no."

Dusty finished his root beer and placed the bottle in the trash box behind him. It clacked against a wealth of tin cans. He gave Maureen a suspicious glance.

She said, "I'm no Soul Flyer, Stewart."

Dusty smiled. "Me thinks the good doctor protesteth too much."

"What is that supposed to mean?"

Maggie touched Maureen's hand lightly. The silence stretched between them before Maggie murmured, "I'm sorry. I shouldn't have said anything. Especially not in front of others."

"You're not telling me you believe in ghosts?" Maureen accused her.

Maggie lifted a shoulder. "Sometimes, Doctor. Sometimes."

Dusty said, "Well, she may not, but I do."

"You, I would expect it of," Maureen replied. "You're full of nonsense, but Maggie has a scientific mind."

"If I'm full of 'nonsense,'" Dusty replied, "it's because I've seen a lot of strange things out here, Doctor. I don't discount any explanation. Unlike you, I don't think science answers all questions."

Maureen picked up the woman's battered skull again and turned it slowly in her hands. The gaping hole, where the sandstone slab had crushed the back, caught the light. "Maybe not, Stewart, but it's still the best way of 'knowing' that we have."

Dusty laced his fingers in his lap. His gaze drifted from Sylvia's wide green eyes to Maureen's stoic authoritative expression and finally landed on Maggie's politely bowed head.

"It's one way of knowing, Doctor. It is not the only way."

Maureen bent forward, as though truly interested in what he'd said. "My goodness, we have a philosopher in camp. I didn't realize you were skilled in epistemology, Stewart."

"He's not a philosopher," Maggie started to defend him, "he's just sensitive to other cultural trad—"

"I am so a philosopher," Dusty cried indignantly. "I can instantly tell the difference between the teachings of Jean-Paul Sartre and Yoda."

Sylvia's brows lifted in admiration. "Wow. I'm pretty good with Batman and Spock, but Yoda is way beyond me."

Another gust of roasting wind battered the camp, rattling the ramadas, and sending Sylvia's empty Coke can tumbling for the hinterlands. She leaped up and ran through the greasewood after it.

When she returned she dropped the can into the trash box behind Dusty's chair and trudged for the ice chest with the beer. As she dug around through the meltwater, she said, "It's definitely time for Coors. Anybody else want one?"

2

A scream split the darkness, echoed from the canyon wall, and dwindled into choking sobs. Browser looked up at the thousands of Evening People glittering across the night sky. A pale blue glow haloed the eastern horizon. Off and on throughout the night Silk Moth had shrieked her husband's name. Peavine, and several other women in the village, had been taking turns, sitting with Silk Moth, trying to comfort her, but it had done little good.

Browser gazed down at his meal. He crouched on the roof of Talon Town eating corncakes and a hot bowl of soup that Redcrop had made for him. The soup, a mixture of squash, roasted pumpkin seeds, and dried yucca petals tasted sweet and flowery. He dipped his corncake into the steaming bowl, scooped up a large chunk of squash, and ate it while his gaze drifted.

He'd posted five guards on Talon Town, including himself. To his left, in the plaza below him, Jackrabbit and He-Who-Flies whispered outside of Cloudblower's chamber. On the toppled fifth story, near the cliff behind Browser, Skink and Water Snake stood, silently surveying the distant canyon.

Browser took a bite of his corncake and chewed slowly. The cold night air carried smells of cedar smoke, damp earth, and the lingering taint of blood and torn intestines.

After the villagers had returned to their chambers, Browser and Catkin had carried Whiproot's body into the newly restored kiva and placed it on one of the long foot-drums. They'd stood in silence, neither saying a word, but both thinking the same thought: Whiproot should have died in battle fighting his enemies, not taken by surprise at home. How could it have happened?

Many things made no sense. At first, Browser had assumed the murderer had attacked Jackrabbit and run to draw everyone away from Hophorn's chamber so that he could kill her—but he was no longer certain of that. The murderer must have seen Browser and Whiproot standing together on the roof before he attacked Jackrabbit. Why had he chosen that moment? If he had waited another finger of time, Browser would have been gone, leaving only two foes to battle.

Browser dipped his corncake again. As he chewed, he frowned out at the dark canyon. It was almost as if the murderer had waited for Browser's arrival. Had *known* Browser would come and wished him to be there when he murdered Whiproot.

Browser's belly knotted. He stared down at his soup. Earlier in the evening, an unthinkable possibility had flashed across his souls. For just an instant, he had feared that the murderer might be using Hophorn against him—dangling her safety in front of his nose like a piece of meat before a starving coyote, luring Browser in, then murdering people while he stood helplessly by.

Browser picked up his horn spoon and stirred his soup. The pumpkin seeds swirled around the yucca petals.

He looked out at the dark zigzagging slash of Straight Path Wash, wondering if the murderer used it to approach the town? Or to escape when he had finished his foul deeds? At first light, he would search for tracks in the frost. If he found none, he would crawl through Talon Town on his hands and knees by himself.

Browser swiveled around and studied the giant half-moon-shaped structure. He saw Skink and Water Snake standing tall, silhouetted against the canyon wall. The roof of each crumbling, stepped-back story, glittered. Collapsed timbers thrust up through the fallen stones like huge spears aimed at the sky gods. Predawn light streamed through gaping holes in the walls.

Many of the holes could not be seen from his current position. The largest, most dangerous openings, gashed the towering rear wall of the town, near the cliff face. A man with a hook tied to the end of a rope might be able to climb in and out of those holes at will, especially given the fallen rocks and deteriorated plaster piled at the bottom.

Browser tipped his soup bowl up and swallowed the last of the sweet broth. As he set it down, he noticed Redcrop trotting up the road to his left. Her long hair fluttered with her stride. She had been up most of the night cleaning, cooking, and running errands for Flame Carrier. The poor girl must be as exhausted as Browser.

She stopped beneath him, and called, "War Chief? The Matron wishes you to come to the Hillside plaza."

"Tell her I'm coming."

"Yes, War Chief." The girl sprinted back toward the village.

Browser slung his bow and quiver over his shoulder and walked along the roof until he stood over Cloud-blower's chamber. At the edge of the roof, he called, "He-Who-Flies?"

The muscular warrior stepped out of the shadows and looked up. He stood twelve hands tall and had a chest like a grizzly bear. His round flat face gleamed in the predawn glow. "Yes, War Chief?"

Jackrabbit leaned against the wall outside of Cloud-blower's chamber. His eyes glinted in the starlight.

Browser said, "The Matron has summoned me. I wish you to take my guard position. I will try to return soon."

"Very well, War Chief." He-Who-Flies reached for the ladder that lay on the ground near Jackrabbit, propped it against the south wall, and started to climb up.

Browser walked to the ladder he'd stowed at his guard position and lowered it over the side to the road below. By the time he set foot on the frozen ground, He-Who-Flies stood tall and straight above him, his bow and quiver over his right shoulder.

Browser removed his war club from his belt and clutched it in his right hand as he headed for Hillside Village.

As he rounded the southeastern corner of Talon Town, he saw two people standing before the small blaze in the fire pit, both small and hunched, wearing long capes. One of them leaned on a walking stick. At the edge of the orange gleam, four guards stood.

Ten paces from the fire, a little old man turned suddenly and called, "My dear grand-nephew!" and hobbled toward Browser in a swirl of feathered cape. He had wispy white hair, a hooked nose, and thick gray brows.

"Uncle Stone Ghost?"

The old man passed between the guards as if they didn't exist and gripped Browser's free hand. He held it to his heart and smiled. "You cannot imagine how happy it made me to know that you had moved here, barely a day's run from my house. Remind me. Which nephew are you?"

"I am not surprised you don't recall. The last time I saw you, I had barely seen eight summers. You came to Faithful Hawk Village after Grandmother Painted Turtle was murdered."

"Painted Turtle! Of course. She was always my favorite sister." A look of old grief touched his expression. In a softer voice he said, 'Then you must be Prairie Flower's son."

"Yes, Uncle."

Stone Ghost started to return to the fire, stopped, and gazed back at Browser with kind brown eyes. He gripped Browser's hand tightly. "I was sorry to hear about your wife and son. Are you well, my nephew?"

"Well enough, Uncle." Browser gestured to the fire. "The Matron is waiting. I think we should—"

"Perhaps later we can speak of this together. I would like to know more about your wife."

Browser nodded. "Of course." He took a breath and steeled himself. How strange that in the midst of his pain and guilt, a flame of anger still burned. She was dead. Why couldn't he let it go?

Stone Ghost affectionately clutched Browser's hand as they walked to the fire. In the wavering gleam, the old man's wrinkles looked like rain-carved crevices. Several strands of tawdry pottery-disk necklaces glinted around his throat. Among the poorer villages a dropped pot became jewelry. They smoothed the pot fragments into round disks, strung them, and wore them. Was his uncle this destitute? From the corner of his eye, Browser scrutinized Stone Ghost's clothing. Patches of feathers were missing from his cape, and his moccasins had holes in the toes.

Browser slipped his war club through his belt and put his hand over the old man's. Before Stone Ghost left, Browser would make certain he had a warm cape, moccasins, and whatever else he needed.

Flame Carrier tapped her walking stick. "Come. Let us get started."

Her gray hair and bulbous nose shone amber as she lowered herself to one of the rocks that encircled the fire.

Browser guided Stone Ghost to the rock beside Flame Carrier and helped him to sit down. Browser took the rock beside his uncle. A teapot hung on a tripod at the edge of the fire. Cups nested beneath it.

Flame Carrier said, "Stone Ghost arrived last night during the insanity. He could hear the commotion from the road and decided to go to my chamber to wait for me." She scowled at Stone Ghost. "After I shoved my liver back down my throat, we spent most of the night talking. I have told him everything I know about the murders. He wishes to question you now, before dawn brings dozens of onlookers."

"I understand," Browser said and turned to Stone Ghost. "What is it you wish to know about the murderer, Uncle?"

Firelight flashed in Stone Ghost's eyes when he jerked. His bushy brows drew down over his hooked nose. "Do you know something about the murderer, my Nephew?"

"Well. Yes. I mean, I saw him last night."

Stone Ghost leaned closer, and his white hair caught the firelight. "What did you see?"

Browser shifted. "A tall man, slender. Though it was hard to tell. He wore—"

"How tall?

Browser shrugged. "Eleven hands, perhaps twelve. I only saw him for a moment, when he was struggling with Jackrabbit, but Jackrabbit is about eleven hands. The murderer seemed taller to me."

Stone Ghost turned to the teapot and said, "May I, Matron?"

Flame Carrier nodded. "That is why I had Redcrop make it."

"I'm grateful." Stone Ghost picked up a cup, dipped it full, and handed it to Browser. Then he filled one for himself. The fragrance of sunflower petals rose.

Browser added, "But the man was wearing a large mask, Uncle. It would have made him at least two or three hands taller."

As Stone Ghost sipped, a veil of steam wavered around his wrinkled face. "What else?"

Browser rested his cup on his knee. "The killer struck

Jackrabbit with a war club and fled through a gap in the wall near Hophorn's chamber. Whiproot and I immediately climbed down and ran to Jackrabbit. I ordered Whiproot to guard the Sunwatcher's chamber and told him that if Jackrabbit recovered, he should send him for help."

"Then you followed the killer, yes?"

"I tried to, Uncle. I didn't make it very far."

Flame Carrier watched them through keen old eyes, her elderly face stern.

Wind fluttered the wisps of white hair clinging to Stone Ghost's spotted scalp. His eyes narrowed. "Inside the town, what did you see?"

"Very little." Browser frowned down at his tea. The firelight dyed the rising steam the deep gold of squash blossoms. "I entered the gap in the wall and proceeded cautiously, listening every step of the way. I heard laughter ahead of me, then I thought I heard something just before Jackrabbit came up behind me, but it might have been a rodent. The crumbling town is filled with them."

"How much time passed between the moment you entered the gap and Jackrabbit appeared?"

"Oh," Browser said through a long exhalation, "four hundred heartbeats, at most five."

Stone Ghost frowned and shifted to peer at Flame Carrier. Firelight flowed across her still face. They appeared to be exchanging thoughts. Flame Carrier tilted her head, and her kinky gray brows twitched.

Stone Ghost turned back Browser. "In those five hundred heartbeats," he said, "did you hear anything from outside?"

Browser's hand arrested in midmotion lifting his tea cup. His gaze darted over the clay-washed face of Hillside Village, noted the coils of smoke rising through the rooftop entries and the way the firelight played on the cliff. "I do not recall hearing anything, Uncle."

"Did you not think that strange? Jackrabbit had just been attacked. Surely he would have been questioning Whiproot, or Whiproot questioning him."

A hollow sensation expanded Browser's chest. He watched the light of the flames sheath his uncle's ancient face and twinkle in his curiously gentle eyes. "What are you saying?"

Stone Ghost smiled. "Tell me, do you think the walls of the town are so thick they eliminate sound?"

"No, because later Jackrabbit and I both heard a voice screaming. It called—"

"It? You did not recognize the voice?"

"No, Uncle, but that is of little import. I have been in battles where my own best friend cried my name, and I did not recognize his voice. Panic twists the souls, makes voices come out in ways they never have before."

"True," Stone Ghost said. He smoothed his thumb down the side of his cup. "When you first entered the Sunwatcher's chamber, what did you see?"

The images flashed across Browser's souls, and he closed his eyes a long moment. "Whiproot lay on his back. His mouth was covered with blood, and his war shirt was pulled up. His belly had been sliced open. Blood streaked the walls and ceiling and pooled on the floor. Hophorn was huddling in the corner, trembling. Blood and stuff from the intestines speckled her face and the blanket around her. Clearly two men had fought. Their sandal prints had tracked through the blood. The way the tracks circled each other, it appeared that Whiproot was trying to protect Hophorn, to keep the murderer from reaching her." Browser shook his head. "As best we could determine, the murderer leaped on Whiproot from the roof and struck him in the head. The blow dazed Whiproot enough that his attacker could stab him. From the cuts, Whiproot tried to defend himself. Then the murderer forced Whiproot to back into Hophorn's chamber and kneel down. But Whiproot must have seen his chance and leaped for the man, knocking him backward. They had overturned the pots on the north wall and stumbled through the warming bowl. Coals and broken potsherds scattered the floor. Instants later, I ran from the passageway where I had chased the katsina and out into the plaza."

"Tell me about the passageways?"

"Well, I—I know almost nothing, Uncle. None of us have spent much time inside. The town is falling apart. Every day we hear crashes and thuds as new sections of walls collapse. No one willingly enters that decaying hive. It is very dangerous."

Flame Carrier added, "When we first arrived, ten moons ago, a twelve-summers-old girl was killed running through the passageways. Browser's wife was with her. She said a roof collapsed on top of the girl. I have forbidden children to enter the town, except with an adult."

Browser could see thoughts churning behind Stone Ghost's eyes. Suspicion glinted.

"We found her body beneath a pile of rubble and fallen timbers, Uncle. It must have been an accident."

"Where did you find her?"

Browser turned, and pointed to the northeastern

side of Talon Town, near Propped Pillar. "There. In a fourth-story chamber."

Stone Ghost gazed at it, then swirled his tea in his clay cup. For a time, only the moan of wind stirred the silence. Stone Ghost pulled the worn softness of his feathered cape up around his throat and sipped from his cup.

"Did you know," he said, "that the last Matron of Talon Town was as mad as a foaming-mouth skunk?"

Browser blinked, wondering what that had to do with the murderer. "No."

"Oh, yes, it was a calamity for the First People. The Blessed Night Sun ran away with her lover, War Chief Ironwood, and the next woman in line was completely daft. Let me see. I think her name was Featherstone. Yes. I believe that's right. As a child, Featherstone had been captured and taken slave by the Fire Dogs. They had beaten her in the head until her souls hung by the thinnest of webs, sometimes in her body, frequently not. She—"

"Uncle," Browser said reprovingly, "what does this have to do with the murderer?"

Stone Ghost looked at Browser with unwavering concentration. "Why, everything, my nephew."

"Why should it concern us that more than one hundred sun cycles ago, Featherstone was struck in the head?"

"Because she was," Stone Ghost responded. "I heard that tale from my own grandmother, the Blessed Orenda. You don't think she lied to me, do you?"

"No, Uncle. I just don't see how the story is related—"

"Oh, all things are related to all other things, my nephew. Whether we like it or not. Yes?"

Browser glanced at Matron Flame Carrier, saw her mouth turned down. He replied, "I wouldn't know, Uncle."

Stone Ghost cocked his head like a curious bird. He pointed to a chunk of sandstone twenty hands away. "Do you see that rock? If we went back far enough, I guarantee you we would discover that it hit someone in the head." He paused to examine Browser's expression. "Humans are like that. We bash each other all the time and for the most trivial of reasons." He lifted a finger. "But, if you make a careful study of bashed heads, you learn a lot about rocks and the people who throw them. Do you see what I mean?"

Flame Carrier gruffly folded her arms beneath her turkey feather cape and gave Browser a disgruntled look. "I told you his souls flitted around like bats."

Stone Ghost swerved to stare at her. "Well, I should think that fact would comfort you, considering that I am here to study people whose souls flit around like bats."

"What?" Browser asked in confusion.

Stone Ghost swung back. "Oh, come, my Nephew. Your wife had no friends, did she? People feared and distrusted her. Many accused her of witchcraft and whispered that she sent her souls 'flitting' about at night to harm others. She suffered violent headaches and on occasion went for days without speaking—"

"How do you know that?" Browser leaped to his feet in sudden fright. The old man's reputation for Power, and possibly even sorcery, dropped on Browser's chest like a landslide. His hand instinctively lowered to his war club. "You never knew my wife!"

Stone Ghost gazed at Browser through strange, glowing eyes. "No, but I know a great deal about her, Nephew. Because I know her Spirit Helper."

Silk Moth let out a wrenching cry, and the world seemed to go still. They all turned to look behind them, toward her chamber at the western end of Hillside Village. Her cries dropped to a series of suffocating gasps.

Browser gripped his club to halt the quaking of his hand. "Is Wolf your Spirit Helper, as well?"

"Mine? No." Stone Ghost shook his white head. "This katsina is a very selective god. It takes him moons of careful observation and much thought before he chooses those he will visit. He makes certain they are outcasts in their villages, and either sick themselves, or with desperately ill family members. He claims he can cure the coughing sickness if only the woman, or girl, will release her souls to him." Stone Ghost rose to his feet and took a step toward Browser. "She tries, of course, very hard. She doesn't wish to die, or to see precious family members die. But she fails. Always. The punishments inflicted by The Visitant for this failure are severe."

Browser's nerves had started to hum. "How do you know these things? Did Catkin tell you about my wife?"

"Catkin is very loyal to you, my nephew. I have a different source of information. The families of the dead in Whitetail Village, Badgerpaw, and Frosted Meadow Village."

"What would they know about my...wife..." Browser's voice faded.

"Each of those villages lost members over the past

sun cycle. Women. Girls. Everyone assumed raiders had stolen them."

Browser stared unblinking at Stone Ghost. "Are you telling me that all of these females were murdered? By the same man?"

"That appears to be the case, Nephew."

Flame Carrier's small brown eyes flared. "Are you certain of this?"

Stone Ghost smiled. "The first rule of investigation, Matron, is that if you are certain, you've probably got it wrong."

Stone Ghost hobbled back toward his rock but before he seated himself he said, "Tell me one last thing. During the turmoil in Talon Town last night, where was the Blessed Cloudblower? Is her chamber not there? In the town?"

"Her chamber is there, yes, but she was not," Browser said. "We have many people ill with the coughing sickness. Cloudblower was in Hillside, Healing."

Stone Ghost nodded mildly. "Yes, I'm sure she was." He sat on the rock and sighed, "It will be dawn in another hand of time. When we have enough light, Nephew, I would like you to show me the passageway where you chased the katsina."

"I will gladly show you, Uncle, but I wish to examine Straight Path Wash first. Before the frost melts."

"Ah." Stone Ghost nodded. "Yes, of course. For tracks. I will wait in the First People's kiva. I must examine Whiproot anyway. I am in no rush."

"Well, I am," Flame Carrier replied. She rose and propped herself on her walking stick. Gray hair fell around her wrinkled face. "The Ceremony of the Long-night begins day after tomorrow. I don't like the idea that a murderer might be moving among us, choosing his next victim." She stabbed her walking stick at Stone Ghost. *"Find him."*

"Oh, that won't be necessary," Stone Ghost said with a smile. He finished his tea and poured the dregs on the hearthstones where the droplets sizzled and popped. "I assure you, he will find me. They always do."

3

Catkin woke at the sound of sandals on the roof. She rolled onto her back and squinted against the morning light that pooled on the western wall.

"Catkin?" Redcrop's young voiced called. "Are you awake?"

Catkin sat up in her buffalo hide. Her breath formed a white cloud in the cold air. Through her roof entry, she could see the girl's pretty oval face and large black eyes. She wore a yellow-and-red painted deerhide cape. Behind her, the dawn sky shone glistening and golden. "What is it, Redcrop?"

"Matron Flame Carrier requests that you meet with her in the First People's kiva. Stone Ghost arrived last night. The clan Elders—"

"What?" She threw back her hide, and lurched to her feet, sleepily looking around for her cape, comb, and a number of other things she knew she needed, but could not think of right now. "Why was I not informed?"

"The Matron knew you were exhausted. She did not wish to wake you. The clan Elders and the War Chief are already in the kiva. They were about to begin but Stone Ghost insisted that I come and fetch you first."

"Please tell the Elders that I will be there shortly."

"Yes, Catkin."

Redcrop's face disappeared, and Catkin heard her steps retreating across the roof.

Disoriented and groggy, Catkin stumbled toward the big red pot that stood in the northeastern corner of her chamber. She opened the lid and surveyed the array of folded war shirts, cotton socks, hair pins, shell bracelets, combs, and pendants. The icy wind last night had knotted her hair. She pulled out a comb, and tugged it through the tangled mass, and winced as she ripped out strands.

She had been up half the night reliving the events, hearing the disturbance, leaping out of bed, and running to Talon Town only to discover no ladder there. Panicked by the cries coming from inside, she had dispatched He-Who-Flies for a ladder and tried to climb the south wall of the town, to no avail. Then, after He-Who-Flies delivered the ladder, and she had made it inside, the sight of Whiproot, the look on Hophorn's face when Cloudblower had entered the chamber... How could anyone sleep?

Catkin pinned up her long hair and fastened it with two plain wooden hair combs. As she slipped off her tan sleeping shirt, she examined the folded clothing in the pot, and selected a knee-length red shirt with white lines zigzagging around the collar and hem. She slipped it over her head, and reached for her buckskin leggings, then stepped into her sandals. She grabbed her cape and climbed the ladder into the morning cold.

Around twenty men and women stood in a whispering ring around the plaza fire pit below, their backs stiff, expressions taut. A group of unnaturally quiet children squatted a short distance away, playing a dice game. Their young eyes kept darting about, as if anxiously waiting to see what would happen next. A half-dozen dogs slept on the warm sand near the fire, their ears pricking when someone got loud.

Catkin climbed down the ladder and headed for Talon Town. As she passed the fire pit Peavine yelled, "Wait!" and shouldered through the crowd. Black-streaked gray hair straggled around her ugly square face, and deep lines cut her forehead, making her appear much older than her thirty summers. Her doeskin cape flapped as she hurried toward Catkin. "I have been talking with the others. We wish to know if the stories are true."

Irritated, Catkin said, "Peavine, I have been summoned by the Matron. I do not have luxury of discussing—"

"Is it true that Stone Ghost has spent the past several days visiting the other villages in the canyon where young women have gone missing?"

Catkin spread her arms. "I have also heard that, but I do not know for certain. I have not spoken with him since I left his house days ago."

Peavine whispered, "Is it true that he is related to the War Chief?"

Catkin hesitated. Peavine would know soon enough, but Catkin did not wish to be the one to stoke rumors. "You will have to ask the War Chief, Peavine."

Peavine's black eyes glittered with suspicion. "How can we expect fairness from the War Chief's great uncle? Surely Stone Ghost will not question his nephew."

Catkin glared. "Peavine, when Whiproot was killed last night, Browser was with Jackrabbit. He could not possibly be the murderer."

"That is not what I heard," Peavine said and cocked her head, peering at Catkin through one eye. "Jackrabbit told me that the War Chief ordered him to stay inside the dark passageways while he went out into the plaza alone. She lowered her voice. "Who is to say what happened in the time the two men were separated." Peavine shrugged. "Perhaps Hophorn knows, but she has told no one."

Catkin took a threatening step toward Peavine and hissed, "If Jackrabbit told you that much, then he also told you the War Chief was standing with Whiproot on the roof when Jackrabbit was first attacked." She jammed a finger into Peavine's chest. "If you are going to tell the story, tell the *whole* story."

Catkin stalked away.

Behind her, Peavine called, "The whole story? How about this? The War Chief bribed someone to attack Jackrabbit to create a diversion, so that he could kill Whiproot!"

Catkin clenched her fists to quell her anger and walked straight to the road that ran in front of Talon Town's south wall. The crushed potsherds on the road shimmered and winked in the morning light. Jackrabbit stood guard on the roof ahead of her. When he saw her coming he lowered the ladder over the side.

"Thank you, my friend," she called.

"It is good to see you, Catkin."

As Catkin climbed, she studied his face. He looked every bit a frightened fifteen-summers-old youth. He nervously brushed his shoulder-length black hair behind his ears and bit his lip, watching her.

Catkin stepped off the ladder onto the roof and said, "How long have you been here?"

"Here? Not long. Two hands of time. I spent most of the night guarding Cloudblower's chamber."

Catkin peered down at the kiva that formed a large circle in the middle of the plaza below. Smoke rose through the hole in the roof, scenting the air with the rich fragrance of cedar. If Jackrabbit had stood guard most of yesterday, then all night long, he must be growing muddleheaded, perhaps even feeling ill.

Catkin pulled up the ladder and lowered it into the plaza. She stepped onto the top rung and said, "How are you, Jackrabbit?"

He gestured awkwardly. "Tired. I—I keep hearing Whiproot's screams."

They stared at each other in shared pain. Whiproot had been a good friend to both of them.

"And your head?" She pointed to the place he'd been struck last night.

He touched it and winced. "The blow glanced off my skull. I have a headache, but it is bearable. Cloudblower made me drink several cups of willow root tea. They lessened the pain."

Catkin said, "Good," but gazed at him worriedly. Jackrabbit should be home wrapped in thick hides and fast asleep. Yesterday, they'd had seven full-time warriors. Now one was dead. Browser had clearly made the judgment that after Catkin's long run, she needed the sleep more than Jackrabbit. She wasn't certain he'd made the right choice. Injured, fatigued men tended to say things they did not mean.

"Jackrabbit, Peavine stopped me near the plaza fire. Did you..." She hesitated, then finished, "Did you say anything to her that might have led her to believe the War Chief murdered Whiproot?"

Jackrabbit's mouth fell open in shock. "No! Catkin, I would never do that! Last night, she asked me what had happened, and I told her. I do not know how she could have misunderstood—"

Catkin waved it away. "Forgive me for asking. Peavine deliberately misunderstands when it suits her purposes. You are tired and have enough to concern you. When I am finished in the kiva, I will take your place here."

Jackrabbit nodded his gratitude. "Thank you. I—I could use sleep."

Catkin clasped him on the shoulder. "I won't be long."

She climbed down and walked across the plaza. Ahead of her the thirty-hand-tall figures of the Great Warriors of East and West peered down. The rich reds, blues, and yellows of their terrifying masks gleamed with an unearthly brilliance in the morning sun. The lightning bolts in their upraised fists seemed to blaze. An eerie gloom hovered in the plaza, like the stench of carrion on a hot day. Catkin's shoulder muscles bunched as she walked.

Long before she reached the doorway that led into the altar room outside of the kiva she heard soft voices.

Catkin ducked low to enter through the T-shaped doorway and stared up at the katsinas painted on the walls. Their gaudy, inhuman masks were hateful, fierce. They had their fangs bared and bows drawn, aimed at the person who had just stepped through the entry. At this moment, her. To her right stood a long rectangular stone altar, freshly plastered in white and painted with the images of mountain lion, coyote, rattlesnake, a rainbow, the sun, moon, and morning and evening stars. To her left, a narrow recessed stairway led down into the subterranean ceremonial chamber. Firelight gilded the steps.

Flame Carrier called, "Catkin? Is that you?"

"Yes, Matron."

Catkin climbed down. Torches burned on either side of the stairs, casting a haunting yellow light over the magnificent circular chamber. They would initiate this chamber tomorrow during the Ceremony of the Longnight and spend the rest of the evening praying that their efforts would open a tunnel to the underworlds, as the Blessed Poor Singer had prophesied.

One hundred hands away, at the opposite end of the kiva, Stone Ghost and Browser tended the ritual fire. Stone Ghost added sticks, while Browser blew on the coals to help them catch. The richness of cedar infused the chilly air.

Four square pillars, painted red, supported the pole roof. In the middle of the pillars that ran north and south, two long rectangular foot-drums stood. During ceremonials, musicians sat 'on the edge of the drums and tapped the leather surface with their feet. Whiproot's body lay to her left on the eastern footdrum, covered with the blanket Catkin had thrown over him last night. Gray-and-black geometric designs banded the top and bottom of the white blanket. Dried blood splotched the center.

Catkin lowered her eyes. *My friend. Gone.*

Somewhere in this room Whiproot's ghost stood and watched, wishing they would proceed with his burial so that he could be on his way to the afterlife.

Soon, I promise you.

Three levels of benches encircled the chamber. The lowest bench had been painted yellow, the next red, and the highest bench shone blue. Above the blue bench, thirty-six glorious katsina masks stared at Catkin through hollow eye sockets. Crypts, filled with offerings, sank into the white walls just beneath the masks. Catkin's gaze took in the bowls of corn pollen, buffalo horn spoons, elaborately carved shell pendants, dance sticks, and beautifully painted gourd rattles. The Katsinas' People possessed little, but they had given their best to these gods.

The four Elders sat in a line on the yellow bench to her left. Catkin bowed to them.

Wading Bird sat closest to Catkin, his bald head shining in the firelight, his gnarled fists propped on his knees. His fringed brown cotton shirt and pants looked freshly washed. Despite his age, he had lost none of his keen sensibilities. He had not taken his eyes from Stone Ghost.

Springbank sat beside Wading Bird in a red-feathered cape. He had his wrinkled lips sucked in over toothless gums. Sparse white hair matted his freckled scalp. After sixty-five summers, Springbank did not see very well. He had to squint to focus his eyes. He seemed to be scrutinizing Whiproot's body.

Cloudblower nodded to Catkin. Catkin nodded

back. The sacred Man-Woman had plaited her gray-streaked black hair into two long braids and left them to drape the front of her white doehide dress. Her triangular face with slanting eyes and sharply pointed nose appeared frozen as though she held onto her emotions with an iron fist.

Flame Carrier sat to Cloudblower's left. Her brown-and-white feathered cape shimmered in the firelight. She had fastened her gray hair over her ears with shell combs. The style did not enhance her appearance. Her bulbous nose resembled a dark brown egg tucked into a wrinkled nest.

"I came as you ordered, Matron," Catkin said.

Flame Carrier gestured at Stone Ghost and Browser. "As soon as we have a reliable fire, we will begin."

Stone Ghost grunted as he rose to his feet and grinned at Catkin. "It's good to see you again, child! I passed you on the road the day you left. You were sleeping, and I didn't wish to wake you. My heart soars to see you alive."

Browser stood and his thick black brows drew together. His round face and black hair gleamed in the flickering firelight. "Were you in danger?"

"No, War Chief."

By noon that day Catkin bad been too haggard to run another step. She had curled into a snow shadow on the lee side of a large boulder and fallen into a dead sleep. She had awakened late in the afternoon, made a watery soup of boiled snow, deer jerky, and cornmeal, then had run until the darkness and falling snow halted her for the night. Had Stone Ghost bulled ahead through the darkness and storm?

"Your dedication surprises me, Elder," she said. "If you hadn't made several stops, you might have beaten me back and shamed me before my people."

Stone Ghost's cheap pottery-disk necklaces clicked as he hobbled forward, a warm smile on his ancient face. Soot streaked the front of his threadbare green shirt. "And terrified your war chief, I fear."

Browser wiped his hands on his buckskin cape. A thin layer of ash coated his flat nose and bushy eyebrows. He smiled at Catkin. "Yes. I would have imagined my finest warrior dead."

Stone Ghost gave Catkin a sympathetic look, apparently sensing how Browser's soft tone must have affected her. "Now that you are present, we may begin. I wish you to assist me."

She stepped forward. "What is it you require, Elder?"

Stone Ghost took her hand and dragged her toward the foot drum where Whiproot rested. "I wish you to be a witness, child. Just watch and remember."

"Of course," she said, but wondered why he needed her when there were five other witnesses in the kiva.

Catkin glanced at Browser, and Browser walked to stand behind her, looking over her shoulder. He moved' in a bone-weary manner. Dark circles swelled beneath his eyes, and his breathing had fallen into the deep tortured rhythms of exhaustion. Catkin whispered, "You need rest, War Chief."

He shook his head.

Did he still have trouble walking into his own chamber? The memories of his beautiful dead son must haunt his sleep. What did he dream of his wife? Did he dream of her at all?

"When we are finished here, I am going to relieve Jackrabbit. I will be standing guard," she said softly. "Rest in my chamber."

He bowed his head as if thankful she understood. "I will. Thank you."

Stone Ghost gently pulled the blanket from Whiproot's corpse and said, "Please come forward, Elders. There are several things I wish to show you."

The Elders whispered among themselves, then Flame Carrier rose and the others fell into line behind her. They filed over and formed a half-circle around Browser, Stone Ghost, and Catkin. Browser backed away allowing the Elders a closer view and leaned against the red northeastern pillar. Springbank took his place at Whiproot's feet, his old eyes squinted.

Firelight fluttered over the katsina masks on the wall fighting carved beaks and bared teeth, feathered head-dresses and fur-shrouded faces. Catkin had the uncanny feeling that they, too, watched, and with an unnatural interest.

"First," Stone Ghost said and tugged on Whiproot's rigid arm, "I wish you to notice the stiffness of the body. Stiffness usually develops within two hands of time after death and disappears within twelve hands of time." He turned to Catkin. "How long has it been since this warrior's murder?"

Catkin hesitated, silently calculating the interval. "At least twelve hands, Elder. Perhaps thirteen."

Stone Ghost nodded. "Heavily muscled people, especially those who die fighting, often remain stiff longer than normal. On the other hand, very slight individuals who die in their sleep may never develop much stiffness. Heat and cold affect this pattern somewhat.

So." He looked at Browser. "Forgive me for asking, Nephew, but I must. Was your wife stiff when you found her?"

Browser's shoulder muscles bulged through his cape. In a tortured voice he said, "Yes, Uncle."

"How long had she been missing?"

"Two days."

Murmurs broke out. Stone Ghost lifted a hand to silence them. "Then your wife was not killed the first night she was gone. She had probably been dead less than twelve hands of time when Flame Carrier found her in your son's burial pit."

Catkin folded her arms, listening, not certain why this was important.

Stone Ghost smoothed wispy white hair from his wrinkled face and tucked it behind his ears, then held his hands out to Browser. "Did you notice cuts or bruises on her hands, Nephew?"

Browser shifted against the red pillar. "No. Why?"

Stone Ghost's hands flashed, cutting the air, as if warding off blows. "When a person fights for his life, he gets injured in the process. For example"—He lifted Whiproot's left hand. One of the fingers had been nearly severed. It hung down over the gashed, bloody palm—"I assume that this warrior was right-handed and holding a weapon in it because he used his left hand to fend off his attacker's knife. That is also why we have cuts on the outside of his forearm."

Catkin's breathing went shallow. She whispered, "He was right-handed."

Browser said nothing, and Catkin could tell from his haunted expression that his thoughts had riveted on Ash Girl, probably asking the same questions as everyone else in the chamber: Why hadn't Ash Girl defended herself? Had her murderer taken her from behind? Perhaps she'd known the murderer and let him get close enough to kill her before she realized what was happening?

Stone Ghost hobbled to Whiproot's head. "Next I wish you to examine the bruises beneath the blood around this warrior's mouth."

"Bruises?" Browser said, astonished. He shoved away from the pillar. "I did not see those last night."

"It was dark, War Chief," Catkin said. "Even when we carried him in here, Jackrabbit stood at the foot of the stairs with the torch. The dim light probably hid many things from our view."

Stone Ghost's brows lowered. "Nephew? Did you not tell me that you thought this warrior had been dazed by a blow to the head, then stabbed, and forced to back into the Sun watcher's chamber, where he fought to protect her?"

Browser nodded. "Yes."

With great care Stone Ghost tipped Whiproot onto his side and pulled blood-stiff black hair away from the rear of his head, revealing the gashed scalp and split skull. Catkin could see the brain inside.

The Elders gasped, and Flame Carrier reached for Cloudblower's arm for support. She whispered, "Blessed gods."

Stone Ghost looked at the Elders one by one. "Which of you imagines that Whiproot could have fought off an attacker after such a blow? This wound was not administered with a war club, but a stone hatchet."

The Elders pushed each other to get closer. Flame

Carrier looked at Browser. She did not utter a word but her eyes accused him of missing the obvious.

Browser said, "He was struck after he was stabbed."

"Long after, Nephew." Stone Ghost let the clump of hair drop. "I suspect he was not quite dead, and the murderer wished to hurry him along. More interesting, though, are the bruises around his mouth. We will know more after he has been washed and prepared, but if you look closely, they appear to be fingerprints."

Catkin could feel the blood draining from her head, leaving her floating on a tide of shock. Her souls pictured the night, imagined it all happening...

Her eyes met Browser's like a clash of war clubs.

She said, "Someone was holding him—"

Browser finished, "—while someone else stabbed him."

Cloudblower let out a small cry and backed away. Her white dress and the silver strands in her braids gleamed yellowish in the fire's glow.

Stone Ghost watched Cloudblower like a coyote at a mouse hole.

"Oh, gods," Cloudblower murmured. Her triangular face flushed and tears sparkled in her slanting eyes. "I—I thought I could stop—" her mouth hung open as if afraid to finish. Then she said, "She tried to t-tell me."

Flame Carrier shouted, "Who did?"

Cloudblower looked straight into Browser's haunted eyes, then ran from the chamber. Her sandals clacked on the stairs and across the altar room above. Flame Carrier swung around to Browser. "War Chief, what did she mean?"

"I do not know, Matron! This is the first I have heard of it!"

"Then go after her and find out!"

Browser bowed obediently and hurried for the stairs.

While Flame Carrier, Springbank, and Wading Bird shouted questions at each other, Stone Ghost took Catkin by the hand and led her away from the Elders. He stopped in the fluttering torch light at the foot of the stairs. His brows arched, silently questioning her.

Catkin whispered, "I'm not certain. Hophorn. I think. It must have been..."

~

"Cloudblower, wait!"

Browser's buckskin cape flapped around his long legs as he ran across the sunlit plaza after her.

Cloudblower ducked beneath her painted leather door curtain and disappeared. The curtain swung.

Jackrabbit, who stood guard on the roof above, gave Browser a puzzled look and nervously glanced around as if fearing some other disaster might befall him.

Browser called, "All is well, Jackrabbit, but stay vigilant."

"Yes, War Chief!" Jackrabbit clutched his war club in both hands.

High on the fifth story near the cliff face, Browser saw Skink and Water Snake put their heads together and talk in low voices. Sunlight burned across the towering sandstone wall behind them and lit the shoulders of their hide capes. Browser could feel the tension rising.

He trotted for Cloudblower's door and stood outside shifting from one foot to the other.

"Come, War Chief," Cloudblower whispered.

Browser ducked under the door curtain into the dim chamber. Larger than most, this chamber stretched three body lengths by five. The warming bowl in the middle of the floor threw a dull reddish gleam over the katsina masks hanging from the white walls. Furred muzzles with sharp teeth shone. Dark hollow eyes peered at him.

Cloudblower's white dress flashed in the shadowed rear of the chamber, but he couldn't make out her face yet. A pile of bedding hides and baskets lined the western wall to Browser's right. To his left black-and-white pots, filled with blue corn, red-and-white speckled beans, and pumpkin seeds, sat in a clump. As Browser's eyes adjusted, he saw Cloudblower cradling Hophorn in her arms. She had her lips pressed against Hophorn's hair. Hophorn wore a long brown dress and badgerhide leggings. The patch of hair where Cloudblower had opened her skull had gone white, as though the roots had been starved and died.

"B-Browsser," Hophorn stammered and reached out to him.

Browser hurried around the warming bowl and crouched beside Hophorn. She sat on a thick pile of buffalo and elk hides. Hophorn looked gaunt. Her broad cheekbones stuck out sharply, making her small nose and full lips seem larger. Long curling lashes fringed her enormous eyes, but fear walked in those black depths.

Browser took Hophorn's hand and held it gently. "Are you well, Hophorn?"

Hophorn tried to nod, but it came out a jittery side-to-side movement. "H-helllp. Me."

Browser glanced at Cloudblower, and the Healer squeezed her eyes closed and shook her head. Browser did not know whether Cloudblower was signaling him not to ask or telling him she didn't understand the plea either.

Browser forced himself to smile, hoping it would reassure Hophorn. "I will help you in any way I can, Hophorn. You know this. You have only to ask."

Hophorn gazed up at him with her whole wounded heart in her glistening eyes. She struggled to say, "C-commming. Ssstop. Them."

"Who is coming?"

"T-Two. The...two."

Browser clutched her hand more tightly. Every muscle in his body prickled. Insistently he said, "Who are they, Hophorn? I must know."

"T-Two." Her strength seemed to fail her. She sank back into Cloudblower's arms, trembling. "C-Coming." Tears traced silver lines down her cheeks.

Browser looked imploringly at Cloudblower. "What does she mean?"

Cloudblower bowed her head and her long gray and black braids mingled with Hophorn's jet black hair. "She keeps repeating the same words about 'the two' coming. I didn't understand until Stone Ghost was explaining the bruises on Whiproot's mouth."

Browser laid Hophorn's hand on her chest and said, "It makes no sense. How could she know the murderers are coming?"

Cloudblower said, "I'm not certain she knows what she's saying. She may mean she *fears* they are coming,

Browser, not that she knows they are coming. The past five days have been horrifying for her. She—"

"For all of us, Cloudblower." Browser slumped to the floor and ran a hand through his smoke-scented hair. "Gods, I am more confused now than when my wife was first killed. What did you think of the things Stone Ghost said about her death? The stiffness of her body? The fact that she did not defend herself? I—"

Hophorn leaned her head against Cloudblower's shoulder, but her gaze remained on Browser, her eyes huge, unblinking, as if anxious for him to say or do something.

"War Chief, your uncle was asking questions, not stating facts. There are many explanations for the things he noted."

He frowned at Cloudblower. "What? Tell me?"

"Perhaps your wife ran for a day, or—or she may have been sitting praying for a day before he found her. She was strong, Browser, but she was also alone and tired. She would have been easy prey." In a strained voice, Cloudblower added, "Especially if there really were two of them."

Browser dropped his head in his hands and massaged his temples. "Yes. One could have distracted her while the other clubbed her from behind. She would not have had the opportunity to struggle against them. Gods, I wish..."

Browser looked up when Hophorn shifted. She pushed away from Cloudblower, shivered, and her trembling arms flopped against her sides, as if they'd gone numb. The horror melted from her expression. Hophorn crawled to her bedding to his right and stretched across a rumpled pile of red blankets like a cat in warm sunlight. Before she closed her eyes a strange ghostly smile came to her face. Then she seemed to be asleep, immediately. Her entire body went limp. Her face slackened.

Browser could not take his eyes from her.

Cloudblower whispered, "Since the injury, she... I can't explain it. Often, she seems to simply leave her body. I will be speaking with her and her eyes go blank. She stares into the distance as though her souls have fled. And, perhaps, that is what's happened. I have sat with her for hands of time, watching. Were it not for the rise and fall of her chest I would think her dead, Browser."

Cloudblower gripped her white doehide skirt and stared at her hands. Her gray-streaked black braids dangled around her triangular face. "I'm afraid for her."

Browser got to his feet and stood looking down at Hophorn's beautiful face. Her long hair streamed across the blankets, creating a shining black halo. She seemed almost too peaceful, her tall, lithe body like a magnificent sculpture.

Outside sandals scraped the frozen dirt and he could hear Catkin speaking softly to Stone Ghost.

Browser murmured, "I am afraid for all of us, Healer."

He reached for the door curtain and drew it aside.

4

B rowser looked out at Catkin and Stone Ghost. The ruined wall behind them resembled a patchwork of red stone and crumbling plaster. Only the First People's kiva, to Browser's left, gleamed with fresh plaster and paint. Strings of red spirals ran around the circumference at the top and bottom of the white ceremonial chamber.

Catkin stood tall, her broad shoulders squared, her face unreadable.

Stone Ghost gave Browser a grandfatherly smile and gestured to the door curtain. "Will the Healer allow us to enter, Nephew?"

Cloudblower called, "Yes. Please, come."

Browser stepped aside, and Stone Ghost hobbled by him into the sage-scented dimness. His white hair gleamed reddish as he passed the warming bowl and went to sit down on a deerhide to Cloudblower's right. The light shone on his long hooked nose and thick white brows. His green shirt showed through the holes in his mangy turkey-feather cape.

Browser continued to hold the curtain aside, but Catkin did not enter. He cocked his head, silently asking why, and she took a step backward, as if she feared to enter the Healer's chamber.

Catkin said, "I promised to relieve Jackrabbit, War Chief. If you need me, that is where I will be."

Browser examined her stiff expression, and an uneasy sensation curdled his stomach. "Very well. I will find you when we are done and tell you what passed here."

Catkin said, "Until then," and strode toward the pole ladder to the roof.

Browser let the curtain drop. Cloudblower sat with her head bowed, as if unwilling to meet Stone Ghost's keen old eyes. The fringes across the breast of her white dress trembled.

Stone Ghost waited, his knotted hands in his lap.

Browser said, "Thank you for what you revealed in the kiva, Uncle. I am grateful for your help."

Stone Ghost smiled and stuck a finger through one of the holes in his cape, as if he'd never seen it before. "And you, Healer, what did you think of my words?"

"You did not come here to ask me that, Elder," she said softly.

"No," Stone Ghost answered. "I came to ask you what it was you could not stop and what Hophorn tried to tell you."

Cloudblower studied her fists. They shone with a crimson gleam. "The day we—we found the War Chief's wife"—she gestured to Browser—"I opened Hophorn's skull to release the evil Spirits feeding in her head wound. Hophorn could not speak at first, but she kept making sounds, frantically trying to tell me something. She would draw two lines on the floor, and repeat words over and over, as if it were urgent that I understand, but I did not, Elder."

Stone Ghost leaned closer to Cloudblower, his eyes shining. "What did you think she was saying? You must have tried to guess."

Cloudblower lifted her hands. "I thought, for a time, the words were *bat* and *fight,* or perhaps *black* and *white*. Something like that." Cloudblower closed her eyes again and took a breath. "Later, I thought she said, 'the bright one,' which made me think that her earlier words might have been *black* and *bright,* but how can I know, Elder?" A pleading expression creased Cloudblower's triangular face. "Hophorn has been too ill to explain, and I—"

"That is true," Browser defended. Cloudblower looked as if she teetered on the edge of a precipice. To give her time to collect herself, he said, "I myself have questioned Hophorn on what she saw the day my wife was killed. The first word she spoke clearly was last night, when she—she called my name."

It had not occurred to him until this instant that it may have taken an overwhelming act of will for Hophorn to find his name inside her, that desperation had torn it from her injured souls.

Stone Ghost's gaze lifted to Hophorn. A lifeless expression slackened her face.

Browser said, "Uncle, when I first entered this chamber, Hophorn told me that 'the two' were coming. She begged me to stop them. To help her."

"The two?" Stone Ghost asked.

Cloudblower shook her head, as if denying what Browser had just said.

Stone Ghost said, "You disagree?"

"No, I—I mean, yes, she did say that, but I think she meant she *fears* they are coming, Elder. It was the tone in her voice; it was not one of knowledge, but terror."

"Perhaps," Browser granted, "but we—"

Hophorn moved. She drew up one knee, and resettled herself on her side, facing them. Her brown dress fell in sculpted folds around her, and her black-and-white badgerhide leggings looked startling against the red blankets. Her eyes opened and fixed on Browser.

Quietly, Browser asked, "Hophorn? Are you awake?"

Her eyes had gone glassy.

Browser returned his gaze to Stone Ghost. "We cannot afford to ignore the possibility that one of the murderers spoke to her last night, Uncle. Spoke to her and told her he would be back."

"You are right, Nephew. Murderers often make threats. Take whatever precautions you must."

Browser nodded. "Later in the day, when people from the distant villages begin arriving for the Ceremony of the Longnight, I will go to Flame Carrier and ask that she speak with the clan matrons. Perhaps they will assign several of their warriors to help guard the village during the ritual. Surely 'the two' will not risk challenging—"

"Surely they will, Nephew. Do you know the faces of every villager who will be here? No? I doubt that they know the faces of every person in Hillside Village either. There will be many strangers present. Two more will be of little consequence." Stone Ghost touched Browser's shoulder. "Though, you are right, of course.

More guards mean more eyes. But do not suppose that more eyes will stop them. They won't."

"I don't understand?" Browser frowned at the old man. "I would not risk killing someone if I thought I might be captured by her relatives."

"No," Stone Ghost answered. "You would not. But you are sane, Nephew."

Stone Ghost grunted to his feet and hobbled across the room, halting five hands from Hophorn. As he knelt, his tattered turkey feather cape spread across the floor. "Blessed Sunwatcher?" he called respectfully. "May I speak with you?"

Hophorn's full lips parted, but her eyes remained on Browser.

"Can you hear me, Sunwatcher?" Stone Ghost waved a hand in front of her open eyes.

Cloudblower's face tensed. She whispered, "It's another of her blanking-out spells, Elder. They come upon her swiftly and often take hands of time to pass. She—"

"I know. She is not well," Stone Ghost sighed, and got to his feet. "I will try again later, when she is rested."

As though some part of her had taken his words as an order, Hophorn's eyes closed, and her head lolled sideways on the red blankets. She appeared to be sound asleep.

Stone Ghost stood silently for several moments, studying her. "Nephew, I wish to walk with the Healer. Alone. Do not consider it a reflection upon you, rather—"

"Do not apologize, Uncle." Browser rose to his feet. "I promised to speak with Catkin. I ask only that you remain in the plaza, in my sight. I do not wish to worry that someone is sneaking up on the two of you."

Stone Ghost turned to Cloudblower. "Healer? Will you grant me a finger of your time?"

"Yes, of course," Cloudblower said but sounded reluctant. She reached for her painted deerhide cape and swung it around her shoulders. "I will meet you outside. I need to cover Hophorn. In a few moments, she will start growing cold."

"Of course." Stone Ghost ducked beneath the door curtain. Browser followed him out into the cool morning air. He could hear Cloudblower whispering to Hophorn and knew from the few words he caught that she was reassuring Hophorn, telling her not to worry, that she would return soon.

He-Who-Flies straightened to his full height, over twelve hands, and a breath expanded his massive chest. He scrutinized Stone Ghost with slitted eyes. His round, flat face showed the strain of a long night. Lines cut deeply around his mouth and across his forehead. "War Chief?" he said to Browser. "A word with you?"

Browser nodded and stepped closer. "Yes?"

He-Who-Flies kept his deep voice low. "What did you find this morning? At the wash? Were there tracks?"

Browser shook his head. "No."

He-Who-Flies grimaced. "I heard what Hophorn said about 'the two' coming. Does that mean you think there are two people working together?"

"It appears so. There are other things, as well, which bolster her words. Whiproot has bruises on his mouth, as though a hand—"

"Clamped his mouth shut while someone else killed him?"

Browser nodded.

He-Who-Flies glanced around. "If the murderers are human, how are they getting in? And out after they commit their crimes?"

Browser searched the enormous crumbling town that surrounded them and the stone and dirt that piled against the walls. "This town is like an ancient rabbit warren. If men are brave enough to risk being crushed by collapsing walls, there are dozens of entries and exits."

"But humans would leave tracks, War Chief. We would see some sign of their passing."

Browser frowned. After Whiproot's murder and Silk Moth's screams last night, no one felt safe. Less than a hand of time ago, he'd heard Peavine tell Redcrop that perhaps Ash Girl's wicked soul had gotten loose and was tormenting the people who'd spoken ill of her during her life. He had not wished to mention that if that were true Peavine would have been the first to die.

"There are tracks, He-Who-Flies, inside the passageway where the katsina fled last night."

"The tracks of two people?"

"No. One. But it tells us we are looking for men, not gods."

"Not gods," He-Who-Flies agreed, "but maybe witches who can transform themselves into gods. Very powerful witches who kill with a word."

Browser replied, "These people prefer real weapons. They struck Hophorn with a club and killed Whiproot with a stone hatchet."

"A hatchet?" He-Who-Flies asked quietly. "I had not heard that."

"I did not know myself until a short time ago."

To his right, high in the rear of the town, Skink and Water Snake watched from the rubble of the toppled fifth story. They clutched war clubs in their hands. On the roof to Browser's left, Catkin stood with her back to him, surveying the canyon beyond. Wind Baby had torn strands of raven hair loose from her combs and fluttered them over her back like the sinuous arms of a dancer. The sight had an odd effect on him, comforting.

Cloudblower pushed her door curtain aside and stepped out. Her graceful brows lowered, accentuating the bladelike sharpness of her nose. She appeared unhappy. "I am here, Elder," she announced and spread her feet as if preparing for a fight.

Stone Ghost slipped his arm through hers and said, "I am not as steady as I once was, Healer. You'll help me, won't you?"

"Yes, Elder. Tell me where you wish to go."

The lines at the corners of Stone Ghost's eyes crinkled as he smiled and pointed. "Let us walk toward the hole in the wall where the killer fled last night. We will talk along the way."

Cloudblower glanced uncomfortably at Browser and He-Who-Flies, then led the old man toward the hole in the crumbling wall.

Browser said, "I will speak with you more later, He-Who-Flies. I promised to inform Catkin of what passed here. Stay vigilant."

"I will, War Chief." He-Who-Flies returned to his guard position outside Cloudblower's door. His eyes scanned the plaza and the cliff that loomed behind Skink and Water Snake.

As Browser climbed the pole rungs of the ladder, he felt exposed, vulnerable. His backbone seemed to turn to ice. The cold sensation spread through him. By the time he'd reached the roof where Catkin stood, he felt as if his insides had frozen solid. Catkin seemed to know. Apprehension strained her beautiful oval face.

"What is it? What's happened?"

"Let us talk away from anyone's hearing." He lifted a hand toward the southwestern corner of the roof.

They walked in silence. Finches flitted through the ruins, chirping and fluttering their wings, hopping from stone to stone. In the distance, the western sky sparkled as though carefully polished.

Browser stopped at the edge of the roof and gazed at the sunlit canyon wall. The pile of fresh earth where they'd buried his son shone darker than the rest of the desert. The boy would be in the Land of the Dead now. Responsibility for his care had shifted from Browser's shoulders to that of the Blessed Ancestors. He prayed that they would care as much for his son as he had.

He forced his eyes away. The grave where they'd found his wife remained a gaping hole. No one had wished to fill it. Nearby, the windswept fire pit Hophorn had stoked lay cold and dead. Large chunks of black charcoal filled the center.

"Hophorn said that 'two' are coming." Browser watched Catkin's face go pale.

"Did she say when?"

He shook his head. "No, but I have known her since we were children, Catkin. The look in her eyes told me she meant *soon*."

A swallow went down Catkin's throat. The morning breeze fluttered her hair around her face. Her eyes lifted to the towering canyon wall. Snow filled the shadowed crevices, and wispy Cloud People sailed through the blue above the tan sandstone.

"What are you looking for?" Browser asked.

Catkin tipped her chin to the rim. "For the place where they must stand."

"Who?"

"Hasn't it occurred to you? The perfect place to watch from is up there. Men could sit on the rim, unnoticed, all day. They could study people's habits, when they rise, when they go for water, how often,' and at what times of day they walk alone. It would take little effort. They could bide their time until they saw their chance."

Browser felt as if he'd been bludgeoned. "Blessed gods," he whispered. "We have to post guards on the rim. Why didn't you tell me this before? When did you first—"

"The day we found your wife," she said. "That was when I..." She paused. A strand of black hair blew across her turned-up nose and tangled with her long eyelashes, but she did not seem to notice. "Browser, how well can a person hear from up there?"

A light-headed euphoria filled him. "The canyon wall seems to magnify sound. I have stood on the rim many times and heard every word spoken by people in Hillside Village. You think—"

"Listen," she finished. "Yes."

The slanting light touched the dark circles beneath her eyes and flashed from her juniper hair combs. She shifted to examine the road that ran in front of Talon

Town, and Browser gripped her hand to make her look back at him. He was conscious of the warmth of her skin and the frail bones beneath her long fingers.

"Catkin, why didn't you wish to enter Cloudblower's chamber?"

The longer he held her hand, the more swiftly her pulse pounded.

As though choosing her words with care, she whispered, "There is something..." A shiver went through her.

"What?"

"I do not know, War Chief!" she hissed angrily. "There is something in her chamber. I have never seen it, but whenever I go near her chamber, I *feel* it, like a serpent slithering through my veins!"

Browser stood rigid. "Is it a—a Spirit, or a thing? Perhaps a witch's charm? We must tell Cloudblower. She may not even know it's there."

In the long silence that followed, Browser saw Redcrop and another slave, an old man named Hawkfoot, walk down to the drainage with water jars swinging in their hands. The shell bells on their sandals clicked. As Father Sun rose higher into the sky, the shadows scuttled back, clinging against the cliffs like dark frightened children.

Catkin whispered, "Cloudblower knows it's there."

"How can you be so certain?"

She disentangled her arm from his grip and walked away into the slanting rays of sunlight that fell through the clouds. She held her head down, as if disinclined to continue their discussion.

Browser matched her stride. "Do you think Cloudblower is involved in these murders?"

"Do you?" she said, and a half-hearted smile touched her lips. "I doubt that either of us do."

He took her hand again, forcing her to stop. "Explain."

Catkin gazed down into the plaza. Two hundred hands away, Cloudblower stood beside Stone Ghost. "Haven't you ever noticed? Whenever I must go to her chamber, she never invites me in. She always comes out to meet me, as if she knows that I know."

"Know what?"

"That she is hiding something. That she has a terrible secret. Something she wishes no one to know."

"Are you accusing her of—"

"Nothing! I would never accuse Cloudblower of harming anyone, War Chief! I love her. She is a good and kind woman. She works very hard to Heal the sick and injured. She loves children and tirelessly cares for the old people. How could I accuse Cloudblower of anything wicked?"

Browser searched her tormented expression. He was not sure if she'd meant that last statement to be taken seriously or if it had been a cry of frustration, meaning no one would believe her if she did.

He reluctantly released her fingers and propped his hands on his hips. "You are not being wholly truthful, Catkin. I know you. Why aren't you sharing your thoughts with me?"

Her eyes evaded his.

Browser fumbled with the polished handle of his war club. Over the sun cycles the wood had absorbed the oils from his hands, the blood of his victims. The club felt solid beneath his fingers: the only thing in the world that did.

He glanced up at Catkin. Loneliness always drove him to her, and he'd never felt more lonely in his life than he did at this instant.

"Please, my friend," Browser said softly. "There are many good reasons for not trusting me, and I know them all. I am often foolish. But"—he looked up and she held his gaze—"you must know that you are the only person in the world I trust completely. I know you keep my confidences locked in your heart, and you must know that I do the same for you."

"Yes. I do."

He spread his arms wide. "Then trust me now. I am worried that there are many things you have kept from me, and I need to hear them. Do you understand? I should have posted guards on the rim the day we found my wife. I was confused and grieving." He tightened his fists and frowned at the rim above Skink and Water Snake. A flock of pinyon jays floated on the air currents, flapping and diving. "I am still grieving. I need you to help me, Catkin."

She looked vulnerable. Her hair combs winked as she turned to look southward, across the canyon. The sparse grasses gleamed like a mottled golden blanket.

Browser moved to stand close beside her, his face no more than two hands away. He could smell the delicate fragrance that clung to her hair and see the sweat that beaded the elegant line of her jaw. "Please. Help me."

Catkin closed her eyes. "The night I—I found you... on the cliff? Last summer?"

"Yes?" he said, but shame filled him. He'd fought half the night with Ash Girl. His son had been huddled in his blankets with his head covered, coughing and whimpering. When Browser had lifted his fist to strike

Ash Girl, he'd suddenly stopped, realizing what he was about to do. He'd run from their chamber like a madman. Catkin had found him on the rim, bent double, sobbing like a five-summers-old child.

"What about that night, Catkin?"

She wet her lips. "What name were you calling?"

Browser frowned in confusion. "What do you mean?"

"You were calling a name. *Shadow* something. I heard you, as I climbed the stairs cut into the cliff."

"I called out to no one, Catkin."

She looked at him as though angry that he would lie to her at a moment like this.

"I swear I called to no one. Why do you think I'm lying?"

"It was your voice, Browser. I would know your voice anywhere. Unless..." Her anger vanished in an instant, replaced by naked fear.

"What is it?"

She whispered, "Did you know that Cloudblower was there?"

"You mean...on the rim?"

"Yes. When I helped you to your feet I heard her whispering."

His bushy brows drew together, not sure he understood why that bothered Catkin. Cloudblower had probably heard his fight with Ash Girl and had been worried about him. "And?"

"She was not alone, Browser. At first I thought she was speaking with He-Who-Flies. The man had a deep voice."

"Go on."

Catkin's eyes scanned the ruins behind them and

the roads in front of them. In the distance, several people walked toward Talon Town.

"Browser, just before we left, I saw eyes flash in the darkness. The man and I stared straight at each other. His eyes blazed, as though I had stumbled upon a private ritual, and he hated me for it. Or perhaps he hated me for being with you, I don't know. I—"

"It was dark, Catkin. If you could not see Cloudblower—"

"I am not finished," she cut him off.

Browser closed his mouth. "Forgive me."

"I have heard that man's voice at least one other time."

"When?"

Catkin shivered. "Last night. The voice that cried 'Help me!' That wasn't Whiproot, Browser. *It was him.*"

S tone Ghost released Cloudblower's arm and peered through the jagged hole in the wall. Fallen pieces of red sandstone scattered the floor. A musty scent suffused the darkness. He could make out the sandal tracks of at least three people in the soft wind-blown dirt.

"Have you ever been in here?" Stone Ghost asked.

Cloudblower's face tensed. "Yes, Elder. Last Moon of Blazing Sun. I came looking for a cool place to sleep."

"The interior chambers stay cool in the summer heat?"

Cloudblower nodded.

Stone Ghost patted the stones in the crumbling wall

and sighed. "My grandmother told me that. She said that winter or summer the temperature varied little in the innermost chambers."

Cloudblower cocked her head, and her long graying black braids fell over the front of her painted deerhide cape. "That is true, Elder. Though few people know it. Did your grandmother live here?"

"No, but she grew up with the Blessed Poor Singer, and he told her many tales of this place."

In a soft, reverent voice, Cloudblower said, "Your grandmother knew the Blessed prophet? I would have given anything to have seen him just once in my life. What was your grandmother's name?"

"I'm sure you've never heard of her. She came from a great people who live far to the east. They are mountain builders. They carry dirt in baskets for hundreds of sun cycles until they've piled up small mountains, then they place their houses on top of them. Her own people called her Orenda, though later in her life she came to be known as The Blessed Mother, because no one was allowed to hurt a child in her presence. She would not even allow a parent to utter a harsh word or give a misbehaving child an unkind look. She spent much of her life loving and protecting children." A fond smile warmed his wrinkled face. "I think she missed her people, though. She often spoke of their magnificent artwork, the brilliant fabrics they wove, the extraordinary stoneworkers who labored for the Sunborn."

"The Sunborn?"

"Her people."

"Curious," Cloudblower murmured. "Why would people do that? Build mountains?"

Stone Ghost stepped inside the dark chamber and blinked until his eyes adjusted. Refuse clotted the floor. A large packrat nest of juniper needles, grass, feathers, and bits of fur filled the corner to his right. Ahead of him, he could just make out a dark T-shaped doorway.

"My grandmother's people believe that Father Sun and Mother Earth were torn apart at the moment of creation and that by building mountains they help Mother Earth to touch fingertips with Father Sun."

"They believe that the earth is their mother?" Cloudblower said disdainfully. "Not their grandmother?"

"Yes. That's right."

Cloudblower folded her arms. "That is foolishness. Our Grandmother Earth gave birth to first woman, then she gave birth to the Great Warriors of East and West who helped the people to climb through the underworlds. The twins ridded the surface world of monsters, in order that we might walk unhindered through the light, and—"

"Yes, that is what we believe. The Mountain Builders would think our stories just as foolish as you do theirs, Healer."

Stone Ghost backed out into the wan winter sunlight and smiled. Cloudblower did not return the gesture. Her expression was that of a man accused of something he had not done.

Stone Ghost sat down on the pile of fallen stones beside the hole in the wall and propped his hands on his knees. A chill breeze blew around the plaza, kicking up plumes of dust. Cloudblower remained standing. Stone Ghost examined the red and yellow images of the gods that danced around the hem of her cape. The Wolf katsina led the procession, followed by the Sun katsina, and Badger.

Stone Ghost hooked a thumb at the wall behind him. "My nephew and I are going to search these ruins this morning. What do you think we will find?"

"I can't say, Elder."

Stone Ghost braced his hands on his knees and gazed up into her troubled face. "On my way here, I visited several villages."

Cloudblower's teeth ground beneath the thin veneer of her cheeks. "Yes, I know."

"I discovered some interesting and terrible things. In the past sun cycle, each of those villages has lost a woman or a girl. Many of the victims were dragged through the villages and left in the plaza for all to see. Then their bodies were stolen. Just like my nephew's wife. Most of the relatives of those women believe raiders are responsible."

Cloudblower did not respond.

Stone Ghost studied the hard set of her lips, as if she were straining against words that longed to be spoken. "The people in Whitetail Village, Badgerpaw Village, and Frosted Meadow Village, told me sad tales of lonely, sick little girls. They also told me that you had been very good to them. They said you ran to their village when they called and stayed up all night nursing the sick. They told me you left only when you believed the girl was out of danger."

"I do what I can."

Stone Ghost smoothed the brown-and-white turkey feathers over his knees. "Yes, but these girls had many problems, didn't they?"

"I tended their head wounds and their coughs,

Elder. I did not notice if something else was wrong with them."

Stone Ghost waited for her to continue. When she didn't, he said, "Shortly after you left, they vanished."

Cloudblower looked up, as if surprised. "What?"

"You knew they were missing."

"Yes, of course, but..."

Stone Ghost scanned her face. "But not when it happened?"

Cloudblower didn't seem to be breathing. Her head trembled.

"Many of them disappeared within hands of time after you left, Healer."

Cloudblower violently shook her head as if to deny it, then, suddenly, the certainty seemed to drain away. She went still. Her eyes darted about, searching for something or perhaps gathering and fitting disparate pieces together.

Stone Ghost gave her more time to think. His gaze drifted over Talon Town, trying to see it as it must have been one hundred sun cycles earlier, filled with playing children, women grinding corn, and traders displaying their wares.

"What did you mean in the kiva, Healer, when you said 'I thought I could stop...?' Stop what?"

"Nothing. I—I meant nothing."

Stone Ghost's eyes narrowed. "You live here, in Talon Town, but you were away last night when your friend was killed. Yes?"

"I was tending Peavine's young daughter, Yucca Blossom. She was ill. I boiled willow bark tea for her pain and Sang to her. She needed me. There were warriors here protecting Hophorn. I thought it was safe to leave." She twisted her hands as if punishing herself for making the wrong decision.

"When did you first learn that something had happened in Talon Town?"

"I heard young Stonehead yelling for help. By the time I reached the town, Catkin and several other warriors had already arrived and were trying to find a ladder to climb over the wall. The screams coming from inside were...were hideous, Elder. I knew a torch would be needed. I ran back to Hillside for one, and when I returned people were frantically pouring over the wall into the town."

"Did you see anyone outside the walls? Perhaps running away?"

"Elder," she said in exasperation, "people were running in all directions."

"Ah." Stone Ghost nodded. "Of course."

The Healer's expression had turned frantic, as if she teetered on the verge of desperate actions.

Clouds billowed over the plaza, pushing westward like a gleaming white army. He pointed. "Did you know that the Thunderbirds build nests of lightning bolts in the Cloud People?"

Cloudblower squinted.

He continued, "It's truly amazing. They weave the lightning bolts into blazing baskets, then tuck them into the soft hearts of the Cloud People. When the hatchlings are born, they shake the baskets apart with their thunder. Lightning bolts fly and the hatchlings soar free."

Cloudblower watched the sky for a few moments, then lowered her gaze to the ground.

"I fear," Stone Ghost said, "that the Cloud People

may be rushing to join us for the Celebration of the Longnight. I hope they do not bring snow with them."

Cloudblower frowned.

"You were captured by the Fire Dogs, weren't you? Many summers ago?"

She flinched. "Why do you ask?"

Stone Ghost rubbed his hands together. The morning air had chilled them. "I have heard they do terrible things to slaves."

Cloudblower stared at him.

"Were you beaten?"

She whispered, "Often."

"Raped?"

She didn't answer.

"You must have a special sympathy for others who have suffered the same fate."

Cloudblower's shoulder muscles swelled through her cape, as if suspecting and fearing his meaning.

Stone Ghost nodded to himself. Her reaction told him a great deal.

She said, "Would that be bad?"

"Not at all. But it might lead you to hide things that you would not otherwise." He smiled. "Do you see what I mean?"

Cloudblower's cheeks flushed. "No, I do not."

"Well, it is a curious coincidence, perhaps, but I often find that murderers have suffered much pain in their lives. Many of them were beaten senseless by their parents or other close relatives. A few endured true horrors, things that sane people could not even imagine. Torture, mutilation. I will not describe the heinous acts for you, because I do not wish those images to live in your dreams as they do in mine. I mention them only because I wish you to understand that I, too, have sympathy for those who have been tormented."

Cloudblower's expression softened. She stood rigidly for a long while, then eased down onto the dirt pile beside Stone Ghost.

The wind changed. The sweet woody scent of roasting pine nuts blew over them. Stone Ghost inhaled deeply. For the next two days, women would be cooking, cleaning, decorating the villages, and preparing costumes for the ceremony. He had lived alone for so long, he hadn't realized how much he'd missed this.

Gently, Stone Ghost said, "Is there something you wish to tell me, Healer?"

She lifted her gaze to the bright colorful paintings of the Great Warriors on the wall to the right. Their terrifying masks glowed in the sunlight.

"Elder," she murmured. "I ask that you listen to me for a time. I do not know if I will ever be able to say these things again."

"I'm listening, Healer."

Cloudblower's words came softly: "You speak about suffering and its results. The Katsinas' People are all wounded souls, Elder. Each suffers in a different way, but that is why he or she is here. We were all desperately seeking a way out of our agony and found it in the teachings of Matron Flame Carrier." She clenched her hands tightly. "I came because I could not bear to live as an ordinary person should. After serving the Fire Dogs, the needs of my souls were different, greater, much more demanding. I craved the companionship of others who understood what it was to be hurt. For many sun cycles I lived as an outcast in my own heart." She lifted a hand to the big warrior who stood guarding her chamber. "He-Who-Flies came because his wife and children had been massacred. He lost everything. When he first joined us, he moved through our society like a man walking in his sleep. He spoke little. He asked for nothing. Except hope, Elder. Hope that the wars would end, that the dead would rise from their graves and walk the earth again. The Katsinas' People give hope, Elder. That is what we do."

Reverently, he said, "I know that, Healer."

Cloudblower paused. "Jackrabbit, the young warrior who stood on the roof this morning? He does not even know where he came from. He woke one morning at the bottom of a cliff, his head bloody and bruised. He could recall nothing. He may have slipped and fallen, or been attacked in a battle and left for dead. He wandered for days before he chanced upon Matron Flame Carrier at Flowing Waters Town two summers ago. She took him in and cared for him. He never left."

Stone Ghost said, "And Catkin? Why is she here?"

Cloudblower fumbled with her hands, lacing and unlacing them in her lap. "I know little of her, Elder. I have heard it said that her husband died, and her clan tried to force her to marry a man she despised. But I cannot tell you if that is true. Catkin is a quiet one. She speaks little of herself. At least to me. She may reveal more to Browser. You might wish to ask him."

They exchanged a glance. Stone Ghost nodded and wondered how many others here knew that Catkin loved his nephew. It might make a difference.

"What of my nephew's wife? What did you know of her? The things I have heard disturbed me."

The painted hem of Cloudblower's cape waffled in

the wind. She seemed to be watching it while she contemplated what to say.

"Elder, she—she often did unkind things to people. Shouting, lashing out with her fists for no reason. For over a sun cycle I feared that her souls had left her body. She seemed to be hovering like Hawk over a precipice of madness."

"Madness?" Stone Ghost asked. "You are the first to suggest that. Why?"

Cloudblower's voice dropped to a whisper. "At night, when she slept, she had terrifying experiences in the Land of the Dead, Elder. Near dawn, two moons ago, she shrieked like a madwoman, and ran to me in terror, claiming she'd heard strange, inhuman voices coming from Browser's mouth while he slept."

"What did you say?"

"I questioned her, Elder, on what had actually happened. I believed, then and now, that she was deep asleep when she heard the sounds. I think something, or someone, in the Land of the Dead was tormenting her, making the voice enough like her husband's that she would think the eerie sounds came from him."

"Why would one of the ancestors do such a thing, Healer?"

Cloudblower shrugged. "The dead are mysterious beings, Elder. I have never been able to fathom their ways."

"Did you perform a Healing for Ash Girl?"

Cloudblower shook her head. "I tried. She wouldn't allow it. She said that her Spirit Helper cared for her and that was enough."

Stone Ghost moved his sandal across the frozen earth. It left white streaks. Why hadn't Browser forced his wife to undergo a Healing? The mad could not make such decisions themselves. They needed others to do it for them.

"And Hophorn?" he asked. "What is her story?"

"Oh, that is easy, Elder." A loving smile came to Cloudblower's face. "She followed Browser. She had taken care of him since they'd been children, soothing his hurts, easing his fears. When Browser and his family joined the Katsinas' People and left Green Mesa Village, she could not stay behind. She loved him too much. Not as a lover, you understand, but as a cherished friend."

"I do understand," Stone Ghost answered. "I had a friend like that once. When the Tower Builders killed her, my souls tore loose from my body. For over a moon, I could not walk, or even feed myself. My body would not move."

Cloudblower gazed at him, concerned. "I have heard that grief can paralyze the souls."

Stone Ghost tipped his wrinkled face to the sunlight, and let it warm him. "It can, Healer. That is why I fear for Hophorn. These 'blanking-out' spells, are a sort of paralysis of the soul. I must find out what she has seen, and why she cannot bear to face it."

"What do you mean? Face it?"

"I think that is why she blanks out. She sends her souls flying to escape."

As though surprised by the suggestion, Cloud-blower said, "She is ill, Elder. Her head injury—"

"Why does it disturb you that she might wish to escape? Is she escaping you, Healer?"

Cloudblower's face slackened.

Five women climbed onto the roof where Catkin

and Browser stood. They carried baskets, pottery jars, and decorations—strips of colorful fabric, ears of corn, strings of bright feathers, and other things Stone Ghost could not make out from where he sat.

As they climbed down into the plaza, Cloudblower bowed her head. Stiffly, she said, "I must get back, Elder. Hophorn cannot care for herself, and she is terrified that the murderers are going to return to kill her. As well, I have preparations to make for Whiproot's burial and the Longnight ceremony. Hophorn usually leads the ritual. Because of her illness that duty has fallen to me."

Stone Ghost nodded. "I thank you for speaking with me, Healer."

Cloudblower rose and her painted cape flapped around her as she walked toward her chamber.

Stone Ghost watched until she had ducked beneath her door curtain, then he stretched in the sunlight.

The women set their pots and baskets down on the long wall outside the First People's kiva and began removing things from inside. One of the women, around thirty summers old with an ugly pocked face and short black-streaked gray hair, watched Stone Ghost from the corner of her eye.

He walked toward them, smiling, and the ugly woman quickly turned away. Harsh voices came from within the kiva. Flame Carrier's panicked tone was accompanied by two scratchy male voices.

"Cancel the ritual!" Flame Carrier cried. *"Have you lost your wits! Hundreds of people are coming. Many have been walking for days. By nightfall their camps will surround Hillside Village. We can't greet them by telling*

them we've decided not to hold the Ceremony of the
Longnight!"

Wading Bird's brittle voice rose above Flame Carrier's, *"Isn't it worse to allow them to stay when murderers
may be stalking their loved ones!"*

Stone Ghost hobbled past and climbed the ladder to
the roof.

When he reached the top, he stood for a time,
enjoying the majesty of the canyon. A large flock of
ravens cawed as they flapped eastward toward Father
Sun, their black wings flashing. Across Straight Path
Wash, he could make out a line of. people coming up
the road. They had packs on their backs. Several children trailed in the rear, surrounded by dogs. He cocked
his head and heard barks and laughter.

Stone Ghost walked east along the roof toward
Browser and Catkin. His nephew looked as if he'd taken
a blow to the stomach. As he turned, his round face and
short black hair shone in the morning's gleam. A new
fear had been born in his dark eyes.

Stone Ghost called. "It is time that we had a long
talk, "Nephew."

Browser's thick black brows drew down over his flat
nose. His weary movements appeared sluggish. He said
something soft to Catkin, then clasped her shoulder,
and came to meet Stone Ghost.

"Yes, Uncle. What is it you wish to know?" His
plain buckskin cape was mottled with the soot of many
campfires.

"First, I would like you to take me to the place
where you found your wife's body, then we must search
this town, Nephew."

Browser seemed visibly shaken by the request. He

swallowed. "I do not have much time, Uncle, truly. Guests are beginning to arrive for the ceremony. I must sleep before the festivities—"

"I understand, Nephew," Stone Ghost said and took Browser by the arm. As he led him toward the ladder to the road below, he added, "I will not take long."

5

Browser could barely feel his sandals striking the sand. He did not know what to think of Catkin's words. He believed that she had heard Cloudblower speaking with a man, but, as one of the village elders, Cloudblower often entertained passing Traders, clan matrons, or even hunters running the roads. She also had many friends, mostly people grateful for Healings she'd performed.

But nothing explained the man's presence in Talon Town last night, or his ghastly pretense of being Whiproot.

Could Catkin be correct?

Cloudblower knew the murderers?

"You are marching like a condemned man, Nephew," Stone Ghost said. The breeze fluttered his wispy white hair, revealing the large freckles on his scalp. His thick brows knitted over his hooked nose. "Why is that?"

Browser did not wish to discuss this with anyone

until he'd had more time to think about it. He replied, "I have not walked this path since my son's burial, Uncle."

"I regret the need to make you relive that day, Nephew. But it's necessary."

The cliff loomed ahead of them, the rim blazing golden against the blue sky. Browser searched every possible lump or shadow that might be a man. An eagle perched on a scraggly juniper that had rooted in one of the crevices. The big bird's head moved, watching them as they approached. But he saw nothing that looked threatening.

At the base of the cliff, his son's burial, marked by a pile of recently dug earth, stood twenty paces to the left of the empty pit where they'd found his wife. Twenty paces to the right, the long-dead ritual fire pit sank into the ground. He still could see Hophorn sitting with her head down, dressed in Ash Girl's red-feathered cape.

"Five days ago," Stone Ghost said, "the Keepers of the Sacred Directions came out here, then you led the procession of mourners, yes?"

"Yes, Uncle. I was lost in my grief, trying just to make it to the end of the ritual. I was watching my feet when I heard Flame Carrier scream." Browser pointed. "You can see the open pit. That is where we found my wife. When I looked up, Flame Carrier grabbed Cloudblower's arm and stumbled backward. Old Woman Up Above wailed like a homeless ghost. I ordered Catkin and Whip...another warrior"—he could not say that name again until Whiproot was well on his way to the Land of the Dead—"to put my son's burial ladder down and follow me. We ran to the pit as quickly as we could."

Stone Ghost walked with his arms folded beneath

his brown-and-white turkey-feather cape. His-hands showed through the holes. "What did you see when you arrived at the burial pit?"

"At first I didn't know what I was seeing, Uncle. I thought it was a man, a tall man. My wife lay on her stomach with her arms and legs sprawled, as if she'd been thrown into the pit. A stone slab covered her head. She wore a white buckskin shirt and pants. Near her feet, the mask of the Wolf katsina rested. When the mourners crowded around the pit and saw the stone, screams broke out. People begin pushing and shoving. Most ran."

"Wise people. What happened next?"

"Catkin realized that something was wrong. She pointed to the places where hands and feet should be. The sleeves and pant legs appeared empty. We feared it might be mutilation. Catkin wished to climb down into the pit to remove the slab, but Cloudblower wouldn't allow it. Catkin had just returned from a walk and had not yet been ritually cleansed in pinyon pine smoke. So Cloudblower climbed into the pit and shoved the stone aside."

Browser's exhausted heart throbbed with the memory. He propped his hand on his war club. "Bloody pulp filled her crushed skull. My wife's long hair had been cut short, as if in mourning. I do not know why a murderer would do such a thing. It makes no sense."

"But thorough work," Stone Ghost murmured. His disconcerting eyes flared a little wider. "How could you tell it was your wife, Nephew?"

In his souls, Browser could see her small, delicate hand, and feel the stiffness. "She was wearing the snake bracelet I gave her at our Joining, Uncle."

Browser stopped in front of the burial pit, and Stone Ghost moved up beside him. He gripped Browser's arm for support. As the old man leaned over, his tawdry pottery disk necklaces swung. Owl feathers scattered the bottom of the grave.

Browser sucked in a sharp breath.

"The feathers aren't witchery, Nephew." Stone Ghost pointed to the cliff. "Owls perch in the crevices at night. I saw their eyes shining early this morning."

Browser squinted at the white splotches of droppings that streaked the wall. His uncle was probably right. Still, the feathers worried him.

"You have had a few days to consider what you saw, Nephew. Why do you think the murderer would dress her in white, cut her hair, and place a stone over her head?"

Browser's gaze returned to the rim. As the day warmed, the scent of damp stone rose. Had the murderers been watching that day? Peering over the edge of the cliff, smiling at the happenings below?

"He didn't want her breath-heart soul to escape, that's why he used the stone. And"—he kicked at a small chunk of sandstone—"perhaps he believed her to be a witch. Many people in the village whispered that she was, but I never saw it, Uncle. A man would know if his wife were a witch, wouldn't he?"

Stone Ghost lightly touched Browser's hand. "I think so, Nephew."

Browser's gaze strayed to his son's burial. From the depths of his souls, he saw Grass Moon smile and heard his son calling, *"Father? Father come and play with me?"* The pain in his chest made it hard to breathe.

"Where was Hophorn sitting, Nephew?" Stone Ghost asked.

He pointed. "Over there. She had her back against the cliff. Catkin noticed the trail of red feathers that led from the burial pit to Hophorn. Apparently, the murderer had taken the red cape my wife had been wearing, carried it over, and draped it around Hophorn's shoulders. Hophorn was also sheathed in ashes, Uncle, and four lines led away from her in the sacred directions. As if the murderer had purified her."

"More likely, Nephew, he was absolving himself of the act of attacking her." Stone Ghost frowned at the fire pit. "What else, Nephew?"

"Two ash-coated eagle feathers stuck out from beneath her sandals."

"Two? Not four? He didn't leave one for each direction?"

"Two, Uncle."

Stone Ghost nodded. "And then your wife's body disappeared, yes?"

"Yes, Uncle."

Stone Ghost said, "Where was Cloudblower when the body vanished?"

Browser grimaced. "She is not the murderer, Uncle. You must trust me about this. I know her. She was in Talon Town, opening Hophorn's skull when it happened."

"Was anyone with her?"

"Yes," he answered. After Catkin's words, how could he still defend Cloudblower? His own emotions churned. "Redcrop was aiding Cloudblower in the Healing."

Stone Ghost scratched his wrinkled cheek. 'The entire time?"

Browser thought about that. "I don't know. Whip— one of my warriors was standing guard over Talon Town that morning."

"And now that warrior is dead."

Browser's belly knotted. "Are you saying he was killed because he knew Cloudblower had left? That he saw her take my wife's body?"

Stone Ghost gave him a lopsided smile. "Why, no, Nephew. You're the one who said that. Were you trying to tell me something?"

Browser frowned, then shook his head. "No."

A brown-and-white feather tore loose from Stone Ghost's cape and flipped away, somersaulting through the air. Stone Ghost smiled and gestured to it. "Was the wind blowing the morning you discovered your wife's body?"

Browser struggled to recall. "Yes. I think so. Just a breeze, but it made the morning seem colder."

"Yet Catkin could follow a trail of feathers, Nephew? Did that not strike you as odd? Surely all such feathers would have blown away less than one-quarter finger of time after being dropped."

As the cliff absorbed the morning sunlight, it warmed and gave off a faintly sweet scent, like a mixture of dust and cactus flowers.

Browser looked down into his uncle's strangely glowing eyes. "Blessed gods. Are you suggesting—"

"No, I'm telling you that the red feathers must have been dropped only moments before the burial party arrived. That's also why you found only two eagle feathers. Wind Baby pulled them loose."

The cawing of the ravens suddenly turned loud, raucous, as if in warning. Browser listened to them with blood pounding in his ears. "Which means the murderer was here. Close by. Probably watching."

Stone Ghost took Browser's arm and guided him toward the ritual fire pit where Hophorn had been attacked. "They always watch, Nephew. If they can. That's their triumph. Why create a pageant if you can't see the audience's reaction?"

They walked into the shade cast by the cliff; Stone Ghost released Browser's arm and carefully walked around the dead fire. Charcoal chunks thrust up through a layer of ice.

"Catkin told me that you found a strange mark near the fire pit where the sand had thawed. She thought it might have been part of a footprint. Is it still here?"

Browser knelt and tapped his finger to the ground. "This is the mark, Uncle."

Stone Ghost examined the arc in the soil: "Did you think this was a heel print, Nephew?"

"I thought it might be. If so, it was made by a big, heavy man."

"Indeed." Stone Ghost got down on his hands and knees and scrutinized the shape with great care. "Was the fire blazing when you arrived? Or burning low, and steady?"

"Blazing, Uncle. I remember because I thought Hophorn must have heard us coming and added wood."

Stone Ghost grunted to his feet. "Did you find anything else?"

Browser hesitated, then reached beneath his cape, to the pouch he wore around his waist. He drew out the turquoise wolf and held it before Stone Ghost on his open palm. "This, Uncle."

Stone Ghost's wrinkled lips parted, as if in awe. "I haven't seen one of those in sixty sun cycles. Where did you find it?"

"There. It was resting on top of a red feather."

Rather than reaching for the precious object, Stone Ghost frowned at the place Browser pointed. "Show me exactly where was Hophorn sitting?"

"In the very back, Uncle."

Stone Ghost skirted the pit and sat down in the same place Hophorn had been sitting, as if trying to imagine what she had seen that morning. His gaze moved from the empty burial pit, to the place where the wolf and feather had rested beside the heel print.

"Have you shown that wolf to anyone, Nephew?"

"Catkin knows, Uncle. She was here when I found it. But I've told no one else. I'm sure she hasn't either."

As he rose to his feet, Stone Ghost said, "That, my Nephew, is why you are both still alive."

Browser searched the rim again and scanned the piles of rock behind Talon Town. "Why?"

"Because he was watching," Stone Ghost said calmly. "He knows that one of you has it."

"But if—if he knows—why doesn't he just kill us and search us?"

Stone Ghost grinned. "He can't risk killing you before he questions you, Nephew. Only a person with the wits of a blood-sucking fly would carry a legendary Power object in his belt pouch."

Browser looked down. The Turquoise Wolf had a curious, unnatural glint in her eyes, as if preparing to leap from his palm and run away like the wind. Browser tucked it back into his belt pouch. "I will hide it as soon as we return to Hillside Village, Uncle."

Stone Ghost affectionately slipped his arm through Browser's and headed him back toward Talon Town. They followed an ancient, overgrown trail that slithered through a garden of toppled boulders.

Stone Ghost stopped in the shadow of the town's towering western wall and released Browser's arm. A curving line of cracked plaster and fallen stones heaped against the base of the wall. His voice went low. "I think these boulders shelter us from view, Nephew. So. Quickly, tell me what Catkin said that upset you."

6

"**M**agpie, could you hold this?"

"Of course, Aunt."

Hail Walking Hawk handed her cane to Magpie and dug around in the pocket of her yellow dress for the two pieces of bread she had saved from their supper of venison chili and biscuits. The pieces of fluffy white bread looked almost silver in the twilight as she withdrew them. She lifted the morsels to the pale blue evening sky and Sang softly. The brightest Evening People had awakened and sparkled on the eastern horizon.

Hail said, "This is for our mother, Iatiku," and bent over to place the bread on the flat slab of sandstone. Her yellow dress billowed around her legs. "And this is for you, Utsiti, creator of the universe." She placed the other piece of bread beside the first. They seemed to gleam against the tan stone.

Hail straightened. The temperature had just begun to drop, and her whole body heaved a sigh of relief. She had spent most of the day in her tent, watching the shadows of the bugs who walked on the red nylon. The pain and the ghosts kept crying out to her, trying to force her to sit up and take notice of them. As the evening cooled, she felt a little better.

"There," she said, "that should do it." She reached for her cane and propped it on the ground. The tip sank into the soft sand.

Magpie took Hail's left elbow and smiled. "Do you realize, Aunt, that if everyone made offerings to the gods each night, all the wars would go away, and no one would ever be hungry again." Perspiration soaked the armpits of her white T-shirt.

Hail grinned. "Especially Iatiku and Utsiti. They'd be as fat as those wrestlers in Japan. What are they called?"

"Sumo wrestlers, Aunt."

"Sumo," Hail tried the name on her tongue. It tasted sticky, like the rice they served in those Chinese restaurants in Albuquerque.

Hail sighed and studied the cliffs that surrounded them. The darkness had turned the tan rock a grayish purple. Owls perched in the crevices, their eyes flashing as they searched the canyon bottom, waiting their chance to dive down and snatch up a juicy mouse or an unsuspecting kangaroo rat.

Hail turned toward the Haze child. He'd been gurgling for the past hour, like a baby blowing bubbles to occupy himself. A black piece of plastic covered the pit. Hail could feel his hope. He knew people had found him, and he could not understand why no one had taken care of him yet. He had been trapped here for a long time.

Not much longer, she promised. *As soon as these*

diggers get you out of the ground, I'll take care of you. Don't be afraid.

Hail's filmy old eyes moved to the top of the pit where the stone rested over the witch's head. She had been a tall woman. Dusty had dug around her long limbs, revealing how her arms sprawled. Washais said it looked like the woman had been hurled into the grave.

Hail glanced at the other pits. All of these women and children had been thrown away like old rags—but from the marks Washais pointed out on the long bones, the muscles had been stripped from them before burial.

That frightened Hail.

When she had been a little girl, she'd heard the Pueblo elders whispering about two *maleficiadores,* enchanters, who dug children from their graves, and cooked their flesh in a large pot in the moonlit graveyard. People could smell the foul odor for miles. Some witches ate only the organs of powerful shamans, to gain their powers. Other witches jerked the flesh of their victims and fed it to their enemies as a way to hide their crimes.

Hail glanced at the square holes.

Many of these women had stones over their heads, but she could sense they weren't witches. Someone had just treated them that way. Nevertheless, evil did live here. They had awakened it with their digging. She could still feel the *basilisco's* malignant presence. Even after centuries of lying in the ground, the corruption was strong. Hail could taste it at the back of her throat, cloying, like the taste of rotten meat.

Dusty would have to get these bones out of the ground soon, so they could all leave, or the corruption would make them sick.

"Aunt," Magpie said, and gently touched Hail's white hair. "I've been having scary dreams."

Hail swiveled her head. Sweat glued Magpie's short black hair to her cheeks, and made her rich brown eyes appear deep and dark. Spirit Helpers often came to people in dreams, delivering messages to help the tribe. "What dreams?"

Magpie tipped her head, as if reluctant to say. "I see terrible things. You and Grandma are talking in the Land of the Dead, and I—"

"Is she letting me get a word in edgewise?" Hail asked seriously. "She could talk a dead rabbit away from a starving coyote."

Magpie smiled, but she gave Hail that look that told her she knew Hail had cleverly sidestepped the part about being in the Land of the Dead.

Hail tucked her cane under her arm and clasped her knobby fingers over Magpie's. At the feel of her smooth skin, love swelled Hail's chest, easing some of the pain. "Help me back to my bottle of iced tea," she said. "We'll talk on the way."

Magpie supported Hail while she searched for steady footing in the sand, then they veered around a thick greasewood bush, and headed east, toward the firelight that haloed the tents and outlined the blocky shape of Dr. Robertson's square camp trailer. He'd towed it in that afternoon behind his shiny red truck.

Dusty sat next to Sylvia before the leaping flames in the fire pit. Washais and Dr. Robertson stood over a table scattered with bones to Hail's right. She could see them in the white sphere of light cast by a Coleman lantern. Frowns incised their foreheads.

Hail and Magpie's red tent nestled between the two

groups; the rain fly that had been set up as a ramada out front waffled in the night wind.

"Please tell me the truth, Aunt," Magpie said hesitantly, fearfully.

Hail smiled up into her niece's dark eyes. "Oh, it's nothing so bad. Not for me, anyway. Death and I have been companions for many years, walking side-by-side, just like old friends."

Magpie's steps faltered. She looked down at Hail with pained eyes.

"Don't mourn me, child. I'm happier than I've ever been. I cherish every moment, every color. When you smile at me, my heart soars like that owl up there." She lifted her cane and pointed to the big bird wheeling silently in the slate sky above them. His body shone blackly as he passed in front of the brilliant crescent moon.

Tears glistened in Magpie's eyes. "Oh, Aunt."

"Listen," Hail said, "I'm going to need you to help me. I don't want anybody else to know about this, and the pain gets really bad sometimes. I have trouble breathing. When it comes upon me, you may have to get me back to the tent before I fall down flat."

Magpie jerked a nod. "Please let me take you home?"

"I need to be here." She gestured at the excavation. "These diggers, they don't know what's slinking around out here. Something old, something evil. I still have things to do. The time's not right yet, but when it comes, I have to be ready."

Magpie tenderly touched Hail's white hair and bit her lip. "But I can't stand to see you in pain."

Hail glanced her way. "I have a bag full of pain

killers in the tent, child. I just haven't been taking them. I get wobbly, and I can't think straight when I do."

Magpie kept silent for a time. "What if your doctor needs to run a test? Don't you need to be close—"

"He can't do anything more, Magpie."

Magpie squeezed her eyes closed, and a tear rolled down her cheek. "Is he sure?"

"Yes, child. It's just my time. Like it will be yours someday. I want to live my last days out in the open, watching sunrises and sunsets, not in a white smelly hospital."

Magpie's jaw quivered. She seemed to be nerving herself to ask the question. "Is it..."

"Cancer, yes. Just like your, grandmother."

Magpie clutched her arm so tightly it hurt.

Hail petted her fingers. "Now I know how packrat feels in Eagle's talons."

Maggie loosened her grip. "Breast cancer?"

"Yes, girl. Which means you have more to worry about than me dying. That doctor in Albuquerque said sometimes this sort of cancer runs in families. *You* have to go get checked. Soon."

Magpie's voice came out low. "How long, Aunt? Did the doctor tell you?"

"A few months. Long enough for me to drive you crazy telling you how much I love you. Now, help me back to my chair by the fire. I want to finish my iced tea, and I don't want you looking like somebody in the family just died, because I'm still here. You see me, don't you?" Hail waved her cane.

"I see you," Magpie smiled, but it looked like it hurt.

Hail gripped Magpie's arm and took one agonizing step at a time. Why did breast cancer make her hurt all over? It didn't make sense. Her chest, naturally burned as if on fire, but her knees and elbows felt like an ice pick had been wedged between the bones. Her sister, Slumber, had never complained about these kinds of pains, but now that she thought of it, Slumber had never complained about anything. Her sister had stayed on her feet and busy to the end.

And so will I. But, unlike Slumber, she had one last battle to wage. And this one, she couldn't afford to lose.

The wind changed, blowing smoke in her direction. The fragrance of the fire pleased Hail. Dr. Robertson had hauled in four bundles of ponderosa pine logs, and the faintly sweet tang saturated the night.

Hail said, "Are you going to be all right?"

Magpie wiped her eyes on her white shirt sleeve. "I'll be fine now. Thank you for telling me straight out."

"I should have done it sooner. I was just being selfish. I wanted to see your eyes shining for me, and I was afraid the truth would dim them."

"It won't. I promise." Magpie suddenly turned and hugged Hail.

Hail stroked her niece's short black hair. "I love you, child. You're the reason I'm still here. You've taken good care of me these past few years."

Magpie couldn't speak. She swallowed and patted Hail's hand.

They walked in companionable silence, smiling gently at each other.

~

Dusty caught sight of Hail and Maggie as they appeared from the darkness." He stopped peeling the label from his Guinness bottle and studied them. Both wore curious expressions, almost desperately loving, as though each feared the other might disappear at any moment. He smiled at Maggie. She smiled back and led her aunt to the lawn chair beside Sylvia. After the elderly woman eased down, Maggie pulled her chair up so close that the aluminum arms touched.

Maggie reached down for the almost empty bottle of iced tea laying in the sand, unscrewed the lid, and handed it to her aunt. "Would you like another bottle, Aunt? This one is almost gone."

Hail shook her head. "I'd just have to get up twice in the night, and the ghosts might get me."

Sylvia's green eyes widened. She had clipped her brown hair up in back, and the style made her face look as lean as a weasel's. She wore a tan tank top, Levi's shorts, and hiking boots. "Did you hear them again last night, Mrs. Walking Hawk?"

"I hear them every night. They're a noisy bunch."

"What did they say?"

"They were shouting at each other and shoving back and forth. I could hear their feet scraping the ground."

Sylvia glanced at Dusty, then whispered, "I wonder what they're fighting about?"

Hail said, "I don't know, but he's really mad. Last night his voice screeched, then her voice went soft, like she was afraid of him, begging him not to hurt her."

"He? I thought we just had women here." Sylvia's

eyes scanned the darkness.

"I heard a man," Hail replied, with a distant look in her eyes. "I think he's the cause of all this. He's really bad. He touched the basilisk. I could feel him in the stone."

"Can you hear the ghosts now, Aunt?" Maggie asked.

Hail cocked her ear to the wind. White hair danced around her wrinkled face as she listened. "No. Even that Haze baby is quiet."

Sylvia sank back into her chair. "Good. I don't want to accidentally get in their way, you know? Getting whacked by a ghost isn't my idea of sacrificing for science."

"Whacked?" Maggie asked. "Ghosts whack you?"

"You betcha." Sylvia nodded. Her freckles looked larger in the firelight. "My mother used to tell me bedtime stories about ghosts when I was growing up. They were always whacking people by throwing chairs and making chandeliers fall on them. I remember one story that scared the bejeesus out of me. The ghost broke an icicle off the roof of the house, then slipped into a young woman's bedroom, and plunged it into her heart, but the woman didn't die right away. She ran around screaming until she stumbled through a window and a piece of broken glass lopped her head off."

Dusty reached for the top log in the woodpile to his left and tossed it into the fire pit. Ash puffed and whirled upward into the night sky. As flames licked around the wood, sparks crackled and shot in all directions. "Your mother told you stories like that at bedtime? And you didn't run screaming?"

"Are you kidding?" Sylvia answered. "I loved those

stories. After one of her tales, I'd pull the blankets over my head and fall fast asleep."

"You must have been suffering from oxygen deprivation. No normal child would sleep after a story like that."

Sylvia took a sip of her Pepsi. "I didn't have oxygen problems until she started telling us vampire stories. I slept with a sheet wrapped around my throat until I was eighteen."

"And discovered baseball bats," Dusty supplied.

"Right."

"I'm surprised you didn't choke—"

"*No, Dale,*" Maureen said sharply, "that's *not* what I mean."

Dusty looked over at them. Maureen and Dale stood behind the table in front of Maureen's tent. Two lines of skulls, and carefully laid out long bones, covered the fake wood veneer top. Dale had come in about sunset, the trailer full of groceries, drinks, and ice. He'd spent his years in tents. These days, he always arrived at an excavation with the old Holliday Rambler trailer in tow.

"Look here, Dale. See these fractures?" Maureen said. "They're all on the right side of the skull." The white lantern light profiled her oval face and flashed in her dark eyes. Her long black braid draped the front of her light green shirt. The silver strands glittered. "These skulls come from burials on the easternmost side of the site. There's a pattern here. As you can see, each fracture is in a different place, as if he started at the linea temporalis, and worked his way back."

"The site as excavated," Dale pointed out. Deep wrinkles etched his elderly face. He wore a faded pair of jeans, and a red-and-black-checked shirt with pearl buttons. His dusty fedora—the kind Bogart always wore in the movies—sat on his head. About the same height as Maureen, his thick gray hair and mustache contrasted sharply with her dark complexion. "There may be more burials we haven't found yet. And, besides, you can't prove it's a pattern."

"Oh, yes, I can. The statistical probability of finding this order of fractures—"

"A *probability,* Maureen. Nothing more." Dale propped his hands on his hips.

Maureen frowned at the top row of skulls. All of them had been carefully placed in Ziploc bags to avoid contamination.

"True," Maureen said, "but based upon what I've seen so far, I can also hypothesize a cause. I wouldn't do it in print. Yet. But I'd tell you, Dale."

Dusty balanced his Guinness bottle on one knee. "I don't get this. If someone's killing slaves, they whack them wherever it's convenient."

Maureen looked up. "If you'll grace us with your presence, Stewart, I'll show you why that's hogwash."

Dusty rose and walked wide around the fire. When he stood opposite Maureen and Dale, he could see that Maureen had left the front of her tent open. Inside lay folded clothing, a microscope set up on a stack of books, and a carefully rolled sleeping bag. He unwrapped a finger from the warm beer bottle. "I'd zip my tent if I were you. This time of night, scorpions, spiders, sidewinders, anything could crawl into your bed. I'm not sure what effect they'd have on you, but I'm sure they'd think you were seriously infringing on their personal space."

"That's interesting, Stewart," Maureen said, as she stepped over and zipped her doorway closed. "You can't imagine how a human being might feel sleeping with a poisonous creature, but you know exactly how poisonous insects and reptiles feel sleeping with human beings. That sums up your character, doesn't it?"

Sylvia snickered, and when Dusty glared at her, she pretended to be choking on Pepsi. She coughed and slapped herself on the back. "Nasty. The carbonation I mean."

Dusty braced a hand on the corner of the table and nonchalantly gestured to the skulls with his bottle. "You were saying about the fractures, Doctor?"

Maureen walked back to the table. "I've arranged these skulls in order of the burials, moving east to west across the site. Notice that the first two skulls show cranial depression fractures on both sides and in two different planes."

"I see that," Dusty said. "So.?"

"*So,* the killer didn't know what he was doing. The blows were random. But look at these." Maureen tapped the bags that held the fourth and fifth skulls. "These women were only struck on the right side of the skull, and these three"—she touched skulls in the bottom row—"were only struck on the left side of the head."

Dusty's blue eyes narrowed. "Your point?"

Maureen gazed at him as if he must be stupid. "It's right in front of your face, Stewart. Don't you see it?"

He studied the skulls more closely. The numerous dents, and radiating fractures, shone oddly yellowish in the firelight. "I see battered skulls. Is there something more here?"

Maureen exhaled hard. "After the first two women, the blows are calculated, strategic." She hesitated, as if waiting for him to supply the rest. When Dusty just stared at her, Maureen said, "The killer was systematically testing brain function, Stewart."

Dale's bushy gray brows went up. The pearl buttons on his shirt flashed as he turned. "You mean the murderer wanted to see what would happen if he struck the head in different places?"

"Of course, he did. Look at—"

"Nonsense," Dusty objected. "You're presuming these burials were deliberately laid out from east to west. We have no way of determining their order. This skull with fractures on both sides may have been the last one buried, not the first. It's more likely that the guy just had the chance to bash both of these women's heads before they could run."

"I'll grant you that's possible," Maureen said, "but I don't think so."

Dusty threw up his hands. "Good God, is this what physical anthropologists call science? I'd be hounded out of the archaeological profession if I openly spouted such baseless garbage."

Sylvia cupped a hand to her mouth, and called, "Let's not forget those who have tried!"

"And failed!" Dusty called. "Jealousy is rampant in this profession, Sylvia. When you're at the top you have to expect a few coup attempts."

In a curt voice, Maureen said, "Dale, I know I've already given you a list of the tests I want performed on these remains, but I want you to add another one."

"All right, Maureen. What?"

"I want a pollen analysis done of the nasal cavities.

There's some desiccated tissue in a few of these skulls. If we—"

"We have a limited budget, Doctor," Dusty replied.

"I want to know what time of year they died, Stewart. If specimen number one has chimaja pollen in her nostrils, and specimen number two has sage pollen, we will know one died in the spring, and one in the autumn. Get it?"

He blinked. "Ah. You mean because that's when chimaja and sage bloom. Sure. I get it. Why is that important?"

"It's important because it might help us to determine the order in which they were interred. Is this coming into focus for you?"

"Oh, yes," he said with exaggerated interest. "Absolutely, your worshipfulness. It's just that the picture I see is a lot different from the one you see." He folded his arms and braced his beer bottle on his left elbow. "You're hypothesizing a prehistoric serial murderer loose among the Anasazi, and I'm saying these women were all tortured by their slave masters and thrown into pits when they were no longer useful. I see it fine. You're the one who's myopic."

Maureen lifted her hands as if in surrender. "If you're going to stick with this slave hypothesis, we should have the bone collagen tested for stable-carbon and nitrogen isotopes."

"What in the name of God is that?"

Dale shoved his fedora back on his head. "Carbon and nitrogen isotope ratios," he explained, "can tell us what types of plants and animals the people were—or were not—eating."

"Be serious, Dale," Dusty said. "I can think of a

dozen alternate hypotheses as to why one woman's diet would be different from another's. Especially if the doctor is right and they really were buried in sequence. Food shifts occur during different times of year."

Maureen braced her hands on the table and leaned toward him. "If there's testable collagen in these bones, Stewart, I'll be able to tell you whether these women were eating watery corn gruel or a lavish diet of deer, turkey, and rabbit. You don't think masters would feed their slaves the good stuff, do you?"

Wind gusted through camp, tousling Dusty's blond hair. He shifted his weight to his opposite foot. "No." He narrowed an eye. "You really can tell that?"

"Maybe. We'll see." She straightened up.

Dale watched them with shining eyes.

Maureen lowered her voice. "I also think I know where to find evidence to support my serial murderer hypothesis."

"Yeah? Where?" Dusty asked.

Maureen pointed to the site. "If I'm right, there's another burial between the Haze child and the woman in unit N4W6." Firelight flickered over her face as she turned to peer at Dusty. "And she has a depression fracture just posterior to the left coronal suture, right over Broca's Area of the brain."

"The what?"

Maureen lifted a slender finger and tapped the side of Dusty's temple, just ahead of his ear. "There, Stewart."

"Hmm," Dale said. He thoughtfully stroked his mustache. "It would be interesting to test your hypothesis. That area is, however, outside the impact area. Maggie?" he called. "What do you think?"

She massaged her forehead. "I don't know. Let me think about it. One pit dug outside of the impact area on the instructions of the Indian monitor is annoying but understandable. Digging another just to prove a hypothesis is going to rankle the Department of Interior bigwigs. The DOI motto is: 'Research is a waste of taxpayer dollars. We do land management, not science.'
"

"But the pit I want dug is closer to the impact area than the Haze child unit that Stewart dug," Maureen said. "Why can't we just excavate the gap between?"

Sylvia called, "I agree! Let's dig it. I think Maureen's right. This is the work of a serial murderer."

Dusty turned toward Sylvia. A crushed Pepsi can lay at her feet. She had a Coors Light balanced on her chair arm. Brown hair straggled around her face. "Yeah? Why?"

"Well, think about it. A few blows to the head is pretty amateurish torture. I mean, the Apache used to build fires in people's stomachs."

Dusty's mouth quirked. "Did you have a point?"

"Well, yeah, boss man. I mean, look at the black slave cemeteries in the South. Some of those people were beat up really bad, and over a long period. Last year, I read about two burials," a man and a woman, who were laid side-by-side behind slave cabins in Mississippi. During their lives, they'd both had their arms broken, their legs broken, several ribs broken. The woman's neck had even been broken once. Now, *that's* slave torture. What torturer would just hit his slaves in the head?"

Dusty walked back and sank into his chair before the fire. "If you want to talk about torture, nobody can hold a candle to the good doctor's people, the Iroquois." Dusty aimed his bottle at her. "They made torture an art. It lasted for days. I remember one entry in the *Jesuit Relations* that described the capture of a British trader. They hacked the guy apart a piece at a time. In the middle of the torture, they stuck his hands in the fire, to cook the flesh, then called the special children forward to chew the meat off the bones. As a reward for good behavior, you understand. Can you imagine watching smiling children eat you alive?"

Sylvia looked fascinated. She gripped her Coors in both hands, and said, "What I can really imagine is all the other kids in the longhouse." In a whining voice, she said, "Oh, Dad, *he's* got one, I want one."

The fire suddenly spluttered, and sparks popped. A haze of smoke rose into the night sky.

Dusty grimaced. "You are a sick woman."

"No," Maureen corrected. "She just doesn't know much about the Iroquois." She gave it the French pronunciation: Irokwah. "They were matrilineal, Sylvia. The kids would have said, 'Oh, *Mom,* he's got one, I want one.'"

Sylvia's green eyes widened. "Hey, thanks for telling me. That's the kind of mistake that could get me killed in the wrong circles."

Dale loudly said, "Getting back to the burials, Maureen. Tell me about the irregularities I see in the squamous portion of this frontal bone. Osteophytes?"

Dusty knew the skull Dale meant. It was the burial Maureen had commented on when she'd first arrived. The crushed skull had come out of the ground in three pieces. After they'd bagged them, Maureen had spent hours looking at them through a magnifying glass. The entire inner table of the skull undulated with white lumps.

Maureen said, "This a classic case of *hyperostosis frontalis interna.*"

Dusty translated, "Which means she had one hell of an endocrine imbalance."

Dale gave Dusty a penetrating look. "Maureen must have told you that. You'd never think of it yourself." He turned to Maureen. "What are the clinical considerations in such cases?"

Dusty made a face and took a swig of his beer.

Maureen said, *"Hyperostosis frontalis interna* is observed almost exclusively in women, primarily postmenopausal women. Several studies have documented it. One of the best known was carried out on women who had died and were being autopsied. In that case, forty percent showed thickening of the skull, and these same bony growths. Another study was done in a home for the aged. Sixty-two percent of the women there suffered from HFI, but none of the men."

Dale seemed to be weighing this, information. His bushy gray brows twitched. "What happens to the women involved? This sounds like a painful condition."

"Not always," Maureen answered. "Sometimes the victims suffer insomnia, urinary difficulties, disturbances of equilibrium, that sort of thing, but nothing severe. On the other hand, some are in agony. They have raging headaches, fainting spells, even convulsions. One researcher discovered a dramatic frequency of HFI in women who were insane."

Sylvia's chair squeaked, and Dusty glanced at her. Her eyes had gone huge. She was listening to the discussion literally on the edge of her seat.

"So these bony growths," Dale said, "must extend themselves into the brain."

"They certainly put pressure on specific areas. The larger they are, the more brain tissue they squeeze."

Dale touched the pieces of skull in the clear plastic bag. "Dusty? Didn't you say you thought this woman's skull had been split by a rock?"

"Maureen matched the fractures to the stone," he said without looking at her. "That's exactly what happened. The rock was thrown into the pit on top of her head, cracking her skull, but—"

"Wow! Hold on! This is coming together!" Sylvia shouted. "Maybe she was crazy, and her people thought she was a witch. Did you ever read that great book by Marc Simmons on *Witchcraft in the Southwest*? In the past four hundred years, lots of crazy women have been accused of being witches. After they were captured, their own people would torture them to get a confession and force them to undo their evil, then they were killed, and in some pretty gruesome ways."

Hail Walking Hawk lifted a frail old hand and the camp went silent.

Wispy hair blew around her ancient face as she propped her elbows on the arms of her chair. "Many years ago, my grandmother told me about two witches who lived over at Zuni pueblo. They could change themselves into animals by jumping through yucca hoops, and once they turned a man into a woman. Everybody said they were crazy, but people were too scared of them to try and kill them. My grandmother said that the oldest witch ran around at night in the body of coyote, howling in pain, because her head always felt like it was going to explode." Hail Walking

Hawk looked at Maureen. "Do you think those women might have had these growths in their heads, Washais? Is that why they were crazy and became witches?"

Maureen's midnight eyes resembled deep dark holes in her firelit oval face. "It's possible. I can't say for certain without examining their skulls, but I wouldn't be surprised."

Dusty asked, "But you said earlier that HFI was found primarily in postmenopausal women. The skull on the table is from a woman in her early twenties. What's the overall occurrence in the general population?"

"About five percent of all adult women suffer from it," Maureen said, "but only ten percent of those are under thirty."

Sylvia flopped back in her chair. "Thank God. I still have a few years before I go crazy."

"Don't be hasty," Dusty said. "What if you're in the ten percent of the five percent?"

Sylvia turned her Coors can in her hands. "I wonder if HFI is related to the incidence of depression among women? I mean, wow, these things grow in your head, and you start thinking crazy thoughts. Who wouldn't be depressed?"

"That's an interesting hypothesis, Sylvia," Dale said. "I think you should do a paper on it next year. In the meantime"—he stretched, and yawned—"it's been a long day for me. I'm going to bed. Good night all."

"'Night, Dale."

He lifted a hand, and walked behind the tents into the darkness, headed in the direction of the Sanolet.

Hail Walking Hawk said, "I'm going to sleep, too. Give me a hand, Magpie," and reached out to her niece.

Maggie helped the old woman out of her chair and tenderly slipped an arm around her shoulders. "Good night everybody. We'll see you in the morning."

"Good night," Sylvia said and lifted her Coors can in a salute. "Don't let the ghosts get you."

Maggie chuckled. "I won't. You either, White Eyes."

Sylvia grinned.

As Maggie and her aunt slowly made their way to the red tent, which nestled between Dusty's tent and Maureen's, Sylvia finished her Coors, crushed the can in one hand, and tossed it into the trash box behind Dusty. It landed with a soft metallic clank.

"Heavy discussion," Sylvia said. "Ghosts, torture, murder, insanity. I'm going to rub my bat with garlic before I go to sleep." She got to her feet and stretched.

Dusty said, "Good night, Sylvia."

"Good night, boss." She headed for her tent.

Dusty used the toe of his hiking boot to rock the pot at the edge of the coals. "There's still coffee in the pot. Are you interested, Dr. Cole?"

Maureen ran a hand through her hair. "I guess." She sat down across the fire and reached for the cup she'd used at dinner. "We need to dig that pit, Stewart."

"I've got to hand it to you, a serial murderer?" He shook his head. "An Anasazi crime scene? They'll be laughing from the Pecos Conference to the SAAs."

"What's the Pecos Conference?" she asked as she poured coffee into her cup.

"The oldest conference on Southwest Archaeology. A. V. Kidder started it back in nineteen twenty-four. It happens every year. People go and talk about their research. The SAAs, I assume you've heard of."

"The Society for American Archaeology." She nodded. "I am going to dig that pit, Stewart."

He sat back. "*You* don't know how to dig, Doctor. If anybody digs that pit, it's going to be me, and I can't scuff the surface without Maggie's approval. Get it?"

She sipped her coffee. "The only thing I get is that the American government is run by antiscience fundamentalists bent on destroying any research that threatens their—"

"Their what?" he demanded, trying to keep his voice low. "Their respect for other traditions? I thought Canadians were all for the 'Cultural Mosaic'? Or did you miss that lecture in Canadian History one-oh-one?"

"The concept of the Cultural Mosaic is based on understanding other cultures, Stewart. We don't take their religious beliefs, turn them into laws, and shove them down the throats of nonbelievers."

He glared at her. "No wonder you're alone. Who in the hell would have you?"

For a moment, she just stared at him as though sideswiped by the comment. Then her lips quivered, she tossed her coffee into the fire, and walked out into the darkness.

Dusty bowed his head and squeezed his eyes closed. "Dear God, I'm an idiot. I've always been an idiot. I will always be an idiot." He opened his eyes and stared unblinking into the fire. He had to find her. He couldn't let her leave thinking he...

"Maureen? Wait!"

7

"I wish to lead the way, Uncle. You understand? If we trap the killer in there, it will be up to me to kill or disable him. I don't want you to get in the way."

Stone Ghost stood leaning into the hole in the wall, surveying the dark interior. His thin white hair fluttered around his head, "I have no objections, Nephew."

Browser poured hot bear grease from a small pot onto the tightly wrapped top of the cedar bark torch, then dipped it into the warming bowl that rested on the ground. Smoky flames curled around the wrapping.

"There is no way that we can travel silently or secretly through these dark warrens, Uncle. The light of the torch, the grating of our sandals on the crumbled floors, will provide plenty of warning to anyone inside. Let us proceed slowly."

Stone Ghost stepped out of the room and gestured for Browser to enter. "I'll be following right behind you, Nephew."

Browser led with the torch, holding it out ahead of

him to light the square room. The white plaster had cracked away from the intricately laid stone walls and crusted the floor. Charred roof beams dangled from the ceiling. Stone Ghost stared closely at the finely fitted rocks, many no larger than the palm of his hand.

"People hide the most curious things. Imagine, this fine stonework, and they covered it with plaster." He canted an eye toward Browser. "Just like people, wouldn't you say?"

"He went this way." Browser walked across the room and ducked through the low doorway into the next chamber.

Sunlight slanted through the gaping hole over Browser's head. He could see a mound of fallen stone resting on the lip of the hole. The beams sagged beneath its weight. "Careful, here, Uncle. A good breath of wind will cause this ceiling to come crashing down.

Stone Ghost entered, gazed up at the hole, and silently followed Browser through two more rooms.

Browser stepped into the next room and the rounded wall of a small clan kiva curved to his right. He hadn't seen that last night.

Stone Ghost whispered, "Is this as far as you went the other night?"

"Yes, Elder." Browser held his torch high, illuminating the litter on the floor. A layer of fine dust and ash covered burned beams, half-rotten wood, old plaster, and torn matting. Footprints had churned up the dust.

Browser identified his own prints, and Jackrabbit's. The third set mystified him. The man had been wearing yucca sandals. Browser knelt and measured the prints against his hand.

Stone Ghost whispered, "My feet are bigger than his."

Browser rose and narrowed his eyes. "His tracks lead around the curve of the kiva."

Browser walked forward cautiously, searching every pile of rubbish.

"Through there," Stone Ghost pointed to a corner doorway, partially obscured by the sagging roof poles. "I would say, Nephew, that's how he managed to lose you the night your warrior was killed. There, behind the fallen timbers, see it?"

Browser walked forward, following the curving wall, until he saw the ladder stuffed into the corner. Above it, a small hole let sunlight into the chamber.

"It appears," Browser murmured, "that the killer climbed back up on the roof, then dropped on Whi— my warrior."

Stone Ghost came up behind Browser and frowned at the doorway. "Let's make sure, Nephew."

Browser nodded, handed the torch to Stone Ghost, and set the ladder into the hole. "Be ready for anything, Uncle," he whispered, and took the torch back.

Browser climbed slowly, listening for sounds from above. He heard nothing. He climbed out into a small rectangular room. The curiously rich and earthy smell confused him for a moment. The floor beneath his feet felt soft. He helped Stone Ghost up and frowned.

"What is this spongy brown layer we're standing on? My moccasins are sinking into it."

Something fluttered on the ceiling, and Browser whirled to look up. No more than an arm's length away, the roof seemed to be moving, undulating in the heat of the torch.

Browser flinched. "Bats."

He hated bats. Creatures of the night, they associated with owls and shared the same skies with witches.

"I don't think they like your torch," Stone Ghost whispered. "It's the middle of the winter. They want to be asleep. Bats are a great deal smarter than people. If you sleep all winter, you don't have to go out in the cold, or store food, and gather wood. Let's leave them in peace."

Browser lowered his torch and picked his way across the droppings into the next room. The entire ceiling had collapsed, covering the floor with crossed beams, stones, and powdered plaster. His haste to get away from the bats almost killed him.

"Oh, dear gods!" he shouted, and stumbled back as the floor beneath his feet gave way and crashed down.

Stone Ghost grabbed Browser's cape and tugged him backward through the doorway.

Dust rose in a smothering veil.

"Thank you, Elder." Browser gasped for a breath and fought to still his pounding heart.

"That was close, Nephew." Stone Ghost poked his head past Browser's shoulder and peered down into the darkness. "Lift your torch. Let's see what's down there."

Nerving himself, Browser stepped back into the doorway and raised the torch. The fallen floor lay in a heap in the center of the room, but beautiful black-and-white pottery lined the walls, dust-streaked and stained with packrat urine. In one corner lay a desiccated coyote, in another, a bobcat, apparently animals that had fallen in and couldn't find a way out.

"Where do we go from here, Uncle?" Browser asked.

Stone Ghost pointed. "The killer went that way. If you will notice, the dust and packrat pellets have been kicked off around the edge of the wall to the right. The dirt has also been polished by someone's sandals."

"What kind of fool would edge his way around this rickety floor?"

Stone Ghost smiled. "The kind who has done it many times, Nephew." Stone Ghost edged out onto the path, hugging the wall.

"Uncle, wait! What makes you think a man made that trail? It might have been a coyote or a bobcat."

"Come, Nephew," Stone Ghost whispered. "If this is the killer's trail, it will support our weight."

"I don't like this, Uncle. It's not safe!" But Browser held his torch low and felt his way around the gaping hole, following in Stone Ghost's footsteps. "If I go crashing down—!"

"You won't, Nephew," Stone Ghost called from where he waited in the T-shape doorway on the opposite wall. "Look around you. The spiders tell us this is the trail of the killer."

Browser finished the perilous journey without falling into the abyss and even more miraculously, without setting himself afire. He slipped into the doorway beside Stone Ghost.

Stone Ghost stuck his head into the next room and sniffed loudly.

Browser gripped his uncle's bony shoulder. "This time, I'm going first, Uncle."

Browser stepped by him into the next chamber. Two ladders led into the chamber above. There was no other way out. Browser lowered his torch to the floor around the ladders.

Ceramic beads from a broken necklace scattered the dust, along with smashed pottery, and pieces of a basket The plaster on the wall to his right had cracked off, leaving only the head and shoulders of the Badger katsina. The masked god stared at Browser through glittering blue eyes. The artist must have mixed ground turquoise with his paint.

Bracing a hand on the ladder, Browser lifted the torch.

Stone Ghost sniffed again. "Wait, Nephew. Notice the air?"

Browser sniffed. "What about it?"

"It's still. No wind." He pointed to the thick spider-webs that filled the corners of the room. "Raise your torch high. No wind penetrates this chamber, but look at the webs. How many have you wiped from your face so far?"

Browser lifted the torch. "None, Elder."

"See, the spiders tell us that someone, at least as tall as we are, walked here before us."

Browser's eyes widened. "I understand."

He tested the strength of the ladder and climbed up into the next chamber. There were two doorways, one on either side of the room. An intact web hung from the lintel in front of Browser. The web on the door behind him, however, was gone.

He reached down to help Stone Ghost off the ladder.

The old man licked his lips and sighed. "Which door, War Chief?"

"This one, Uncle." Browser led the way.

As he stepped into the small, dark chamber, the

light of his torch gleamed over corncobs, a splintered war club, and shreds of dusty cloth.

A path had been kicked through the clutter into the next room. Browser followed it. When he ducked into the next room, he stopped suddenly. "Uncle, come and see this."

The sound of Stone Ghost's steps crunching on broken pottery seemed loud in the stillness.

Browser walked forward. The man's skeleton lay hunched in the far corner, propped against the wall, and covered with a crumbling stack of mats. Mice had gnawed the extended leg bones, but a single patch of hair clung to the rear of the skull.

Browser lowered his torch and pulled back the mats to examine the man. A broken arrow shaft, partially packrat gnawed, lodged in his ribs like a malignant sliver.

Stone Ghost bent over Browser. "He's been here for a long time."

Browser let the mats down and straightened. "Do you think he was one of the First People?"

"Perhaps. But if so, someone in the past one hundred sun cycles stole his turquoise wolf pendant. All of the First People had one." Stone Ghost gestured to the next doorway. "Have you looked in there yet, Nephew?"

"No, Uncle."

Browser walked to the entry and thrust his torch inside.

Behind him, he heard Stone Ghost whisper to the dead man, "No, I'm sorry. I haven't seen the Blessed Sternlight."

Browser's grip tightened on the torch handle.

"Uncle, isn't Sternlight the priest who first brought word of the Katsinas? Back in the days before the Blessed Poor Singer became a prophet?"

"Yes, that's right," Stone Ghost answered, and casually stepped by Browser into the next chamber. "He was captured and killed by the Fire Dogs."

Browser's skin prickled as he followed the old man through the chamber toward the ladder that stood in the hole in the floor. The air had a musty, heavy feeling.

Stone Ghost gripped the poles of the ladder and started to step onto the rungs.

"Uncle, please don't do that," Browser said and trotted forward.

His breathing had gone hoarse, as if he'd been running for days. Despite the cool air, perspiration soaked his war shirt.

"Very well, Nephew," Stone Ghost said and stood aside.

"Thank you." Browser climbed down two rungs and extended his torch into the chamber. In the corner to his right, a shining mass of what looked like wet rope lay. The opposite corner was filled with over a dozen standing poles, as if someone had brought them in to shore up the roof, but hadn't used them yet.

Browser climbed down and waited.

Stone Ghost panted as he descended, and his legs were shaking.

Browser gripped his arm and supported him to the floor.

Stone Ghost smiled and turned.

He froze.

Browser spun around, searching the room for some threat he'd missed.

"Easy, Nephew," Stone Ghost whispered. "It's the middle of the winter. I think if we stay away from them, they won't bother us."

"What?" Browser held out his torch.

"I wouldn't do that, if I were you. They are dormant now, but like all of their kind, heat brings them to life."

"Blessed Katsinas!" Browser leapt back with his heart in his throat. "I didn't see them!"

His torch sparkled from a hundred eyes. Their triangular heads rested on gleaming scales. The diamond patterns on their backs resembled mottled weavings.

"I don't think the rattlesnakes arrived here the same way that we did, Nephew." Stone Ghost looked around. "There must be another entrance."

The old man picked his way through the crumbling matting that scattered the floor and headed into the blackness to the left.

Somewhere above them, a rodent scurried across plaster, its claws clicking.

"Ah," Stone Ghost barely whispered. "Here, we have it."

Browser followed. Only the faint hissing of the burning grease, and the sputter of the flames could be heard.

Stone Ghost walked behind the upright poles and vanished. Browser ran after him.

As he stepped into the chamber, a cold shaft of light shot across the room to illuminate a spiral painted on the far wall.

"It's a solstice room," Stone Ghost said as he walked toward a large oblong bundle in the middle of the floor. It was wrapped in yellow cloth, and two small pots sat on either side of it. Each pot had a flat piece of sandstone waxed to the rim to seal the pot. "Since we are nearing that day, the spiral behind you is illuminated. At any other time of the year, however, this room will be in shadow."

The old man bent down next to the bundle and frowned.

"What is that, Uncle?" Browser examined the room behind them, then turned back.

"You wouldn't have to ask if you were closer. The smell of rotting flesh is very distinctive, even wrapped in thick fabric."

Browser leaned against the door frame, where he could watch their back trail. "Human, or animal?"

"I don't know yet."

Stone Ghost began unwrapping the yellow fabric.

He had to tug the last layer loose from the blood-caked skull. The bones of the nose, cheeks, forehead, and jaw had been crushed. The hair was cut short in mourning.

Browser suddenly felt lightheaded. Blood pounded in his ears as he stepped forward. "Uncle..."

Stone Ghost ripped the cloth away to expose the ribs, the empty gut, and hips. The bones had been stripped. The thigh bones were welded stiffly to the pelvis by dried ligament and tendon. Even the thin strips of muscle between the ribs had been cut out.

"Curious." Stone Ghost reached down, and slipped off the anklet that adorned her foot. Made of carved jet beads threaded on a braided yucca string, it was beautiful. He slid it onto his own wrist and reached for the bracelet.

"Blessed Katsinas," Browser whispered.

He ran forward and bent over the corpse. The familiar jet bracelet, carved into the shape of a serpent, caught the weak solstice light.

"Uncle, this... I-I..." he stammered and stared at the desiccated body, searching for any feature that looked familiar. "That bracelet belonged to my wife. Do you think this woman is actually... I mean, maybe the woman in the grave was someone else?"

"It's possible, Nephew."

Browser's knees went weak. "If this is my wife, what happened to her? Uncle? Why is her—her flesh gone?"

"Perhaps there is a more important question, Nephew. Perhaps you should be asking if either of the women was your wife."

His breathing seemed to stop. "Are you saying she's alive?"

"Not necessarily. Not in the way you think."

"I don't understand. What are you talking about? If my wife were alive, she would have come home."

A solemn expression came over Stone Ghost, as though he were pondering something too monstrous to imagine. "Yes. Of course, Nephew."

The dawn horizon glowed with an eerie luminescence that only a desert could spawn. Maureen tipped her head back, enchanted by the sight, wondering at the diffuse pastel aurora. The lilting calls of coyotes rang from the canyon walls.

All night long, she had walked down the dirt road,

alternately cursing Stewart, and teetering around the edges of the abyss left by John's death.

Around midnight, she had ended up in the huge ruins of the giant pueblo where she now sat on a low sandstone wall, shivering, hunched over for warmth. How could a place roast you during the day, and freeze you at night?

Whether she looked inside herself or out at the grease-wood, chamisa, and sagebrush, the view was the same: Dry, empty, and lonely.

The first plaintive songs of the morning birds filled the air. Bats fluttered around the dark face of the cliff to her left. She watched them in an odd haze of memory, seeing John's body sprawled on the kitchen floor, his wide eyes staring sightlessly into hers, feeling his hand, all the strength and warmth gone. The stench of burning spaghetti sauce mixed poignantly with the fragrances of the desert and dawn. She'd come home late from a faculty meeting. The shock of finding him still numbed her.

Maureen rubbed her arms.

She wanted to go home. This wasn't her place. None of her ancestors had ever trod this sere landscape. Her place was faraway. Cool, with slow, dark rivers, and billowing white clouds. The spirits of her ancestors, Seneca and white, moved in the Ontario shadows, not here.

She surveyed the ruins. Tumbled, ghostly walls— the wreckage of ancient dreams—thrust up around her. To her right, the gaping circle of a kiva yawned. A wooden marker bearing a white "10" indicated that she had stopped at some tourist point-of-interest. She rose from the stone wall and stared into the giant subterranean ceremonial chamber. Eyes seemed to peer back at her from the shadowed depths. For the briefest of moments, she could have sworn she heard singing, then the booming of a jet high overhead drowned it out.

She rubbed her eyes. "You're tired. Hurting. You've been up all night wandering around with ghosts. No wonder you're hearing things."

After John's death, she'd worked herself pitilessly, never missing a class. Weekends had been the worst. She'd rushed to her car after her last class, driven down Queen Elizabeth Way to her favorite liquor store in Niagara-on-the-Lake, then gone to their lonely home, locked herself in, and drunk herself into oblivion. Beyond feeling. Beyond any...

The sound of gravel crunching under a boot made her turn.

He stood silhouetted against the dawn, tall, his blond hair shining. A stab of fear went through her in that instant before she placed the rumpled straw cowboy hat.

"Get away from me, Stewart."

He thrust his thumbs into his jeans' pockets, as if cowed. "I'm truly sorry, Maureen."

"You certainly are."

He winced, shifted uneasily, and looked at the sunrise. The iridescent sky glittered with bands of indigo and orange. "I've been tracking you all night. It's given me a lot of time to think."

"You? Think? Did it give you a headache?" She crossed her arms, not wanting to shiver against the cold. Not in front of him.

His face was in profile, but she saw his brow line. "Tracking you wasn't so bad at first. In the moonlight, I could follow your tracks down the dust to the road. After that, I had to search every room in Kin Kletso and Pueblo del Arroyo. You wouldn't believe the size of the rattlesnake I stepped on. I guess he lives in the Mesa Verdean addition over at Arroyo."

She looked at the ruins to the south. "Mesa Verdean addition?"

He nodded. "Anasazi migrants. They reinhabited the canyon around A.D. twelve-fifty." He pointed behind her. "They also rebuilt the great kiva behind you. Roofed it, plastered it, painted it. We think it was a messianic movement, maybe the start of the kachina religion."

She took a deep breath. "What's the name of this place?"

The massive stone walls had solidified in the growing light. "This is Pueblo Bonito. Up until about eighteen-thirty, it was the largest building in North America. As best we can guess, it stood five stories tall and had over eight hundred rooms. When it gets a little lighter, I'll take you around. The masonry will stun you."

She could see the regret in his eyes. He really was trying hard to apologize.

"You're an enigma to me, Stewart. I can't figure you out."

To her surprise, he said, "That's all right, I'm an enigma to myself. I have this black place inside me. I don't like to admit it, but it's there. Sometimes, it opens up, and I say outrageous things like I did last night. Then I spend the rest of my life kicking myself for it."

"For the sake of efficiency, I hope your knees are double-jointed."

He peered down into the shadowed depths of the kiva. After a long silence, he added, "A lot of Power was concentrated down there. You can still feel it. Some good, some bad. The old gods still dance, echoing the beginning times and the journey up from the underworlds." He paused. "That black place inside me, it's my own kiva, I guess. I keep the past locked up in there."

As though uncomfortable, he bowed his head. "I'm going to dig that unit you want me to."

Maureen frowned, trying to figure his angle. "Why?"

He vented a deep sigh. "If we don't, we'll never know which of us is right. Is it a slaves' burial ground, or a murderer's hiding place?"

She gave him an askance look. "Can we dig the unit? Will Maggie authorize it?"

"Well," he said and scanned the brightening sky. "It's about three miles back to the site and asking her that exact question. Which means we ought to get started." He held out a hand. "If you're ready."

"Do you need to rest?" Little Bow asked
Marsh Hawk.

She stood bent over, her beautiful
round face twisted in agony. Marsh Hawk's cough had
grown worse. She could barely take ten steps before
another fit doubled her over.

Marsh Hawk shook her head. "No, I am well
enough, husband, and it—it isn't much farther. When
we get there I will have all night to rest." The curly
brown hair on her buffalo cape looked black in the
twilight.

Since noon, they had been falling farther and
farther behind, straggling at the rear of the Frosted
Meadow procession. His brother, Singing Mantis,
walked just ahead of them, his bow in his hand,
anxiously studying the canyon bottom.

Little Bow stroked Marsh Hawk's shoulder-length
black hair. "Very well, but I am planning to rest on the
other side of the wash."

She smiled. "All right, husband. I will do as you say."

As Sister Moon rose higher into the sky, her silver gleam flooded the canyon, shimmering in the twisted junipers and outlining every dark crevice in the sandstone walls. Shadows draped the rocky rim like a string of polished black beads.

Ahead of them, Talon Town gleamed. The fifth story had collapsed into a heap of jutting timbers and fallen stones. Most of the plaster had cracked off and scattered the ground around the enormous half-moon-shaped structure like a dirty white apron, but torches burned everywhere, and he could smell the scent of cedar fires and frying bread. To the right of the town, Hillside Village sat against the cliff, white and rectangular. A large fire burned in the plaza.

Many small camps scattered the flats, and he could see groups of people standing in the wavering firelight.

"Hallowed Ancestors," he murmured. "I would not have believed it if I hadn't seen it with my own eyes. Talon Town looks alive."

His great-grandmother, the Blessed Horned Bird, had told him many tales of the rise and fall of the grandest town in the Straight Path nation. On cold winter nights, she'd held Little Bow close and whispered of the wicked First People and their evil courtship of the lost ghosts who roamed the canyon.

She had often spoken about the Blessed Cornsilk. Her father had been a great warrior, one of the Made People and her mother had been the highest Matron in the land. Horned Bird had vowed that if Cornsilk had only taken her rightful, place as Matron of Talon Town when Night Sun left, the Straight Path nation would still be strong: "The Blessed Cornsilk would have built alliances, not waged wars. She would have extended the trade routes so her people would have had food in the dark times. Cornsilk would have sniffed out the plots and stopped the First People before they started hiring assassins to take each other's lives."

Then, immediately after telling this story about the great and Blessed Cornsilk, Horned Bird would speak in low tones about the death of the last of the First People, and the celebration that lasted for a full sun cycle.

Marsh Hawk started down the road into the steep, jagged ravine, and Little Bow followed. Gravel grated beneath his sandals.

"You don't think that crazy old man will be here, do you?"

Over her shoulder Marsh Hawk called, "Everyone else is coming. I don't see why Stone Ghost wouldn't."

Little Bow leaped the trickle of water flowing in the bottom of the wash and started up the opposite side of the drainage. Marsh Hawk weaved in front of him and started coughing, the sound raw and wet.

He trotted to her side and wrapped an arm around her shoulders, holding her up while she trembled and gasped. The effort coaxed tears from her eyes. Marsh Hawk leaned against him until the fit passed, then she gulped air and wiped her face with her hand.

"I'm sorry, husband. I know I'm the reason we have fallen so far behind."

She rested her chin on his shoulder, and Little Bow hugged her. Her swollen belly pressed comfortingly against him. He patted her back. "In a finger of time, we will catch up."

He held her as they climbed up out of the wash and onto the sandy flats. Moonlight sheathed the desert, casting odd shadows. Mixed with the flickering amber glow cast by Talon Town and the fires of the smaller camps, the shadows seemed to crawl toward them in a rush, then scamper away as if frightened by their human scents.

"I want you to sit down and rest, my wife. You are ill and with child. A few moments will harm no one."

Marsh Hawk sank to the ground and heaved a tired breath. "Just a few moments, Little Bow, then we'll be on our way."

"Rest as long as you need to. We are in sight of the town. This night will be filled with nothing but reminiscences and feasting anyway. Tomorrow, the holy work begins."

As he knelt by her side, an uneasy sensation crept through Little Bow. He squinted for a long moment at the darkness, wondering what had happened to everyone else. They must have descended into a dip, or perhaps the firelight had blinded him. A large boulder tipped precariously over the bank to his left. Little Bow reached for his club. The boulder cast an oddly shaped shadow. His souls could conjure the shape of a tall man's shoulder, and a leg almost hidden by the rock. He stared at it.

"Look, husband. The rest of the village is almost there," Marsh Hawk said and tipped her chin toward the fire blazing in front of Hillside village.

The first in a straggling line of people walked into the crowd, and voices rose. Matron Corn Mother strode directly toward a woman wearing a red-feathered cape, and they embraced.

"That must be Flame Carrier."

"Yes," Marsh Hawk said. "The new Matron of Talon Town."

Little Bow smiled at the irony. Flame Carrier was one of the Made People, a member of the Ant Clan, masons, architects, and artists. The First People's ghosts locked inside Talon Town must be shrieking at the insult.

He dragged his gaze away. Inside Talon Town, he could just see the upper torsos of the Great Warriors. The eye sockets in their fierce masks gleamed with a curious fire, as if anxiously gazing beyond the people, and the camps, to the desert where Marsh Hawk and Little Bow knelt. Little Bow had the discomforting feeling that they saw something he did not.

He put a hand on Marsh Hawk's shoulder. "If you are rested, wife, we should go."

She looked up. "I thought you told me to take as long as I wished, husband?"

"I did, but..." he paused, his senses suddenly on alert. An owl hooted in the darkness, and he caught sight of a dark body sailing over their heads. "I think we should leave."

Marsh Hawk shoved to her feet and scanned the moonlit desert. Barely audible, she murmured, "Why? What do you—"

He cut the air with a fist. *"Walk."*

She did.

Little Bow drew his war club and held it at his side. He followed on his wife's heels, protecting her back.

"Shh," someone hissed from behind them.

In one fluid movement, Little Bow shoved Marsh

Hawk to the ground, and whirled around with his club up. "Who's there?"

A shadow detached itself from the boulder, and hoarsely whispered, *"Run away before it's too late!"*

Little Bow took a step toward the man. "Who are you?"

"Great evil lurks in these ruins, Little Bow. Did they not tell you?" He sucked in a desperate breath, as though he'd been running for a hand of time to get here. The shadow seemed to turn around, as if fearfully gazing over his shoulder. *"If you do not leave, you will have to do battle with the Wolf Witch, the most powerful witch in the world. Leave. Now!"*

Little Bow's mouth dropped open, but no words came.

The shadow hissed, *"Ask them about the ashes. Ask them, Little Bow."*

"What ashes? What are you talking about?"

The man seemed to dissipate into the air. The shadow vanished.

"Wa-wait!" Little Bow called. "Who are you? I don't understand!"

Marsh Hawk cautiously sat up, her eyes wide with fear. Pale sand caked the front of her buffalo cape. Neither of them spoke for three or four hundred heartbeats, then Marsh Hawk whispered, "Hurry. Let's go."

Little Bow wavered. If he'd been on a war walk, he would have run the man down, and demanded an explanation at the point of a deerbone stiletto, but he couldn't leave his pregnant wife alone in the darkness.

Little Bow reached down and helped Marsh Hawk to her feet. She was shaking, her gaze on the place where the man had vanished.

"Stay to my right," Little Bow instructed. "Walk quickly, but do not run. I must watch and listen. If you get too far ahead of me, I cannot protect you."

Marsh Hawk nodded.

They started for Hillside village.

He heard nothing. No steps. No breathing. No leggings catching on brush.

But the owl's shadow wheeled over the ground, as if circling them.

Little Bow dared not look, but his heart fluttered. What if the man were a witch? Witches were canny. They could change themselves into whirlwinds, and careen around villages unnoticed, or leap through magical hoops of twisted yucca fibers, and turn themselves into animals.

They were especially fond of night birds.

It took all of his strength, but he kept his gaze on the surrounding brush, searching for a human foe. Ordinary flesh and blood could be killed. He did not know about enchanted witches.

When they came to within fifty paces of the crowd in Hillside village, Little Bow turned to Marsh Hawk and shouted, *"Run!"*

She gripped handfuls of her long skirt and ran hard, her hair flying out behind her.

Only when she had entered the crowd, did Little Bow grant himself the luxury of flight. He whirled and his muscular legs drove into the ground. He blasted into the crowd, and shouldered through the sea of people, following his wife.

Marsh Hawk saw him behind her and stopped. Little Bow waved her ahead. "Go on!" he called. "Tell Corn Mother."

Marsh Hawk headed for her.

Corn Mother halted her conversation with Flame Carrier. Her wise old eyes fixed on Marsh Hawk.

Marsh Hawk knelt before Corn Mother, and breathlessly said, "Matron, forgive me, but we must speak with you."

"What is it, child?" Corn Mother clasped the hood of her blue-and-white-striped cape at the throat. Thick gray hair stuck out around her hood, and her skeletal face, with its jutting lower jaw, appeared unnaturally pale in the fire's sheen.

Flame Carrier, who sat beside her, frowned. She had small narrow eyes, and a bulbous nose. A few kinky gray hairs made up her eyebrows. She sat on a deerhide, dressed in a beautiful red macaw-feather cape.

It took Little Bow a while to work his way through the two hundred or more people in the plaza. Some sat in small groups, others stood, talking and laughing.

"Forgive us, Elders," he said as he bowed to the matrons, "but this is urgent."

Corn Mother searched his face, then Marsh Hawk's, and said, "Tell me."

"A man stopped us at the wash, Matron. Well, I—I think it was a man," Marsh Hawk corrected herself. "It seemed to be a man."

Flame Carrier's expression turned grave. She quietly asked, "What man?"

"We could not see him, Matron," Marsh Hawk answered, "but he called to us from the shadows."

"Yes?" Corn Mother asked. "What did he say?"

"He said that great evil lurked in these ruins, Matron, and told us if we stayed here we would have to do battle with the Wolf Witch, the most powerful witch in the world."

"He said something else, Matron," Little Bow added. "He told us to ask about the ashes."

"Then vanished into the night."

Corn Mother mouthed the words: *the Wolf Witch*.

Flame Carrier gripped her arm. "Do you know what that means?"

The people closest to them went silent, and their gazes riveted on the matrons. A din of whispering broke out.

Corn Mother said, "Stories. I remember stories from when I was a child."

The crowd rearranged itself, creeping forward, forming a ring around the two old women.

Another coughing fit struck Marsh Hawk. She tried to cover the sound with both hands. The fit affected her like a seizure, her whole body tensed, and quaked.

Little Bow slid over, put his arm around Marsh Hawk's back, and drew her against him.

Matron Corn Mother waited until the fit had eased then began slowly, as if the words took effort. "It began about one hundred sun cycles ago. They knew they were in trouble. They began sealing exterior windows and doorways—actually walling them up with stone and mortar. Talon Town was originally open in the front, allowing people to come and go as they wished. Did you know that?"

"No, Elder," Little Bow answered.

"Yes, when they first grew scared, they built that string of rooms on the south side, but they left two gates. Then they closed off the gate to the eastern half of the plaza and narrowed the western gate to the width of an ordinary doorway. Finally, that gate, too, was walled off. They even closed the small vents that allowed air to circulate through the town. The only way in or out was over the walls by ladder."

"It must have been difficult for the elderly and the sick," Marsh Hawk said.

"That was the least of their concerns. The First People who lived in Talon Town were being murdered one by one. Their bodies were thrown into shallow graves. Stones were dropped over their heads to keep their wicked souls locked in the ground forever. When the town was abandoned, the bones of those people became priceless. To witches." She laced her hands in her lap and gazed into the faces of her listeners. "About —oh, let me see—it must be fifteen summers now—the most powerful witch in the land moved into Talon Town. He was called the Wolf Witch, but his real name was Two Hearts."

"Two Hearts?" Flame Carrier said.

"Yes. Blessed gods, he was evil. Common witches gather putrefying corpse flesh to make their corpse powder, but legends say that Two Hearts made his from the bones of stranded ghosts. By grinding the bones, and carrying the powder with him, he could force a ghost to do anything—even kill entire villages of people. He—"

From the rear of the crowd a man shouted, *"His corpse powder was always lethal because he made it from the bones of First People!"*

Villagers began shuffling back, shoving each other to get out of the way. In the narrow alley that formed, Stone Ghost appeared, wearing the same ratty turkey-feather cape he'd worn days ago at Frosted Meadow village.

Little Bow gaped.

The old man was covered head to toe with gray ash. He hobbled forward, and extended his cupped hands, as if silently asking people to look at what he carried. "Even a single grain of Two Hearts' corpse powder could kill. Several people in nearby villages had this powder sprinkled in their hair and died writhing like clubbed dogs." More loudly, he added, "And it was rumored that Two Hearts stashed entire pots of corpse powder in the burials of people he truly hated. To drive their souls mad for eternity!"

A roar went through the gathering.

Little Bow shuddered. He could imagine no more terrible curse. Even in death the witch's enemies could not escape his evil.

As Stone Ghost came closer, Little Bow craned his neck, trying to see what the old man held.

Stone Ghost grinned, stopping often to allow puzzled people to look into his hands. His sparse white hair stuck out as though he stood on a high mountain during a lightning storm. The dark age spots on his scalp showed through the thick layer of ash.

"What's he been doing?" Little Bow whispered to Marsh Hawk. "Sleeping in the trash mound?"

As Stone Ghost came closer, he spied Corn Mother and a look of genuine excitement brightened his face. "My dear Corn Mother!" he called. "How good to see you again. I hope you buried that footprint as I instruct-ed." He shouldered between Little Bow, and Marsh Hawk, dumped his rocks at Corn Mother's side. Then he reached out, seized her hand. "We wouldn't want to have it running around trampling people's souls."

"I buried it properly." Corn Mother jerked her hand away. "What happened to you? You look like someone shoved you face-first into an old fire pit!"

"Well, that's almost right," he said, and flopped down on the hide beside Corn Mother. As he brushed at his filthy cape, a choking veil of ash rose.

Corn Mother waved at it. "Where did you find so much ash?"

"Hmm?" Stone Ghost said, and his eyes narrowed, as if he'd no idea what she meant. "What? Oh! It's remarkable what a man must do to dig out the truth. You see, I thought it was very odd that there was no woodpile beside the ritual fire. Wouldn't you think that odd? The Sunwatcher knew the burial would last for another hand of time, and she would be responsible for burning the boy's clothing, and then smoking the burial participants in pinyon smoke to cleanse them. Why wasn't there a woodpile?"

Corn Mother turned to Flame Carrier. "What's he talking about?"

Flame Carrier's face turned a mottled crimson. "I knew there was something strange that day, but the woodpile...gods, I should have noticed."

Stone Ghost scooped up the rocks he'd dropped, gathering them into a pile before him. As he began to arrange them, he said, "After I thought about the missing woodpile, another thought occurred to me. You know how, on a freezing night, snow falls into a fire, melts, puts out flames, then freezes over the ash bed?"

"Of course. What of it?" Corn Mother squinted.

Flame Carrier released her blue-and-white hood

and bent forward to point at the white rocks. "What are those?"

"That," he said, and shook a finger, "is the question, Matron."

Stone Ghost lifted a rock, turned it on end, and tried to fit it to another rock, as if reassembling a shattered pot.

Little Bow gestured to the rocks. "Where did you find them?"

"Beneath the ice in the ash bed. That's why the mysterious messenger tonight told you to ask about the ashes. It took half the day, but I finally sifted them out."

The hair at the nape of Little Bow's neck tingled. "How did he know you would be looking through an ash bed?"

"He watched me until well after sunset. He knows what this is, of course."

"What?"

"I said *he* knows, Little Bow, I don't."

Little Bow gave Marsh Hawk an askance look. The rocks had broken jaggedly, along the tiny white lines that veined the stones. Such fractures appeared when you threw a chert cobble into a very hot fire and it exploded.

"You think this was once whole?" he asked. "Like a hammerstone?"

"I think it was whole, yes. Here." He shoved several rocks toward Little Bow. "Help me piece it together."

Little Bow squatted. The white chert cobble had probably been pulled from a creek bed, but what it had been used for, he could not tell. "Who is the man who spoke to us, Elder?"

"How would I know?"

"Well, if you saw him watching you, you must know—"

"I never saw him."

Little Bow's mouth quirked. He debated asking the old fool how he could possibly have known he was being spied upon if he never saw the spy, then decided against it. He suspected Stone Ghost would just spout something equally ridiculous.

The evening's merriment had faded to an eerie anxiety. Only the people on the farthest edges of the plaza continued to talk and laugh. At least one hundred people ringed them, listening.

"Tell me, Little Bow, the man who stopped you tonight, was he tall?"

"Yes, Elder."

"Slender? Or a heavy, broad-chested man?"

"We could not see him very well, Elder. He clung to the shadows. But I would say heavy."

Moonlit clouds massed over the towering sandstone wall behind Hillside Village, blotting out the Evening People. Thunderbirds slept in the clouds, their deep voices rumbling.

"Elder, is it possible that the man who spoke to us is the Wolf Witch?"

Stone Ghost fitted six pieces together, and the object began to take shape. It resembled an elongated egg, a little more pointed on one end than the other. "I cannot answer that. If so, he has seen the passing of at least fifty-five sun cycles."

Marsh Hawk said, "This man was much younger, Elder. He—"

Corn Mother interrupted, "Witches can prolong

their lives by removing their relatives' hearts with a spindle and putting the hearts into their own chests."

"Yes, that's true," Stone Ghost said, "but it is difficult for me to believe that Two Hearts is alive. I have not heard anyone speak of him in at least fifteen summers. Witches are vain. They take pride in their despicable acts. If Two Hearts is alive and working evil, he would make certain people knew."

Little Bow picked up a rock and fitted it in place. "Hmm," he said, "this piece is grooved. Do you see this?"

Stone Ghost's eyes flared. He pulled Little Bow's hand close to examine the groove. "Where does it go? Can you tell?"

Little Bow turned it over, tipped the rock up, and placed it in the middle. It wasn't connected to any other pieces, but that's where it went. The smooth outer edge of the stone fitted the curving line of the "egg."

"Elder," Little Bow said, then paused while he thought about Talon Town and Two Hearts. "Why did the First People seal up every window and door? Were they afraid of witches? Fire Dogs?"

Stone Ghost looked up, and their gazes held. "Neither, warrior. Humans can fight witches. Humans can fight Fire Dogs. What they often cannot fight are the shadows that whisper to them from their own souls. That's what they were afraid of. As we all should be."

Little Bow tilted his head, wondering what that meant. Shadows whispering from the souls? Lofty sounding nonsense. He fitted another rock into place.

As he drew back his hand, he paused. "Elder," he said, and studied the emerging shape. "This is the head of a war club."

Stone Ghost froze with a rock halfway to the blanket. White hair fluttered around his face and tangled with his stubby eyelashes. He did not bother to brush it aside. His dark pained eyes lifted to Flame Carrier.

"Matron, would you send for my nephew?"

The sharpened edge of the shovel caught on roots as Dusty lifted and tossed the dirt into Maureen's screen. She threw her weight into rocking the mesh-bottom box. Dirt cascaded through onto the back-dirt pile.

All in all, it hadn't been too traumatic. Maggie had reluctantly agreed. Dale had crossed his arms and firmly forbade them to make further excavations outside the designated impact area. His bulldog jaw had been set, his wiry gray hair poking out from under his fedora.

Dusty had immediately set up the transit, and while Maureen held the rod, shot in the elevation for the control corner. He wanted to get it down before anybody had time to reconsider. After they'd measured out the two-by-two unit, he'd started digging.

Sylvia knelt in her unit ten paces away, continuing the slow process of skeletal removal. Maggie and Hail sat under the ramada, sipping tea, talking softly.

Dusty took a minute to pull the line level tight and extended his tape measure to check the depth of his pit floor while Maureen sifted through the root mat, gravels, and small stones in the screen.

"This is hard work." Maureen sighed, flipped the junk out of the screen, and wiped her forehead on her white T-shirt sleeve. "I'm going to have great arm muscles when I get back to Ontario."

"And every other kind of muscle," Dusty said, as he jotted notes on his clipboard. "There are no out-of-shape, pudgy women archaeologists. Unless they're *academicians*," he said the word like a five-syllable curse.

Maureen leaned on the screen. "Did your mother excavate or just do cultural fieldwork?"

Dusty hesitated, his pen hovering over his clipboard. Without looking up, he said, "If I talk about my mother, I don't want any flippant comebacks from you, all right?"

"Sure."

Dusty took a deep breath. "She never sank a trowel. She never washed a potsherd. Her kind of fieldwork was walking around a village, taking notes about what people were wearing or eating. If she ever got dirty, she went into town and took a shower, so she'd look 'pretty' the next day. The Zuni used to make jokes about her behind her back. They called her 'The-Woman-with-No-Eyes,' because she never looked at them, just her papers."

Maureen toyed with a root that had lodged in the hardware cloth of the screen. "She must have had a knack for languages though, if she could understand what they were saying."

"She did." He left it at that.

Maureen worked the root out of the screen and

tossed it onto the dirt pile. "How did you end up with Dale?"

Dusty finished making his notes, closed his clipboard, and set it aside. "There wasn't anybody else. After Dad..."

"When did he die?"

He met her gaze. "Actually, that's the wrong word. He didn't just die. He killed himself."

To his surprise, her voice softened. "Were you the one who found him?"

He shook his head. "No. A nurse in the hospital did."

Maureen rubbed her fingers along the wooden rim of the screen. "I found John. He'd been making dinner. He was in the kitchen. I came home late."

She had said the words matter-of-factly, but he heard the buried pain.

"My father electrocuted himself. The nurse said that he didn't give any sign. Just took off his slippers, jumped up on the sink, and by the time the orderly got the door open, Dad had unscrewed the lightbulb, and stuck his finger into the socket. He had his bare foot on the metal faucet."

Dusty sank his shovel again, and Maureen extended the screen to catch the dirt. She sifted it back and forth, before reaching down and lifting something. "Potsherd," she said, and flipped it to him.

Bracing the shovel handle on his hip, Dusty rubbed it clean with his thumb, and studied the decoration. "Mesa Verde Black-on-white. I'd say we're coming down on our cultural layer. You're going to have to go over and fill out an artifact bag for this level."

"On my way." She let the screen down, and walked for the green ammo box where Dusty kept supplies.

He studied the ground, looking for the soil discoloration that indicated the old ground surface. Root casts —the places where brush had grown, died, rotted, and been refilled with dirt trickling down from above— spotted the soil.

Maureen pulled a Ziploc sandwich bag from the dig kit. She used a Sharpie pen to mark it with the unit provenience, and level depth.

She was a striking woman.

He smiled grimly at himself. He'd known a lot of striking women. They tended to gravitate to him. They usually hung around for about two weeks, just enough time to peel back his good looks and see what lay beneath.

"Did he..." Maureen proceeded slowly, as if moving through a mine field. "Was it a terminal illness? Is that why your father was in the hospital?"

Dusty used his shovel to scoop up loose sand and tossed it into the screen. "It wasn't that kind of hospital."

She set the artifact bag down and gripped the handles of the screen. The muscles of her slender forearms tightened. "I'm sorry to hear that."

"It was a long time ago." He knelt down to retrieve his notebook, blew the sand off the page, and jotted his level notes. He made a quick description of the soil, the root casts, and the single potsherd. Setting the notebook aside, he glanced up at her, and an odd prickling sensation went through him. The veil that generally covered her eyes had vanished. She was gazing at him somberly.

"I don't think I'll ever be able to look back at John lying on the floor, and say, 'It was a long time ago.'"

"Yes, you will. Pain goes away, Doctor. Eventually. That or it tears you apart."

He focused on the pit floor, trying to gauge where he'd most likely come down on the burial. If the soil horizons continued to slope, he ought to hit it just to the left. He made his first shovel scrape, then a second. They worked in silence, him shoveling to the *shish-shishing* of her screening.

He had almost dug another ten-centimeter level when he noticed the discoloration, a subtle distinction of color and texture. He stopped. "Curtain time."

She set the screen aside and knelt on the lip of the unit. "What did you find?"

Dusty indicated the changing soil horizons with a finger. "This," Dusty told her, "is the darker stain from the organic content of the old site surface. That's from the ash, organic trash, and stuff left over from the occupational phase of the pueblo. This," he indicated a lighter soil that curved in an irregular arc, "is intrusive. Younger silt and sand washed in."

"The grave?" She looked at him with sudden anticipation.

"Apparently."

She started to get down into 'the pit. "Let's get her uncovered."

Dusty held up a hand. "How about you stand back and let me map this in first? You know, do a little *real* science along the way."

Maureen sank down on the edge of the pit with a disappointed expression. "Just don't take too long, Stewart."

Dusty measured in the soil discoloration, took notes, and began troweling, pulling out the intrusive soil until he encountered jumbled dark soil, several chunks of stone from the toppled pueblo wall, and three sherds of pottery.

"What is all this?" Maureen asked.

"Trash. He shoveled it on top of the grave to cover her up." Dusty took a soil sample and bagged it. "Do you see the ragged edge of the grave?" He pointed to the irregular pattern. "Normally we'd see long scars left by the digging sticks as they levered the soil loose. This is choppy, as if the digging was difficult because the ground was frozen."

"Pollen in the nasal sinus will tell us, but I'll bet you're right."

He worked quickly but diligently, troweling for a time, then mapping in the broken sandstone rocks, potsherds, and stone flakes. When he finally stood up to stretch his back muscles, Dusty studied the outline of the soil discoloration, the grave, and tried to imagine how the skeleton might be laid out below. If this burial followed the pattern set by the others, her body should be laid out with the head to the north.

For a reason unknown to him, Dusty suddenly said, "My father was committed for his own safety."

Maureen's eyes tightened. She frowned at the ground. "By your mother?"

"She was long gone by then."

"Your grandparents?" she asked gently.

"They weren't on speaking terms with Dad. He was supposed to become a lawyer, or doctor, or something productive. I don't know the history of it. Just bad blood between them."

"Then who?"

"Dale did." He rolled the trowel in his fingers. "I think it's one of the toughest things he's ever done. God knows, because of it, I've hung like an albatross around Dale's neck for years."

"What happened to your mother?"

"She teaches at Harvard, manages a big collection of Australian Aboriginal and Māori artifacts at the Peabody. That's where she made her name for herself."

Maureen sat back, stunned. "You mean, Ruth Ann Sullivan is *your* mother?"

Dusty knelt and started troweling dirt again. "You know her?"

"Everyone knows her. Her books are classics. After Margaret Mead died, Ruth Ann Sullivan filled her place, writing about culture for the popular audience." She frowned at the top of Dusty's blond head. "You really hate her, don't you?"

"If I gave her any thought, I probably would. But I don't. In fact, I—"

Bone grated beneath his trowel. Dusty's blue eyes narrowed. He slowly pulled back the darker earth, exposing the rear of a skull.

"My God," Maureen whispered. "There she is."

Dusty stood, smacked sand from his hands and pants, and said, "I need to get the camera. Would you like to *gently* excavate around the skull while I do that?"

"Would I!" She jumped into the pit and grabbed for his trowel.

Dusty got out and walked over to the ammo box. By the time he'd removed the camera, placed the North arrow and scale, and snapped a couple of shots, Maureen had excavated around the side of the skull.

He'd just started walking back to the ammo box to put the camera back when Maureen called, "Dusty?"

It was the first time she'd ever called him by his first name.

She stood up in the pit and looked at him. Her breathing was coming fast, and her voice had a higher pitch than normal. "You'd better take a look at this."

Dusty hurried back and knelt, looking down at the skull. "What did you find?"

Maureen used her trowel to point to the dent in the woman's skull. Fractures radiated out from the temple on the left side. Just where she'd predicted. "Language skills, Stewart. He was trying to find the source of language in the human brain."

He got into the pit with her. "Amazing," he said in awe.

Beside the skull, Maureen had exposed a small patch of what looked like ground stone. "Can I have my trowel back?"

"Why?"

"This looks like a metate, but it doesn't seem to be very big. It may be a fragment of a broken metate."

He took the trowel and cleaned the dirt away until he could see the metate fragment had been inverted, its smooth grinding surface carefully stuck to the top of a pot with what looked like beeswax.

'This is curious," Dusty said and wiped his forehead with the back of his hand. "The person who did this was taking special precautions to preserve whatever's inside this pot."

"Can we open it?"

Dusty's trowel hovered over the pot. "I don't know

if that's wise. This is an unusual burial artifact. First, we'd better..."

He heard Hail Walking Hawk's cane tapping the ground and Maggie's soft voice: "We can see it once they get it out of the ground, Aunt."

"I want to see it now, child," Hail answered.

Dusty shielded his eyes against the sunlight and looked up at the old woman. Gray hair framed her wrinkled face.

"Did you find that woman, Washais?"

Maureen said, "I think so, Mrs. Walking Hawk. We also found a pot that's covered with a grinding stone. The stone is held in place by wax. Do you know what it might be?" Maureen pointed to it.

Hail squinted her ancient eyes, as if trying to see the pot, but not quite able to. "Might be food for the afterlife."

Dusty asked, "Is it all right if we take it out and open it?"

Hail didn't answer for a time. Wind blew her hair around her face. "Do you think it will tell us something about the murderer, Washais?"

"It might. We won't know until we open it."

Hail's head tottered in a nod. "Open it up, then, and let me know what you find."

～

Maureen slid behind the cramped table in Dale's camper and carefully placed her microscope and dissecting kit on the Formica top. A Coleman lantern sat in the middle of the table, hissing softly. As she reached into her travel bag for slides and stain, she looked around. A tiny gas stove and cupboards filled the space to her left. To her right, a small window reflected the lantern's silver gleam. The booth had once been upholstered in reddish brown fabric, but years of dust, spilled coffee, and sweaty archaeologists had turned it gray. The battered old trailer possessed the faint metallic smell of mice.

Dale opened the camper door, and the hinges complained as he stepped inside, followed by Dusty. Dale cradled a black-on-white ceramic pot in his hands, the heavy sandstone cap still in place. The trailer rocked as they came to stand over the table.

"We just lifted it out of the grave. Ready?" Dale asked.

"Ready." Maureen turned on the battery-driven light of her portable microscope.

Dale settled the round-bottomed pot on a fabric donut, a device used to support either human skulls or fragile pottery.

"I have plenty of bags." Stewart reached into his back pocket and produced a roll of translucent Ziplocs.

"Good." Maureen opened her dissecting kit and' removed a scalpel, then she studied the dark brown wax. "The wax apparently once covered the entire top, as though the person who sealed it melted the wax and poured it over the metate cap." Brown splotches mottled the cap, filling the depressions in the stone. "My God, there are dermatoglyphics in this wax. I'm going to try and pry the wax around the edges loose, so we don't destroy them."

"What?" Stewart raised a blond eyebrow.

"Fingerprints," Dale said. "If Maureen is correct

that these women were murdered, the prints probably belong to the killer."

"Well," Maureen said, "in that case, the murderer was a woman."

The camper went silent. The hot wind outside seemed suddenly loud, shrieking and whimpering as it rocked the camper.

Maureen frowned at their stunned faces. "What's the matter?"

"A woman?" Dusty whispered in awe.

"I can't say that for certain yet, of course, but look at the palm width demonstrated by these fingerprints." She pointed. "It's small. The size a woman, or a child, would make. Maybe a small man, but I doubt it."

Maureen took her scalpel, and carefully pried on the sandstone cap. It didn't budge. "This stuff is like concrete."

"It's had eight hundred years to harden." Dusty said. "Here, let me help." He reached out, grasped the sandstone cap, and wrenched it free with a twist.

Maureen barely caught the pot before it spilled. "Good Lord, Stewart! Who do you think you are, Indiana Jones in the tombs of Venice? Too bad you didn't have a stick of dynamite and jackhammer, eh? Maybe some rare thousand-year-old fabric to make a torch so you could melt it off?"

Dale gave Dusty a reproving look, then picked up the sandstone cap, and held it to the lantern light. "Open a Ziploc for me, William. We can probably obtain good pollen, phytolith, and maybe even some macrobotanical samples from the protected surface within the wax ring."

Stewart opened a gallon Ziploc, allowed Dale to

slip the cap inside, then promptly "zipped" the bag closed.

Maureen tipped the pot to the light and frowned at the contents. At first glance, the stuff looked like shredded jerky. A thin gray layer of mold gave it a silvery look.

Dale peered at it and shook his head. "I thought it might be food or precious gifts for the afterlife. Apparently not."

Dusty took a Sharpie pen from his green T-shirt pocket and labeled the bag containing the stone cap. "It still might be food. Shoshonean tribes in the Great Basin and Plains dried squirrels and rabbits and then ground them up on metates. Sort of a flaked meat. The prehistoric precursor to hamburger."

"Give me a minute and I'll settle this discussion." Maureen used forceps to lift a thin brown strand from the pot, then pulled scissors from her dissecting kit, and clipped off a tiny sample. She dropped the rest of the strand back into the pot and fixed the sample to a slide. "Let's see what we have here."

She started at ten power and grunted.

Dale said, "What?"

"Muscle tissue," she replied.

The memory of striations on some of the earlier burials caused her forehead to line.

"What are you thinking?" Stewart asked.

"Hold on." She rummaged through her kit, located a test tube, a small vial of clear liquid labeled "Human Juice," and a length of string wrapped around what looked like a heavy cigar tube.

"What's that?" Stewart asked.

"This is my traveling physical anthropologist's

down-and-dirty field lab. Dale, I need a *clean* porcelain surface. Have you got a saucer? A plate?"

"I do." He unsnapped the latches on one of the cabinets. Reaching in, he pulled out a plastic bag of china saucers. "I bag them straight out of the dishwasher because I don't like the taste of mouse droppings. Will this do?"

"Fine," she said. She turned the saucer over and set it on the table in front of her. From her kit, she took a rag and two more small plastic bottles. "Bleach," she explained, and dripped two drops inside the ring on the bottom of the saucer. "Stewart, I see a roll of paper towels hanging from the bottom of the cabinet behind you. Unroll three squares and give me the fourth. Tear it off by holding it at the corners, and don't let it touch anything as you hand it to me."

Steward obeyed, frowning as he handed her the fourth towel. "I want you to explain this to me."

Maureen took the towel by the edges and curled it into a cone so that the unhandled portion of the towel made the point. "All right, the center of the saucer is glazed, and, for the most part, protected from scratches. There might be a fingerprint, so I'll use the bleach, and spread it around with the clean paper towel. Bleach denatures protein." As she spoke, she used the towel to swab the interior surface. "We'll leave that to set for a moment. Stewart, hand me another towel. Same procedure."

He carefully ripped another clean towel from the roll and handed it over.

Maureen used the towel to wipe the saucer bottom clean. "Now,"—she dribbled a little liquid from the second plastic bottle—"we'll apply distilled water and ask for yet another paper towel."

"You must have stock in a paper mill," Stewart said and gave her another towel.

"No," Maureen said, "I'm doing my best to minimize contamination."

She scrubbed the surface with the latest paper towel. "I'm trying to remove any of the remaining bleach." She squinted at the gleaming surface. "That's as good as we'll get out here." With the forceps she lifted the bit of tissue from the microscope slide and dropped it into the center of the plate. "Now comes the fun part." She carefully cleaned the scalpel handle and used the metal butt to mash the bit of tissue flat. For long minutes, she rocked the rounded end back and forth, flattening the bit of tissue. Finally, she picked up the test tube, unstoppered it, and used a needle from her dissecting kit to flick bits of pulverized tissue onto the scalpel blade, then she dropped them into the test tube.

"All right, we have a sample in the test tube." She lifted the little vial marked, 'Human Juice.' "This stuff is an antihuman antigen. It reacts with human tissue. I carry it around because it often comes in handy in the field."

She carefully measured out two drops and set it aside. She added distilled water, stoppered the test tube, and dropped it in the weighted cigar-shaped holder. "Science time, archaeologist," she said to Stewart as she handed him the tube. "You're a big muscular man. I want you to go outside, let out the string to its full length and spin the tube around your head for the next five minutes while Dale and I make ourselves a cup of coffee."

Stewart lifted his brows, hefted the weighted holder, and asked, "Why don't you do this?"

"Because I've done it before. You haven't."

"Right," he nodded. The camper door squeaked as he stepped outside. Wind slammed the door closed.

Dale gave her a smile and lit a match. When he turned on the gas burner, blue flames burst to life.

Maureen leaned back and smiled. "God, this is fun, Dale. I haven't enjoyed myself this much in years."

Dale's gray mustache quirked. "You and Dusty seem to have come to an agreement of sorts."

"Of sorts." She tilted her head, and watched Dale pour water into the coffeepot. "He's a curious character. One minute he seems like a perfectly rational adult, and the next minute he displays the emotional development of a twelve-year-old. What's the thing between him and Ruth Ann?"

Dale dumped coffee into the old fire-blackened pot, pushed the lid down, and glanced at her from the corner of his eye. "Did he tell you about that?"

"Not much. Just that his father committed suicide in an asylum."

Dale set the pot on the flames and turned around. He folded his arms and leaned against the counter. "That's more than he's told anyone in years, I think."

"Why did she leave?" Maureen lowered her voice, glancing cautiously at the door.

"Another man. His name was Carter Hawsworth. He was out here studying social structure at Zuni Pueblo. Ruth offered to show him around. Professional courtesy, you know. Sam was working in Blanding,

Utah, at the time. When he got back a week later, Ruth had a one-way ticket to Cambridge. She waved it at him when he walked through the door."

"That quick?"

Dale nodded, reached into his pocket for his pipe, then went through the careful ritual of filling the bowl, tamping it down and lighting it with a match. After puffing it alight, he looked at her from the midst of a hazy blue cloud. "Sam worshiped that woman. Her betrayal destroyed him."

"If their marriage could be broken that easily, whatever got them together in the first place?"

"Oh, who can say? I think Sam was new and exciting to her. They came from the same roots, old money, East Coast high society. She was young, out on her own for the first time, and here was this handsome young archaeologist living a romantic life in field camps. She was pregnant before they were married and, from her perspective, trapped, because Sam wasn't going back East to a university. He'd virtually come to blows with his parents when he turned down a teaching job at Harvard and left for what they called 'The Wild West.' Sam was a field man, one of the best. His soul would have died in a university."

Maureen laced her fingers on the table. "How old was Dusty when this happened?"

"He'd just turned six. For most of those years, Ruth had endured. She never showed him the kind of love that a child needs to survive. I remember one night in December"—he gestured emphatically with his pipe stem—"I came over to show Sam a curious artifact I'd found and couldn't identify. Dusty was four. He'd done something, I never knew what, but Ruth had locked the boy in the basement. It was pitch black down there and icy cold. He'd been there since early morning. I could hear him screaming her name, telling her he was sorry, begging her to let him out." Dale blew out a stream of smoke. "I couldn't stand it, Maureen. I had to leave."

Her heart clutched up. "Why didn't Sam do something?"

"He was a good man, Maureen, but he wasn't a strong man. I think he knew, even then, that he was going to lose Ruth, and was trying so hard to keep her that he let her do things to his son that no sane man would have." He paused and frowned at his pipe. "After she left, Sam disintegrated before my eyes. He attempted suicide three times the first month. He couldn't take care of himself, let alone a six-year-old boy."

"Was Dusty there?" She shot a glance at the door and lowered her voice. "When he tried to kill himself?"

"Every time."

"My God." Maureen bowed her head. "That's why you committed him and took Dusty?"

He nodded. "Somebody had to. I called Sam's parents, and they didn't want him. I tried to find Ruth's parents, but couldn't. I didn't know it at the time, but they'd both been killed in a car accident the same week that Hawsworth showed up at Zuni. I'm sure Ruth was dazed, hurting—"

"That's no excuse..."

Dusty opened the door and stepped in, followed by a filthy Sylvia. Her green T-shirt and khaki shorts were covered with dust. Half-moons of mud arched beneath her armpits. She'd pinned her brown hair up, but wet brown locks straggled around her freckled face.

Dusty panted slightly as he walked forward. "That's more of a shoulder workout than I'd have thought."

"Careful Dusty," Maureen warned. "Don't shake it up."

"Of course not, Doctor. I may have never acted as a centrifuge before, but I'm smart enough to understand the process."

Maureen lifted her brows in surprise. "What are you doing? Impersonating a scientist?"

He gave her a bland look. "Yeah. Right. I thought I'd give it a try. Were you convinced?"

"No way," Sylvia said as she slid into the booth across from Maureen. "You'd be better at impersonating a woman. It wouldn't take as much effort."

Dusty scowled at her as he handed the tube to Maureen, perfectly upright. "I'm going to buy you a nice batch of anthrax to go with your cheezy fishies, Sylvia."

Her green eyes widened. "Thanks, boss. After the Hezbollah pays me for it, you can come visit me on my island."

"After you sell it to the Hezbollah there won't be any islands, you dope."

Sylvia sighed and sank back against the booth seat. "Wow. I figured there'd be something upwind of D.C."

"Yeah, well, trust me. Santa's headquarters at the North Pole isn't all it's cracked up to be. Ask Rushdie."

Maureen gave them a disgusted look, then unscrewed the cap, extracted the test tube, and held it up to the lantern light. "Well," she whispered.

"What is it?" Stewart squinted at the little red blob in the bottom of the test tube.

"A positive reaction," Maureen said. "The precipitation we've just completed tells us that this pot is full of powdered people."

"Uh-oh," Sylvia whispered.

Dusty gave Dale an uneasy glance. "Jesus. We're in trouble."

"That's an understatement," Dale said.

"I don't understand." Maureen propped the tube on the table. "In many cultures around the world, people macerate their dead and save the flesh. It's a variation of keeping your husband's ashes on the mantle. Among the Chocktaw, Chickasaw, Cherokee—"

"This is the southwest, Maureen," Dale said, and his gaze locked with Dusty's.

Dusty nodded and exhaled hard. "Well, at least we know something more about Maureen's serial murderer."

"What?" Maureen asked.

Dusty looked at her with bright blue eyes. "He was into a lot of things. He specialized in young women, did a little basic experimentation in neurophysiology with a war club. After he killed his victims, he stripped the flesh from their bones, and..." He let the word hang and turned to Sylvia.

Sylvia finished, "And used it to make corpse powder."

"Right."

"Corpse powder?" Maureen said. "You think that's what this is?"

"No question about it," Dale replied. "And we've opened it up without taking any precautions. The evil is loose."

Dusty ran a hand through his blond hair. "Let me

be the one to tell Maggie and Elder Walking Hawk. This will probably shut the excavation down for a few days while we undergo a cleansing, but—"

"A few days if we're lucky," Dale said. "Things like this can *end* an excavation."

No one seemed to hear the coffeepot as it began to perk.

10

Sister Moon's gleam penetrated the gathering clouds and streaked the cliffs with soft dove-colored light. Where it fell upon patches of ice, they shone like glassy eyes.

Browser sat with his elbows propped on his knees, throwing pebbles into Straight Path Wash. He had deliberately taken the guard position farthest from the village. If the murderer wanted to find him alone, now was the time.

He longed to see the man face-to-face, with his war club in his hand.

And he could think out here. All the conversations, the laughter, the running children, and the barking dogs had frayed his nerves.

He drew his buckskin cape more tightly around him. Seven warriors walked the torchlit tiers of Talon Town, and another six perched on the roof of Hillside Village. Most of them, he did not know. After Flame Carrier had approved his plan, Browser had gone to the newly arrived matrons from the other villages and explained that he needed additional warriors to maintain the "harmony and sanctity" of the celebration. Everyone knew that large gatherings tended to provoke arguments. Two summers ago in Rowing Waters Town, a man had been killed. The matrons were happy to oblige. He had posted half of the warriors, sixteen men and four women, in strategic locations: on roofs, the mounds in front of Talon Town, and three men on the rim. They would stand guard through the night. Tomorrow, while they slept, he would post the other sixteen warriors.

Wind Baby ruffled Browser's hair with icy fingers and whistled in his ear, as if taunting him, trying to get him to rise and return to the village.

Browser tossed another pebble into the wash. Moonlight gleamed from the stone as it fell, then he heard it splash into the water.

Dozens of campfires sparkled at the base of the northern canyon wall, running like twisted strands of beads from Kettle Town on his right and well past Talon Town on his left.

At least two hundred and twenty guests had already arrived, and Flame Carrier expected another forty before dawn. Many of the visitors had moved in with friends from Hillside Village. Others had settled into the cleaner rooms in Kettle Town. No one would brave Talon Town. They all knew the legends about the ghosts and witches who roamed the abandoned chambers at night.

Most people had made simple camps in the flats. They'd dug a fire pit, spread out their hides, and arranged their belongings around the camp's perimeter. Large water pots, painted with tadpoles and baby snakes, stood close to the fires. Beside them sat small-handled pots painted with the sacred images of the Corn Dancers; they contained white cornmeal for making the sacred breads they would share tomorrow night.

A prayer pole stood at each camp. Four perfect ears of yellow corn clothed in glittering beadwork topped the poles. Below them hung magnificent masks draped with necklaces of Olivella shells, red coral beads, carved jet bears, and obsidian mountain sheep, as well as fans of mallard, macaw, downy eagle, pinyon jay, and crow feathers. At the base of the pole, a rawhide basket nestled on a willow twig mat. The basket held all colors of corn kernels, squash seeds, pine nuts, sunflower seeds, tobacco, and red-and-white beans. Each was a promise forgotten, but not abandoned. Tomorrow they would be presented to the gods. Gods remembered every vow a person had made to their clans or families and, if properly asked, would gently remind the penitent, so that his loved ones would not know he'd forgotten.

Browser picked up another pebble. He had promised to make Grass Moon a yellow dance stick for this celebration.

His son had seen two summers when Browser first told him the story of the journey through the dark underworlds. *"When humans finally stepped into Father Sun's blinding light, it hurt them, my son. Tears ran from their eyes, and each place a tear fell, yellow lilies, and sunflowers grew."*

From that instant, Grass Moon had loved yellow. Ash Girl had dyed all of the ties on their clothing yellow, because it pleased their son.

Browser picked up another pebble.

Ash Girl.

His rage had melted, but he could not describe the emotion that had replaced it. He felt numb, drained of everything human in his souls. After seeing her mutilated body, he could barely think. A part of him still loved Ash Girl, and the realization brought him pain. He also remembered the adoration in Grass Moon's eyes when he'd looked at his mother.

Browser clutched the pebble and whispered, "I needed her too much. That's what drove her away. And that's why she's dead."

The sicker Grass Moon became, the more demands Browser had made, and the more time Ash Girl spent searching for a Spirit Helper—as if desperate to ease both his, and their son's, hurts.

Why hadn't he seen that?

He'd interpreted her long absences as neglect. Proof that she really hadn't cared about them at all.

He hurled the pebble into the drainage.

Stone Ghost had said that Ash Girl's Spirit Helper was a very selective god, only choosing desperate women who were sick themselves or with sick families. He'd said that this "Visitant" promised to cure the illness if the woman would release her souls to him, and that when the woman failed, he killed her.

But now it appeared there were two murderers, not one.

A single madman, Browser could understand. But two? What purpose could they have? What goal would their brutality achieve?

Cloud People sailed in front of Sister Moon, and a

well of darkness enveloped Browser. Movement caught his eye.

Across the drainage, a tall dark figure wavered against the firelight. It had no depth, like a cutout of black cloth.

He eased his club from his belt. The blood rushing in his veins turned hot. Sweat ran down his chest. As always before a battle, he felt lightheaded.

As the Cloud People passed, moonlight drenched the canyon again.

Very softly, a voice called, "Browser?"

"Gods, Catkin!" he said, and got to his feet. "Call out to me earlier next time! I was ready to bash in your skull!"

She halted on the opposite bank. "Call out? So the murderers can hear me?" She folded her arms.

He vented a tingling breath. "I thought you were resting?"

"Not anymore."

Browser stiffened at her tone. "Why not?"

"Come over here, and I'll tell you about it."

He trotted for the trail across the wash. As he ran down the slope, and up the other side, some of his tension fled.

Catkin met him at the top of the trail. A black blanket covered her tall lanky body from throat to knees, and she wore black leather leggings, and sandals. Her long braid fell down her back. When Browser got close enough to see her oval face, with its turned-up nose, he noticed how quickly she was breathing.

"Hurry," he said. "Tell me."

"Your great-uncle found something interesting. Come and see."

Catkin turned and headed back for Hillside Village. "Tell me! I want to know now."

"He wants to tell you."

They walked in silence to the edge of the crowd, then Catkin extended a hand. "Stone Ghost is sitting by the plaza fire with Flame Carrier and Corn Mother. Go. I will take your guard position until you return."

Browser pushed through the crowd, saying, "Forgive me...I'm sorry, I must reach the matrons...Pardon me, please."

He shouldered through the last throng of about thirty people who blocked his way and stepped out into the firelight.

Stone Ghost sat on a blanket with a pile of rocks between his scrawny legs. Ash coated his wrinkled face and mangy cape and even caked in the creases of his eyelids. The resulting black line gave him a bizarre appearance.

Flame Carrier looked grim. Wet gray hair framed her small narrow eyes, and bulbous nose, as if she'd been perspiring despite the cold. The beautiful red-feathered cape that Ash Girl had made for her glimmered in the wavering firelight.

Corn Mother, from Frosted Meadow Village, sat to the right, whispering with a young man. A woman sat next to him, her face pale and strained from the coughing sickness.

"Nephew?" Stone Ghost called. "Come. See what we've discovered."

Browser walked wide around the fire and squatted in front of the old man. People must have been waiting for Browser's arrival. The throng pressed closer, hissing and pointing, their eyes wide.

Browser frowned down at the rocks on the blanket.

It took several moments before he understood.

He reached out and touched the fragments. 'That's the head of Whip—of a dead warrior's club, Uncle. The way it's cracked, you must have found it in a fire. Where?"

"Catkin said it was his, too," Stone Ghost answered in a calm voice. "It had been cast into a blazing fire, a fire built up so high and hot, it would be certain to shatter chert. The murderer, or murderers, never thought anyone would sift through the bed of ashes to dig out the tiny pieces that remained."

Browser drew his hand back and clenched it in his lap. "You found this..." His voice faded as his souls started to ache. "In the ritual fire pit? The one where Hophorn was sitting?"

Stone Ghost's dark gaze affected Browser like a lance in his heart. He seemed to sense that the news about Whiproot would wound Browser deeply.

Stone Ghost clasped Browser's wrist in a gesture of sympathy. "Matron Flame Carrier has set a pot of pine pitch on to boil. As soon as it is ready, we must glue these pieces back together. Will you help me?"

"Of course. Yes, Uncle."

"Good," he said, "then we will see if the shape matches."

"Matches? You mean the—the dent in Hophorn's skull?"

Stone Ghost shook his head sadly. "No, Nephew." He prodded the pieces of the rock, shoving them closer together. "I am more concerned about the strange mark by the fire pit. The one you thought might be a 'heel' print."

Confused, Browser said, "I don't understand."

"Don't you?" Stone Ghost asked gently, and his smile warmed as he cryptically added, "That's good."

~

"Let me fetch a torch, Uncle." Browser's voice sounded hollow, as though his insides had been kicked out. He could not take his eyes from the fractured head of the war club. "I will meet you at the southwestern corner of Talon Town."

Stone Ghost rose to his feet, and two more feathers fell out of his ash-coated cape and fluttered to the ground. His brown socks showed through the holes in his moccasins. "We will be there shortly, Nephew."

Browser bowed to the matrons and shouldered through the whispering crowd. People watched him with worried eyes.

He took the trail that curved around the eastern wall of Talon Town. Each time his sandals landed he felt as if another chunk of his souls had shaken loose and shattered to nothingness.

It couldn't be true. Not Whiproot. Not the man he'd warred besides, and relied upon, even entrusted with his life.

When Browser ran beneath the enormous images of the gods, he glanced up at Badger. The magnificent katsina's eyes gleamed. He seemed to watch Browser as he hurried around the corner of the town and onto the road. At dusk, he'd staked two juniper bark torches on either side of the ladder to the roof. He ran for the closest one and pulled it out of the ground.

Jackrabbit crouched on the edge of the roof, his

wide brown eyes and pug nose glowing orange in the wavering gleam. He'd tucked his shoulder-length hair behind his ears. His doeskin cape flapped in the wind.

"War Chief?" he yelled. "Is all well?"

Jackrabbit turned when a long line of people filed around the corner and marched up the road toward Browser. Stone Ghost and Flame Carrier led the procession.

"What's happening?" Jackrabbit hissed. He wet his lips as if his mouth had suddenly gone dry.

Browser called, "Stone Ghost found the head of a war club in a fire pit. We—"

"Whose war club? Why was it in a fire pit?"

The procession, at least one hundred people, stopped, and began shoving on the road behind Browser, trying to peer around each other to hear what Browser was saying. As they moved, the brilliant reds, blues, and yellows of their clothing appeared to be a fluid rainbow.

"Everything is well, Jackrabbit. This is just another thing we must look into."

Jackrabbit gazed down at the crowd. He could tell from people's expressions that it was not "just another thing," but he said, "Yes, War Chief."

Stone Ghost hobbled by Browser with the glued chert cobble clutched in his right hand. It resembled an oddly shaped black-and-white egg. The pitch had not taken long to set in the cold, but the head of the club was not whole. Many small gaps remained. Stone Ghost had filled them with pitch as best he could, but one end of the cobble had a deep notch in it. The piece that fit there had probably exploded into a thousand tiny fragments in the blazing fire. Browser suspected they'd never find it.

Flame Carrier stopped beside Browser and pulled the torch from his hand. "I'll carry this. You lead the way, War Chief."

"Yes, Matron."

Browser pulled his club and caught up with Stone Ghost in four long strides. "Uncle, allow me to go first. Just in case there is someone—"

"I would rather you walked at my side, Nephew. So that we may talk."

"The Matron asked me to lead—"

"Then do not get too far ahead of me."

"Yes, Uncle."

Browser walked in front. The whispers and rustles of clothing made it impossible to listen to the darkness. Browser prayed the murderers were not...

From behind him, Stone Ghost said, "They are, Nephew. Be certain of it. They're out here watching us right this instant."

His fingers tightened around his club. "How do you know? Do you see them?"

"No, but less than a hand of time ago, one of them spoke with stragglers coming in from Frosted Meadow Village."

Browser's steps faltered. He had to force his legs onward. "What did he say?"

"Nothing important. He spoke to them to let me know that he'd been watching me all day. But I knew that already. Of course, he didn't know I knew that."

Frustrated, Browser said, "Uncle, just tell me what he said."

"Very well, Nephew, no need to growl. He told

Little Bow and Marsh Hawk that they might have to do battle with the most powerful witch in the world and urged them to ask about the ashes."

"The ashes?" Browser glanced at the old man over his shoulder. His uncle's wispy white hair bore a thick coating of gray. "The ashes in the ritual fire pit?"

"Of course, Nephew. He was just threatening me. Do not let it disturb you."

Flame Carrier walked up beside Stone Ghost, and said, "What are you two whispering about?"

"I was just telling my nephew—"

"Well, hush! People are frightened. They're like a covey of quail back there, ready to burst into flight at the sight of their own shadows!"

Browser said, "Yes, Matron," and led the way to the fire pit near the canyon wall.

People started to rush forward, coming in like a wave. Browser shouted, "Stay back! You'll destroy what we're looking for!"

Shouts and curses rang out as the crowd settled into an irregular semicircle. People shuffled and jostled for position but stayed about five paces away.

Stone Ghost knelt beside the curious mark in the soil, and Flame Carrier bent over him. Her red cape glittered in the torchlight.

"Bring the torch closer, Flame Carrier," Stone Ghost instructed as he held the mended chert cobble over the mark.

Flame Carrier lowered the torch.

Browser tried to watch the crowd and Stone Ghost, shifting his gaze back and forth.

Stone Ghost rotated the cobble onto its side and compared it to the mark, then grunted unpleasantly. He spun the cobble in his hands, tipped it on end, with the point aimed at the sky, and tried again.

"Ah," he said softly. "Nephew, I wish you to see this."

Browser knelt opposite Stone Ghost and watched as his uncle lowered the heavy end of the cobble to the ground and inserted it into the impression. "You try," Stone Ghost said and handed the cobble to Browser.

Browser took the cobble, bent down, and carefully placed it into the niche in the soil. The right side sank more deeply than the left, but it fit perfectly. Browser lifted the cobble and handed it to Flame Carrier. "Matron, do you wish to see?"

"I have seen all I care to, War Chief," she said. "Tell me what this proves? One of our warriors dropped his club here before your son's burial. That does not mean he used it to strike Hophorn. Or that he is the one who harmed your wife."

"No, Matron. But if not, why was the club thrown into the fire? Someone obviously did not wish for it to be found."

"Perhaps it was destroyed, War Chief. That does not prove that our warrior harmed people with it first."

Stone Ghost shoved up on wobbly legs. "Matron Flame Carrier is correct, Nephew. We have proven nothing. All we can say is that it looks as if the club struck the ground here, and then, at some point, all of the wood was thrown into the fire, along with the club. Now that we've determined that, let's return to the plaza and rejoin the festivities. I'm thirsty for more of Flame Carrier's excellent yucca blossom tea."

"But, Uncle—"

"Come," Flame Carrier ordered and walked back up the trail.

The crowd turned and followed her, casting backward glances at Stone Ghost and Browser.

Stone Ghost slipped his arm through Browser's and fell in line at the rear of the assembly.

Stone Ghost whispered, "I wish you to consider something, Nephew."

"Yes, Uncle?"

"The voice Catkin heard that night on the rim, and the voice she heard in Talon Town last night..." He looked up at Browser, as if expecting him to finish the sentence.

Browser said, "Might have been—that warrior—after all."

Stone Ghost nodded. "I'm not saying it is so. Only that you should think on it, and on the reasons that warrior might have had to murder someone."

"There were times when I thought he wished to murder his wife, Elder, but I never heard him wish anyone else ill."

Stone Ghost stepped around a rock in the trail. "The warrior had difficulties with his wife?"

"Moons ago, Uncle. You saw how badly his face was scarred. It happened in a battle last summer. When he returned home, his wife would not touch him. His heart was crushed. For three moons, he moved into one of the chambers in Talon Town. He did not stay long. Silk Moth asked him to come home in early autumn."

"I see."

Browser glanced down at the thin old man beside him. Stone Ghost had said the words slowly, deliberately, as though he really did see something Browser did not.

Browser said, "Uncle, that warrior returned from a war walk late the night before the burial. He helped carry my son's burial ladder to the grave. He was my friend. I cannot believe in my heart that he—"

"Hmm?" Stone Ghost said as though he'd just noticed Browser was speaking. He blinked owlishly. "Oh, well, of course not, Nephew. I don't believe he did it either."

Browser stopped, letting the procession move on ahead of them. They stood near the southwestern corner of Talon Town, just beyond the gleam of the torches.

"Why did we just take the cracked head of his war club out to the fire pit if not to prove that he—"

"Not he. His war club. Did he ever mention to you that it was missing?"

Browser sifted his memories. Had it been missing, Whiproot would have demanded that Hillside Village be searched, and 'the culprit punished severely. War clubs were not weapons, they were alive and part of a warrior's souls.

Browser said, "No."

"Then he loaned it, or gave it to someone, didn't he? Who? Why? A warrior and his club are usually inseparable. I doubt he would have given it to a passing stranger."

"You think the murderer was a friend of his?"

"Or a relative. Maybe someone powerful enough to demand he turn his club over. One of the elders in Hillside Village? Who would you give your club to, Nephew? And why?"

Stone Ghost started walking again.

As they rounded the corner and headed up the road, Browser said, "My wife, perhaps, if I thought she were in danger, and I knew I wasn't going to be there to..."

I was never there. Ever.

He let the sentence hang and grimaced.

Stone Ghost stared at him with unnerving concentration, "What?"

"Nothing, Uncle."

Browser lifted a hand to Jackrabbit, who stood on the roof, and said, "I must tell my warriors this news, Uncle, before they hear it from someone who does not know the facts."

"Of course, Nephew."

Stone Ghost started to walk away, then stopped and turned. "Catkin is standing guard in your position, is she not?"

"Yes, Uncle."

"When you go to relieve her, Nephew, take great care. The two of you, together in one place, and away from the village fires—"

"I understand, Uncle. I will. Sleep well."

Stone Ghost inclined his head, smiled, and walked up the road.

Browser looked at the two guards, one standing on each of the mounds to his right, then cautiously went to the ladder and climbed.

Jackrabbit extended a hand to help Browser from the ladder to the rooftop, and said, "I don't believe it! Our friend would never—"

"That's right, he wouldn't."

Jackrabbit stared openmouthed at Browser. "But I

heard people talking *as* they passed. They said our friend—"

"His club, Jackrabbit, not him. Do you ever recall him loaning it, or giving it to anyone?"

At the very thought, Jackrabbit clutched his own club in both hands. "No, War Chief."

"Well, he must have. Start asking around among our people. *Quietly.*"

"Yes, War Chief."

Browser gazed out across the moonlit canyon to the place Catkin should be standing. Dark cloud shadows roamed the canyon bottom, flowing like water over the low hills.

"I must return to my guard position, Jackrabbit. Remain alert. He-Who-Flies will relieve you at dawn."

He jerked a nod. "Yes, War Chief."

Catkin rolled on to her back in her buffalo hides and gazed at the big fluffy flakes of snow tumbling through her roof entry and onto the coals in her warming bowl. A soft sizzling filled her chamber. A few Evening People gleamed through the gaps in the clouds, sparkling against the indigo blanket of night.

Catkin stretched. The rich scents of ritual cooking filled her nostrils. For the past two days women had cooked rabbits, band-tailed pigeons, deer, and a variety of corn flour breads. They'd roasted gourds, pine nuts, sunflower and pumpkin seeds, boiled enormous pots of beans, and made a delicious jam by boiling dried yucca fruits and chokecherries until they became a paste. All of those scents clung to the village. Her stomach growled.

Catkin sat up and tossed a few twigs into the bowl. The wood crackled and spat, and flames licked up around the tinder.

She rose in the soft yellow gleam and walked to the

big red pot across the chamber. On this, the shortest day, and longest night of the sun cycle, she had sacred duties to perform.

As she pulled her tan sleep shirt over her head, she Sang:

> *My breath-heart is calling to you Father*
> *Sun,*
> *Hear me calling,*
> *I am coming,*
> *I am coming,*
> *Dark purple rises in the east,*
> *I am coming,*
> *Begging you to awaken, and light the*
> *world,*
> *I am coming, Father Sun.*

She drew out her long blue war shirt, a white dance sash, her white feathered cape, polished slate mirror, and a small pot. Beautiful red, black, and white paintings of the katsinas covered the pot.

She hung her cape on the ladder that thrust up through the roof entry, then shrugged into her blue war shirt, and tied the white sash around her waist. As she slipped on two pairs of cotton socks and her sandals, she thought about Cloudblower. Catkin had never known anyone as kind or caring. Or secretive. She did not know what to expect today. They might simply climb the cliff, perform the sacred Turning-Back-the-Sun ritual, and return to Talon Town for the morning Dances. But Catkin had the uneasy feeling that, after all that had happened in the past few days, Cloudblower would feel obligated to speak with

Catkin. And Catkin did not know what she would say.

She laced up her red leather leggings, then combed and braided her long hair.

As she lifted the lid on the small painted pot, the sweet perfumes of corn flour and ground evening primroses encircled her. Catkin dipped her fingers and rubbed the fine white powder over her face.

"In memory of White Shell Woman," she reverently whispered, "grandmother of Father Sun. We thank you for giving us light and warmth."

She studied herself in the polished slate mirror. The powder shimmered a ghostly white, and her dark eyes looked huge.

Catkin tucked the pot and mirror back into her big red jar and stepped to her buffalohide bedding.

Her war club, as always, rested to the side within easy reach. She picked it up and tested its familiar weight. It felt comforting in her hand. She tied it to her dance sash and yawned.

As she walked to the ladder and swung her white-feathered cape around her shoulders, snow fell around her, landing on her hair and hands. Climbing the stairs cut into the cliff would be treacherous, especially in the darkness. They would have to go slowly.

Catkin started up the ladder and stepped out onto the roof. Tendrils of blue smoke rose from the other roof entries of Hillside Village, and she could hear people talking softly, readying themselves for the sacred activities of the day.

Her sandals crunched snow as she walked across the rooftop. A few fires gleamed in the flats below. Her gaze landed on the place Browser stood guard. He would be tired and hungry, probably thinking about Whiproot's war club, speculating on how it had ended up in a roaring fire.

As she had all night.

She walked to the ladder and took the slick rungs down one at a time. Scattered patches of starlight lit the canyon, gleaming from the freshly fallen snow.

When Catkin reached the ground, she turned and saw Cloudblower waiting for her near the plaza fire pit where a bed of red coals glowed. Cloudblower had her hands extended to the warmth. She wore her buffalo-hide cape, painted with the red images of wolf, coyote, eagle, and raven, the Blessed Spirit Helpers of the Katsinas' People. Feathers and seed beads knotted the ends of the long fringes on the bottom. Cloudblower had coiled her long gray-streaked black braid on top of her head and fastened it with carved deerbone pins. Her triangular face, slanting eyes, and sharply pointed nose looked somehow softer beneath the layer of sacred white powder.

She turned when Catkin neared, and said, "A Happy Longnight to you, Catkin. Are you ready?"

"I am ready, Elder."

Cloudblower nodded and led the way.

They walked in front of Hillside Village and out onto the dark trail that ran eastward along the base of the cliff. The massive bulk of Kettle Town, almost as large as Talon Town, loomed huge and black in the distance. Orange gleams lit a few of the chambers near the front of the town, and Catkin saw the dark shapes of people moving about on the rooftops. After they'd eaten, and sung their morning prayers, they would dress for the celebration, and make their ways to Talon Town.

Only the Dancers would be allowed into the newly restored kiva. Spectators would sit in the plaza or on the roofs and wait for the Dancers to emerge from the subterranean ceremonial chamber.

They walked behind Kettle Town to the ladder that leaned against the rounded tower by the cliff. Cloudblower climbed up first and waited for Catkin. When she stepped onto the tower's roof, Cloudblower took the next ladder. The cliff here was too steep for stone stairs. The ladder, coupled with handholds, took them to the slope in the cliff where the stairs had been cut a hundred sun cycles ago.

"Careful," Cloudblower said as she stepped off the ladder onto the stairs. "The steps are icy."

"I will be, Elder."

Catkin climbed slowly, actually it was more like crawling. She braced both hands on the top step, found a handhold, then slid her knees up, and reached for the next step.

Father Sun had just opened his eyes in the Land of the Dead. A deep blue gleam arched over the eastern horizon, lighting the tallest ridges and dying them an unearthly shade of purple. From this vantage, Catkin could see vast distances. Blunt buttes jutted up here and there across the eroded country. The early morning light threw their shadows across the uplands like arms stretched out in longing. Black slashes of drainages cut the hills and zigzagged into the bottomlands.

Cloudblower crawled onto the rim and extended a hand to Catkin.

Catkin grasped her fingers and allowed Cloudblower to pull her up. Golden spikes of grass grew in the rocky crevices. They swayed gently in the morning wind.

To the south, in front of her, the lands of the Fire Dogs rose in cool blue layers, the grass-covered flats giving way to pine-whiskered Thunder Peak. Billowing black clouds sailed over the canyon, trailing gray veils of snow beneath them. Turquoise Maiden formed a black hump on the eastern horizon, to her left. Westward, the fires of Starburst Town glittered like fallen stars.

Catkin inhaled the beauty and exhaled a prayer of thanks.

Cloudblower walked across the canyon rim, her head bowed, Singing softly.

Catkin followed. Father Sun would be very weak this morning, his strength exhausted from a sun cycle of rising to light the world. If he could not pull himself into the sky, he would stand still on the horizon, and Cloudblower would have to perform the sacred Turning-Back-the-Sun ritual. She would have to offer her own strength to Father Sun.

Two summers ago, in Flowing Waters Town, Catkin had played the flute for Hophorn while she'd performed the ritual. Hophorn had been fasting for sixteen days, drinking only dried squash blossom tea. Yet she had lain on her side and wretched into the winter grasses for two hands of time. By dawn, the vomiting had turned to dry wrenching heaves. But her strength had been enough. Father Sun had risen and chased the cold and darkness from the land.

Cloudblower walked around a shoulder-high pillar of wind-carved sandstone, then turned, and looked eastward across the point of the pillar. As she pulled out the four small bags she wore as a necklace, snow coated the shoulders of her buffalo cape. Melted flakes glistened like tears in her hair.

Catkin folded her arms beneath her white-feathered cape and waited.

Cloudblower opened the first sack, and her deep beautiful voice echoed across the canyon, *"In beauty we begin. In beauty we begin."*

She tipped the sack and poured white cornmeal to the east. Wind Baby caught the meal and carried it out over the rim in a fog. It shimmered among the snowflakes and fell.

Cloudblower turned and emptied the red cornmeal to the south, the yellow to the west, and the blue cornmeal to the north.

Then she lifted her meal-covered hands to the sky, and finally, bent over to touch Our Grandmother Earth, as she Sang: *"In beauty we finish. In beauty we finish."*

Catkin looked eastward. Usually, at this time in the ritual Father Sun crested the horizon, but it appeared they had some time.

Cloudblower said, "Forgive me. I am not as adept at this as Hophorn. She always knows the exact moment to empty the last sack."

"She has had more practice, Cloudblower. I don't think Father Sun cares if our prayers are a little early."

Cloudblower smiled and walked to stand beside Catkin, gazing eastward. A translucent lavender halo marked the place where Father Sun would first show his face. The Cloud People seemed to be waiting, hovering in the purpled light, with their bellies gleaming.

The longer they stood there, the more uncomfortable Cloudblower seemed to be. She finally walked a few steps away.

Catkin said, "Are you well, Cloudblower?"

Cloudblower's mouth tightened. She knelt and gently touched an ice-sheathed blade of grass that protruded through the thin layer of snow. "Beauty is such a frail thing, Catkin. I often wonder if humans understand how precious it is. Every time we love, or touch someone tenderly, or laugh in genuine delight, we should be deeply grateful. Each should be a prayer. I have always tried to live that way, but often, more of late"—Cloudblower gave Catkin a tremulous smile—"I fail."

"We all fail, Elder. It is allowed on occasion."

Cloudblower rose to her feet and shook her head. "Not for me."

Wind Baby gusted across the rim, kicking up snow, and whirling it over the edge in a luminous haze.

"Why not, Elder?"

Cloudblower frowned at the eastern horizon. Father Sun had still not shown his face.

"I have made too many errors, done too many terrible things in my life, to be allowed to fail ever again."

Cloudblower took a step toward Catkin, and Catkin 'felt suddenly anxious. Sweat broke out beneath her arms and trickled down her sides.

"I have only seen you do good things, Cloudblower: I think, perhaps, you demand too much of yourself."

Cloudblower tipped her head to the right and stared at Catkin. The lines around her dark eyes deepened. "I can do many good things, when I—I live in my female soul. But often my male body takes over, Catkin, and you cannot imagine the things I long for. The things I do."

She took another step closer, and Catkin backed away toward the rim. Two hundred hands below, she could see Talon Town. The plaza fire blazed, and people had already begun to line the walls. Old people sat with blankets pulled over their heads, and parents clutched children in their laps. Even in the dim blue gleam, the bright colors and elaborate designs on their clothing made a gorgeous sight.

Catkin said, "What's wrong, Cloudblower?"

The sacred *Kokwimu* turned away, but not before Catkin saw the anguished expression on her face. "You see, it is because I understand the twists of male and female souls that I try so hard to help people."

"I can understand that."

Cloudblower turned back, and tears blurred her eyes. "No, Catkin, you can't. You see, not even I knew until a few moons ago, the—the violence—of the male soul." She held out a hand to Catkin. Her voice went low and shaky. "In that time, I have learned a terrifying truth."

"What truth?"

Cloudblower clenched her hand to a trembling fist. "Have you ever felt... I mean, has it ever occurred to you that there might be more than one person inside you? That someone else lives in your body without your permission?"

Catkin shrugged. "Often. When I am engaged in battle, I am a different person. I will catch myself about to slice a man's throat and wonder who it is inside me who can do this terrible thing. But if that other 'me' were to ask my permission to take over my body during a fight, I would give it without hesitation, Elder. 'She' is the one who keeps me alive."

Cloudblower kept silent, staring into Catkin's eyes. Finally, she whispered, "May I tell you a story?"

"Yes. Of course. I love your stories."

Cloudblower checked the horizon again and folded her arms tightly across her chest. The red paintings of wolf, coyote, eagle, and raven swayed. The birds appeared to be flying.

"I know a woman. When she was a child, she had a very wicked father. He hurt her, Catkin. She does not remember what I am about to tell you, but I swear it is true. When she'd seen two summers, he started lying with her, forcing things inside her. When she cried, he used to make her play a game he called 'beetle,' where he forced her to lie on her back, then push up with her arms and legs until she'd arched her back as far as she could. She had to stay that way for hands of time. When she couldn't, he beat her in the head with a fire-hardened digging stick. By the time she'd seen four summers, she fell asleep every time he came into their chamber. Just"—Cloudblower shook her head—"fell on the floor sound asleep. She would wake up bleeding and imagine that some monster had harmed her while she slept. She envisioned hideous creatures with deep growling voices and sharp claws."

Horrors stirred in Catkin's souls. She could see a small, helpless little girl reaching out to a man who should have been protecting her, caring for her, and instead, he...

Cloudblower shuddered.

Catkin said, "Elder, if the girl cannot remember these things, how do you know about them?"

"There is a—a boy—a man. He comes by here often, to see the woman. He worries about her. We talk."

The man I heard you speaking with here on the rim? The man in the plaza the night Whiproot died?

"He lived in her village when she was little?"

Cloudblower nodded. "Yes."

"What else did he tell you?"

"Oh, many things," she exhaled the words. "He told me that the girl said something to the old women in the village, something they understood, even if the girl didn't. She was barely two at the time. All four of those old women were murdered, Catkin. They were horribly mutilated." She hesitated as if expecting Catkin to remember hearing about the event. It did strike a memory chord, but Catkin couldn't quite recall the context of the stories. She frowned, and Cloudblower continued, "In the girl's fifth winter, her mother finally discovered the truth, and her father ran away before he could be punished for incest."

"Did anyone ever tell her what he'd done to her?"

"Gods, no, Catkin. Do you think her mother wished for her daughter to be Outcast from the clan at the age of five summers? You know the incest laws. Everyone involved is tainted with the evil and has to be punished. It does not matter whose fault it was. The little girl would have died."

"Did you ever perform a Healing on the woman, Elder?"

Cloudblower squeezed her eyes closed. "I never had the chance. I..."

A tiny sliver of gold rose over the eastern horizon. Cloudblower walked back to stand behind the Sun

Pillar. As she lifted her hands to frame the image tears traced silver lines down her cheeks.

"Father Sun rose in a different place," she said and let out a relieved breath. "He does not need our strength to journey across the sky today. We can return and join in the celebration."

Strands of graying-black hair worked loose from her braid and fluttered in the wind. She gave Catkin a pleading look. "Please do not mention these things, Catkin. I love this woman. I think it might harm her to hear my words repeated."

"I would never repeat anything you tell me, Elder."

Cloudblower steepled her fingers over her mouth. "Thank you, warrior. I had not planned on burdening you—"

"It is not a burden to ease someone else's hurt, Elder. It is a privilege."

Cloudblower touched her shoulder and softly said, "If we hurry, we can be back in time for the morning Dances."

12

Lavender thunderheads walked across the dusk sky on willowy iridescent legs of rain. Hail tipped her head back and inhaled the sweet scents of damp earth and dry grass. Thunderbirds rumbled in the distance, bringing the storm closer.

She groaned softly as she bent over and picked up a branch to prod her pinyon pine fire. A hand of time ago, Hail had boiled juniper needles in Magpie's big chili pot, poured equal amounts into five plastic bowls, and instructed each of them to take a ritual bath—which meant they had to dip a cloth in the water and wash every part of their skin and hair.

Behind her, in the red tent, Magpie, Sylvia, and Washais whispered. Dusty and Dr. Robertson had already been purified and returned to Dr. Robertson's trailer to dress.

Hail couldn't see the bottom of the fire too well, but the flames looked high enough. She used her stick to lift the pile of Dusty's and Dr. Robertson's clothes and dropped it onto the fire. Thick greasy smoke rose as the flames licked up around the edges and gradually worked their way to the center.

She leaned on the stick while she gazed out at the site.

Evil rode the air with silvered wings, flashing around, studying the camp and the people, waiting its chance to slip inside them and make a nest in their souls.

The Haze boy had been very quiet, as though afraid to breathe.

Hail had to purify everyone who'd been there when the pot was opened, then she had to figure out what to do with the pot itself.

When the fire had burned through the clothes, Hail threw another pine log onto the flames, and said, "All right, Magpie, you can come out."

The three women emerged carrying their plastic bowls, and bundles of clothes. Blankets covered their naked bodies, and the tang of juniper surrounded them. Washais had unbraided her hair, leaving it long and free. It fell over her pale blue blanket in a shining rippled wealth. Magpie and Sylvia stood in matching ivory blankets.

"All right," Hail said, "no one may ever use those bowls again. They've been tainted with the evil. Toss them into the fire." She tapped a heartstone with her stick.

The white plastic bowls landed in the flames and shriveled up into black knots. An ugly acrid smell rose.

"Sylvia," Hail said, "you first. Go stand over there, downwind from the fire."

"Gotcha." Sylvia walked to stand directly in front of Hail.

"Now you two"—Hail gestured to Washais and Magpie—"stand on either side of me."

Magpie stood on Hail's right and Washais on her left.

The coffeepot, filled with water, sat on the ground in front of Hail. She propped her branch and reached down for the battered black handle. "Okay, Sylvia, take off your blanket."

Sylvia tossed the ivory blanket aside and spread her arms. As skinny as a Cottonwood twig, the white skin she kept covered looked corpsish against her deeply tanned face, lower arms, and legs.

"I'm ready, Mrs. Walking Hawk. Cleanse me."

Hail poured a little water from the coffeepot onto the coals, and a blue haze of smoke billowed up. "You and Washais help out, Magpie."

"Yes, Aunt. Follow me, Maureen." Magpie used the blanket around her shoulders like wings to fan the smoke across to Sylvia.

"I see," Washais said and fanned her blanket in rhythm with Magpie's.

Sylvia closed her eyes as the cleansing smoke blew over her. "I love this smell. Feels hot though."

Hail said, "You'll feel a lot hotter if that corpse powder gets inside you and starts eating you alive. Turn around, Sylvia."

"Okay." Sylvia spun on one foot, military fashion.

Magpie said, "My God. That's the whitest butt I have ever seen in my life."

Sylvia grinned over her shoulder. "Blinding, ain't it?"

When the smoke dwindled, Hail poured a little

more water on the fire, and Washais and Magpie blew it across to Sylvia.

Hail said, "Make sure it touches every part of you, Sylvia. Smoke is a cousin to the Thunderbirds who bring us rain and life. The Spirit of the smoke will drive away any evil that lived in that corpse powder."

"Cool," Sylvia said, and fluffed her shoulder-length brown hair out so the smoke would penetrate it.

"Good. You're done, Sylvia. Go put on clean clothes."

Sylvia picked up her blanket and walked for her tent. "See you soon."

Hail gestured. "Washais, your turn."

Washais took up Sylvia's position, except that she stood solemnly with her head bowed, as though saying a silent prayer.

Hail waited until Washais lifted her head, then she said, "Take off your blanket, child."

Washais pulled it away from her shoulders and dropped it at her feet. A tall woman, Father Sun had roasted her in the past few days. Her chest had gotten it the worst, though. A scoop of reddish-brown curved down over the tops of her breasts.

Hail poured water on the fire again, and Magpie fanned the billowing smoke across.

Washais lifted her face to the sky, and started singing, a beautiful lilting song that soothed Hail. Magpie smiled broadly. Neither of them understood the strange words, but they both knew it was a blessing song, asking forgiveness, praying for good things for her people.

'Turn around, Washais," Hail instructed. Washais turned and spread her long arms and legs. When she finished the song, she feathered her hair in the smoke, and started speaking in a new language.

"En archay ayne ha logos, kai ha logos ayne pros ton theon..."

Hail looked at Magpie and they both shrugged. You didn't have to understand words to know when somebody was being reverent. It was the softness of the voice, the posture.

Hail poured more water on the fire, and Magpie fanned smoke over Washais.

When Washais went silent, Hail said, "You're done, Washais. You can put on clean clothes now."

"Thank you, Mrs. Walking Hawk." She picked up her blanket and headed for her tent.

Before she ducked through the flap, Hail asked, "What language was that last prayer, Washais? It was pretty. I don't think I've ever heard that before?"

"New Testament Greek. That's the opening of the Book of John." Washais smiled and entered her green tent.

Hail turned to Magpie and lifted a hand. "Give me your blanket, Magpie. I'll fan you."

"Thank you, Aunt, but I don't know why I have to be purified. I was with you when they opened the pot."

Magpie handed over her blanket and went to stand across the fire. Short black hair framed her round face. Even her arms, used to the sun, had tanned more deeply since they'd been here.

"I know, child," Hail said, "but I don't want to take any chances with you. When you talked to Dusty, you might have breathed in some of the powder on his clothes."

Magpie gave Hail a soft look, smiled, and closed her eyes. "All right, Aunt, I'm ready."

Hail poured water onto the fire, laid her stick down, and fanned the smoke over her great-niece.

Magpie gathered the smoke in her hands and rubbed it over her arms, and face, then the rest of her body. Next, she turned around and ran her hands through her short black hair.

"All right, child, you'll be fine now."

"Thank you, Aunt." Magpie picked up her blanket and headed for their red tent. "I'll be right back."

"Good. You and me need to figure out how to catch the evil that's running loose around us."

"I know, Aunt. I have some ideas about that."

From inside her tent, Washais called, "So do I!"

Sylvia ducked out of her tent dressed in faded blue cutoffs, a red tank top, and hiking boots. "Wow, I feel like a million dollars. I think it worked."

Hail smiled and used her stick to lift Magpie's contaminated clothing and dropped them into the flames.

Sylvia came to stand beside her. "Can I do that?"

"Yes." Hail handed her the stick. "But don't let the end of the stick touch you anywhere, and after you've burned all the clothes throw the stick in on top of the flames."

"*No problemo,*" Sylvia said,

As Sylvia lifted Washais's old clothing into the fire, Hail hobbled over to one of the lawn chairs and eased down. It felt good to sit. Sweat trickled down her neck and soaked the collar of the blue-flowered yellow dress. Magpie had insisted she take a pain pill about two hours ago, but Hail wasn't sure she felt better. The pain had lessened, but a groggy, off-balance, sensation had replaced it. For no reason at all, the world would just go out of focus, and Hail would stumble. She'd almost fallen into the fire when she'd been cleansing Dusty. If he hadn't snatched her sleeve and dragged her back, she'd have been scorched. She didn't like feeling this way.

Sylvia *tsked* to herself as she lifted her own clothes, a pair of shorts and a T-shirt, into the flames. "That was my favorite buffalo shirt. I guess I'll have to get back to Wyoming someday to find another one like it."

"You should get a real buffalo hide to make a shirt out of," Hail suggested. "It would keep you warm in the winter."

"I wonder where I'd get one. I've never seen them at Wal-Mart."

Hail chuckled. "I think you ought to call one of the buffalo ranches in New Mexico. Some of them sell hides. I had a cousin who..."

The door to the camp trailer squealed as Dusty and Dr. Robertson came down the steps. Dusty wore a yellow T-shirt, and pink shorts. They'd been white at one time, Hail thought, but he must have washed them with something red. His reflective sunglasses glinted as he walked. Dr. Robertson looked like a flag in his red-and-white-striped shirt, and blue jeans. They were talking in low tones as they approached the camp. Frowns incised their foreheads.

"Hey," Sylvia called. "I figured you two would be the first back into camp. What took you so long?"

A gust of wind whipped across the site, rattling the tents and trash box. Dr. Robertson pulled down his fedora to fend it off, and Dusty turned his head. Blond hair flipped around his face.

"We were discussing what to do with the pot of powdered people," Dusty said. "Before the cleansing, we put the cap back on and double-bagged it in Ziplocs, as Elder Walking Hawk instructed, but—"

"But!" Washais said as she ducked out of her tent. She'd replaited her hair and the braid hung down the front of her tan T-shirt to the waist of her jeans. "Now we have to get rid of it, right?"

"Right," Magpie said as she joined the group. She'd dressed in a white T-shirt and brown shorts. "The question is, how?"

"I'm not sure," Hail said in a frail voice and laced her arthritic fingers in her lap. "Maybe we should find another place, far away from here, and bury it again. That would keep wicked people from finding it and using it to hurt others."

As Dusty sifted through the ice chest, Dr. Robertson and Sylvia unfolded lawn chairs and sat down across the fire.

Washais pulled up a chair next to Hail. "Mrs. Walking Hawk, I have an idea that might sound strange to you, but I would like to take the pot back to Canada with me, for further study—"

"You're joking, right?" As Dusty turned, sunlight reflected from his glasses. He had a bottle of fruit juice in his hand. He twisted off the cap, and said, "Doesn't Canada have laws about the disposition of human remains?"

"Yes, of course. There will be a lot of red tape, but this is such a rare opportunity, I think—"

"We can't, Maureen," Magpie said. She dropped into" a chair beside Sylvia, to Washais's left. "There are strong traditionalists here who will want to see the pot, and its contents, destroyed—or as my aunt suggests, at least put in a place where it can't hurt anyone."

"Well, we can't destroy it," Dusty said. "We'd be in violation of every historic preservation law on the books. Not only that, we'd be destroying federal property. So let's figure out something else to do."

"Give it to me," Washais said. "That's what else we can do. I'll take the evil far away."

Wind blew wispy hair into Hail's eyes. She tucked it behind her ear and said, "We have to respect the Power there, Washais. People can die just from touching that pot."

Washais bowed her head and seemed to be marshaling her arguments. In a soft voice, she said, "I know this is difficult, but the contents of that pot might tell us how that woman lived, how she died, why this terrible thing happened to her. Isn't that important? Isn't it more respectful to learn from her? Elder Walking Hawk, I think she's just another, older Elder, one who can teach us new lessons."

Dusty said, "I don't agree."

"Why not?" Washais turned and glared.

"If they were just slaves, like I thought in the beginning, I might have sided with you. But you've proven your point. These women were murdered, and at least part of this last one was turned into corpse powder. She's better off covered up. According to traditional beliefs—"

"Hold it," Washais said. "I don't understand this. Four years ago, I went to the rededication of an ossuary. We held our Feast of the Dead and invited our ancestors to come visit us from the Village of the Souls. When it was all over, we each took little containers of earth from the burial pit, because we believe it contains bits of our ancestors. My container sits by my bedside table. That's *traditional,* isn't it?"

"Your tradition, not theirs," Dusty said, and took a sip from his juice bottle.

"What makes one traditional belief more important than another?" Washais's brows lowered.

Gently, Hail said, "Washais? I don't understand your ways, but I'm glad your ancestors hear you and help your people. This place is different, though. Our ancestors lived and died here. Their blood runs in our veins. We have different ways. That *stuff* you found today is dangerous." She blinked her white-filmed eyes at the clouds building in the sky. The scent of rain had grown strong. "It's bad enough that those NOAA people want to put a weather station here. With all the bad things that happened on this spot that weather station is never going to work right." She looked back at Washais. "I think we have to take that pot away and cover it up. Maybe put a big rock on top so that the evil can never get loose again."

Dusty nodded. "I agree."

Dale pushed his fedora back on his head. "If that's what our Indian monitor wants, then that's what we'll do. Just tell us where to bury it, Maggie."

Magpie's brow furrowed. "I'll have to think about it."

"But, Dale," Washais said. Disbelief crept into her voice. "I *need* to do more work on this burial."

"I know it would be nice, Maureen, but it isn't going to happen. We're over the budget already, and I hate to keep bringing it up, but she's outside of the impact area."

Washais's gaze went from Magpie, to Dale, then rested on Dusty. She looked at him as if for support. He slowly shook his head.

"Not this time, Doctor," he said. "Sorry."

"I don't understand either of you." Her hot gaze went from Dale to Dusty. "You're telling me that you are willing to stop scientific inquiry based on religious fundamentalism? Do you realize the precedent this kind of decision sets? What happens if next week a group of Cherokee fundamentalists come out, say that the contents of that pot are the sacred remains of their ancestors, and claim it as a holy relic? Will you let them have it based solely upon religious mythology? What if a Navajo witch claims it because he wants its Power? Will you give it to him? How do you decide *which* religious beliefs are more valid than others?"

Dusty leaned forward. "I agree it's difficult, but—"

"Difficult? It's *insane!* And you're as nutty as your father if you let it happen!"

Dusty seemed to turn to stone. He stared at her through glittering blue eyes.

Washais rose to her feet and stood quietly for a long moment. "I need to get away for a while, Stewart. To think about this. Would it be possible..."

Dusty fished in his pocket with his free hand. The keys rattled as he tossed them to Washais. "Drive carefully, obey the speed limit signs, and don't trust the gas gauge. Fill up at Crownpoint going and coming."

Washais nodded, said, "Thanks," and stiffly walked to her tent. She dragged out her purse and headed for the Bronco.

As the engine roared to life, and she backed out, dust filled the air.

Hail watched the blue truck jounce down the dirt road for town. "I hope she's all right," she whispered in concern. "I didn't mean to hurt her."

"She'll be all right, Aunt," Magpie said, and came over to sit in Washais's chair. She took Hail's hand and stroked it. "Don't worry about her."

Dusty peered at Hail over the rims of his sunglasses; she could see a mixture of hurt and rage in his eyes. "She's fine, Elder," he said in a clipped voice. "She's just not accustomed to making decisions based upon real life cultural taboos. Physical anthropologists work with sterile facts. Life has just taught her a valuable lesson."

"Really?" Dale asked with mock interest. "What?"

"Sometimes science is irrelevant." Dusty adopted an authoritative posture, his broad shoulders squared, his chin up.

The first drops of rain started to fall, stippling the ground and hissing in the fire.

Dusty finished his juice and threw the bottle into the trash box. It clattered through the other garbage. He stabbed a finger at Dale. "If we have trouble over this, I want you to remember that you're the one who invited her out here. I was against it from the start. A lab rat in a field camp! God forbid."

Sylvia examined Dusty through squinted eyes for several seconds, clearly on the verge of defending Washais, then as if she'd reconsidered, she smiled, and her gaze dropped to Dusty's pink shorts. 'Tell me something, boss? Do those come with the panties built in?"

13

The hollow thumping of the foot drums in the First People's kiva echoed through the twilight, slow, steady, like a sleeping person's heartbeat.

As Browser and Cloudblower walked across Talon Town's crowded plaza, Cloudblower said, "Hophorn is afraid, Browser, but I think it will be good for her to watch the Dances. This is her favorite ritual of the sun cycle. If she does not attend, I think in a few moons, she will wish she had."

Cloudblower wore her painted buffalohide cape, red leggings, and moccasins covered with shell bells. They clicked pleasantly. She had coiled her long gray-black braid on top of her head. The style made her face appear starkly triangular.

Three lines of people encircled the plaza. Children sat in front, with the elderly behind them. Other adults stood against the wall. The bravest people perched on the flat roofs of Talon Town, wrapped in many-colored blankets. The village elders, along with Stone Ghost, sat on the roof of the great kiva. Each group of elders had their own colors and styles of ritual capes. The Hillside elders wore red-painted buffalohides; the Starburst Village people preferred yellow deerhides; the elders from Frosted Meadow adorned themselves with rabbitfur capes, covered with a thick layer of blue-gray pinyon jay feathers. The capes adopted by the Badgerpaw Village elders had an intricately woven layer of cotton lace draped over the top of finely smoked leather. Stone Ghost, of course, wore the same mangy brown-and-white turkey-feather cape. His wispy white hair looked as if it had been teased just for this occasion; it stuck out like a frizzy halo.

In the northernmost corner of the plaza, beneath the enormous paintings of the Great Warriors of East and West, an array of blankets had been spread. Haunches of roasted venison, whole cooked turkeys, and a variety of smaller game, hung from racks above steaming pots of beans, plates of breads, baked gourds, bowls of roasted pumpkin and sunflower seeds, large fabric bags filled with popped corn, and several water jars. People were free to help themselves throughout the celebration.

Peavine walked through the gathering, speaking to people. She had an annoyed expression on her ugly face. Her white doehide cape shone in the torchlight.

"You have spoken with Hophorn about this?" Browser asked.

"This morning. She agreed to try. I don't know how long she will be able to sit outside. The only place she feels safe is in my chamber. But even if she sits for less than a hand of time, it will help her, Browser."

Dusk fell over the canyon like a gray opalescent

blanket, gleaming from the snow that had fallen at dawn. The towering cliff behind Talon Town shone faintly blue. Above the rim, the first Evening People sparkled.

The booming of the foot drums grew louder, and the high wail of a flute joined in. The note hung like a hawk in midair, before it lightly swooped down and fluttered.

Cloudblower stopped before her door curtain and called, "Hophorn. We are here. Are you ready?"

A stammering voice responded, "Y-yes, I—I am."

Cloudblower drew back the curtain, and Browser saw Hophorn sitting just inside the entry. She gazed at Cloudblower and Browser as if terrified by the sight of them. She was trembling, her long black hair moving as if alive.

Softly, Cloudblower said, "Don't be afraid, Hophorn. I'm going to spread your hides right in front of the door in case you wish to go back inside. And Catkin will be standing guard on the roof above you."

"Yes, she will," Browser said.

Hophorn wet her lips, nodded, and reached for the black blanket that lay folded beside her. She drew it to her chest. She wore her usual Longnight ritual clothing, a scarlet macaw cape elaborately decorated with bone beads, and tiny red shale figurines carved into the shapes of frogs, birds, deer, and wolves. Her strange jet pendant, the serpent coiled inside the broken eggshell, hung down to the middle of her chest. "R-ready," she managed, and extended a trembling hand to Browser.

He helped Hophorn outside and held her up while Cloudblower ducked into the chamber to grab an armload of hides.

Cloudblower carefully spread the hides out next to the door curtain. "You'll be safe, here, Hophorn. I swear it. I—"

"Have, you seen my daughter?" Peavine said as she strode up. Her pocked face had mottled with what appeared to be anger. "She was supposed to be here a half a hand of time ago."

"I haven't seen Yucca Blossom, Peavine," Cloudblower said. "But she is eleven. Several of the older girls gathered near the Hillside plaza fire to talk. Perhaps she is there."

"Well, she isn't supposed to be!"

"Do you wish me to send someone to fetch her?"

"No," Peavine replied irritably. "If she isn't here by the time the Dances begin, I'll fetch her myself. And she'll be sorry."

Peavine turned and stalked away.

Cloudblower exchanged a bewildered glance with Browser, then reached for Hophorn.

But Hophorn turned to search the roof, as if for Catkin.

Catkin lifted a hand and walked over. "It is good to see you, Sunwatcher. Are you well?"

Hophorn smiled, weaved on her feet, and sank to the hides as though her legs would no longer hold her.

Browser called, "The Sunwatcher will be sitting here for the Dances. You'll watch over her, won't you?"

"Of course, War Chief. And when Jackrabbit takes my place in another hand of time, I'll tell him to do the same."

An expression of relief slackened Hophorn's pretty face.

Cloudblower gently pulled the black blanket from

Hophorn's hands. "Let me help you." She shook the blanket out, then draped it over Hophorn's head, and tied it in a knot in front. "There. You should stay warm now. I must go into the kiva to purify the Dancers, Hophorn, but I won't be away for long, and Browser will be close while I am gone."

Hophorn looked up at Cloudblower with huge eyes.

Cloudblower gently touched her cheek. "Browser? I know you are charged with maintaining harmony in the plaza, but if you are able—"

"I will stay as close to Hophorn as I can, Elder."

Cloudblower gave him a grateful look, backed away, and strode for the kiva.

Hophorn gripped a handful of Browser's buckskin pant leg and held tight.

He knelt beside her, and whispered, "You don't see them here, do you, Hophorn?"

She scanned the faces in the plaza, and on the rooftops, then she did it again, with great patience, before she shook her head.

"Good. I asked the village matrons to personally identify each person before we allowed him or her into Talon Town. People will, however, be coming and going all night long." Browser pointed to the ladder that stood ten paces to Hophorn's left. "If you see *anyone* come down that ladder that you think might be—"

She gestured to the roof. "C-Catkin."

"Yes, good, Hophorn. Call out to Catkin, or to me if you see me. We will have those people face-down in the dirt before you can shout again."

Browser patted her hand where it gripped his pant

leg. "I'm going to have trouble breaking up fights if I have to drag you with me."

Hophorn gazed at her hand, and slowly, a finger at a time, let go.

Browser said, "If you need me, I'll be close. Just call. Do you understand?"

The black blanket hid her face unless she was looking directly at him, but he saw her nod.

"Good. I'm going to go stand over there." He pointed to the door that led into the kiva's antechamber. "That's thirty paces away, Hophorn. I'll be there the entire time. I promise."

Hophorn gazed up at him with terrified eyes, but she nodded.

Browser smiled and walked across the plaza to his ritual position beside the door. A total of two hundred and forty-three people had come for the ceremonial. Villagers from Starburst Town, the last to arrive, had trotted in just after dawn. Conversations and laughter filled the night.

Browser glanced back at Hophorn. Her eyes had not left him.

He waved.

Her expression didn't change. She watched him as if her life depended upon it.

Catkin stood tall on the roof right above Hophorn, her club resting on her right shoulder. Her long black braid draped the front of her white-feathered cape.

Their gazes met and held.

The lines around her eyes had tightened.

He braced his feet and tried to get a full breath into his lungs.

The flute and drums inside the kiva went silent.

The crowd hushed.

Like a wave rolling toward shore, people turned as one, to watch the door beside Browser.

Cloudblower stepped out with a feathered prayer stick in one hand, and a red pot of sacred cornmeal in the other. As she walked she Sang in a deep melodic voice:

> *"I am planting the northern mountains.*
> *I am planting the western sea.*
> *I am planting the southern deserts.*
> *I am planting the eastern trees."*

She knelt in the middle of the plaza and planted the prayer stick in the snow. The downy eagle feathers on the top fluttered and swayed in the cold evening breeze.

As she rose, she tipped her pot and poured a line of blue cornmeal at the base of the prayer stick, then backed up toward Browser and the door to the subterranean ceremonial chamber. The Dancers would follow that line, symbolically retracing the path of the First People from their emergence from the underworlds to their arrival at Straight Path Canyon. They would Sing of the long journey in the brilliance of Father Sun's light.

Cloudblower halted on the other side of the door, and a haunting chorus crept from the kiva, soft howls, and yips, hawk shrieks, and the low roars of mountain lions.

Cloudblower lifted her meal-covered hands to the Evening People, and at that instant, a line of unearthly figures emerged from the firelit womb of the kiva.

They shuffled forward with their arms swinging

and their sandals kicking up a haze of snow. Their Song was hushed, like the chirping of newborn birds. Their glorious masks, part animal, part astonishing god, bore sprinkles of raindrops, shining stars, and feathered halos. Ruffs of buffalo fur encircled their throats; and their bare chests, painted pure white, gleamed with black zigzagging lightning bolts. Their turkey-feather capes swayed as they trotted down the road of emergence, tossing their masked heads, and staring at the crowd through dark, empty eye sockets. They carried red-and-yellow dance sticks and gourd rattles.

When they reached the planted prayer stick, they broke into four lines and veered outward in the sacred directions, showing the different paths people had taken after they'd reached Straight Path Canyon.

Hophorn clutched the black blanket beneath her nose covering most of her face, but a reverent glow lit her eyes.

Browser smiled.

The Dancers shook their rattles, circled, and formed two concentric circles.

Each breath they released, each thump of their feet, called to Our Mother Earth, telling her that after this long night, Father Sun would hold her longer, love her more, and warmth would seep back into her bones.

The Dancers stopped circling and tilted their heads, as if listening.

The flute sounded again, the note so sweet and high it brought tears to Browser's eyes. He bowed his head.

Four women emerged from the kiva, their white doeskin dresses and boots shining as they trotted very close to the crowd—but hallowed, untouchable. Eagle feathers adorned their long black hair, twisting and bobbing in the breeze. The Deer Mothers circled the plaza four times, Dancing through the soft torchlight, their arms reaching for the sky, supernatural beings that had just emerged from the misty cloud of legend. Their hoarse breathy voices resembled those of deer in the forest, calling warnings to each other.

The masked Dancers bleated or howled in terror. Some ran for cover in the crowd. Others hunched down and waited for the sacred Mothers to pass.

Spectators put their hands over their eyes and watched through the weave of their fingers. No one could look directly upon such Power and beauty.

Browser glanced back at Hophorn.

She was gone. The hides empty.

Panic went' through him, then he saw the door curtain to Cloudblower's chamber swinging.

Had she only been able to watch for a finger of time?

Browser looked up at the roof. Catkin knelt with her back to him, speaking to someone below. Probably one of the warriors standing guard on the mounds.

Several people perched on the roof near Catkin, watching the Dances, smiling.

Browser heaved a sigh and lowered his head again as the Deer Mothers passed by.

My white buckskin shirt and pants blend with the snowy ground, but Shadow's dress is the darkness.

She paces behind me, her steps silent, black eyes glittering. She is an abyss in the night, invisible, dangerous.

A single flute wails.

It begins low, a shrike's whistle.

People line both sides of the Dancers' path. Old people grin and clutch squirming children to their chests. The Dancers' moccasins shish as they prance through the snow. The light of creation lives in their hooves, claws, furred muzzles, and polished wooden beaks.

I rub my cold face, stunned by the beauty. As the Dancers sway and dip, they watch me with the ancient eyes of long-dead heroes, ancestors, the spirits of clouds.

The flute grows shrill and breathy—like a strangled scream.

And I know it is time.

Shadow creeps up behind me.

I can feel her eagerness.

On the fabric of my souls, I see her smile. Death lives in the elegant curves of her lips, the quivering of her nostrils. She is magnificent.

Her fingers sink into the muscles of my arm like blades.

"Wait," I whisper.

She is trembling, the longing so strong it is a physical pain.

"Go to the pottery mounds," I say. "I will bring her to you."

She backs away.

After several moments, I turn, but I see only darkness and starlit snow.

Distant buttes are black blocks on the horizon. The scent of burning cedar rises from the sacred fires, bathing my face.

I scan Talon Town and Hillside Village.

I wonder if my daughter sees me. If, even now, she is shouldering past the onlookers, hurrying to meet me. The face of death and the face of the beloved are often indistinguishable.

I have experienced this myself when Shadow becomes intoxicated with the kill and turns on me. The instant before she attacks, there is a moment when I would willingly throw myself into her arms and allow myself to be consumed by the fires of her lust.

Ah. I see her.

Running away from the plaza fire in Hillside Village. She is achingly beautiful.

"Yes," *I whisper.* "Come to me. Have I not told you that you must be bathed in blood to be saved?"

Already I can feel it on my hands, warm, sticky, the scent pungent. I shiver.

As I rise, I gaze down at the dead guard. The gaping hole in his chest resembles a red-lipped mouth open in a final scream. He was standing on the edge like the others, watching the Dances. The firelight had blinded him.

I take no pride in such kills. They are like slaughtering coyote pups in their den.

The night is clear. By morning, we will all be freezing, ready for the bowl of life. The sacred meal. Hot. Steaming. We will shudder as we eat.

I tiptoe along the rim and halt near the top of the cliff stairway.

There is another. She follows the first, though the girl does not know it. Her mother?

I crouch like a cat.

Two of them.

One for each of us.

Shadow will be ruthless.

He stood on the sandstone rim one hundred hands above Yucca Blossom, his white buckskin cape and pants glowing in the torchlight. She clung to the sandstone steps, breathing hard. Gray feathers haloed his wolf mask, rising like silver rays behind the pointed ears. For a time, he crouched so still and calm, the shells sewn around his collar caught the night's gleam and shone like mirrors.

The world died around Yucca Blossom.

Her ears no longer heard the ritual chanting or flute music that echoed across the canyon. Her eyes no longer sought the Dancers in the plaza. The magnificent dresses, turquoise and shell jewelry. The ornately decorated war shirts which had flashed brilliantly moments ago, vanished as her world became the canyon rim.

Two Hearts lifted his right moccasin and extended a hand to the Dancers in Talon Town.

Yucca Blossom glanced back and forth between them.

He mimicked the steps of the Dancers who snaked around in Talon Town, shaking rattles, Singing in deep resonant voices. Like the Serpent of the Heavens who guarded the skyworld, his body glittered and swayed.

She reached for another handhold and pulled herself up. The stones were slick, icy with snow. But she hurried.

He stood like a dagger of silver flame. His long white cape blazing.

The shell bells on her cape scraped against the rock, and her white kirtle flashed around her blue leggings, as she scrambled up the cliff.

His breathing seemed loud, hoarse, his need for her unbearable.

Yucca Blossom climbed the last step and ran to him. Her two braids, woven with strips of red cloth, hung down to her waist.

He reached out, almost as if afraid, and stroked them.

She could barely hear his tight voice. *"Afraid?"* he asked.

"No. I want to be with you."

He nodded, but spread his white cloak and enfolded Yucca Blossom anyway, protecting her from the darkness and cold.

They stood close for several moments, and she smelled an odd scent, musty, metallic, like the dust that rises from fallen buildings.

He whispered, *"Do you know where the pottery mounds are?"*

"Yes. I have been there many times."

"Go. Wait for me. I will be along very soon."

Yucca Blossom obediently trotted away, heading north. She turned only once to look back.

At first she didn't see him, then the feathers on his mask quivered.

He lay stretched out on his belly in the snow just above the stairs, as if waiting for someone else.

14

Catkin saw the seven warriors from Frosted Meadow coming up the road, laughing and playfully shoving each other. They wore red capes with the hoods pulled up. Several weaved on their feet. Catkin had seen them earlier, gobbling blue corn bread, and drinking copious amounts of fermented juniper berry juice.

As they climbed the ladder to the roof, she walked down to meet them.

The first man, built like a grizzly bear, stepped off, smiling, and Catkin whispered, "The Deer Mothers have arrived."

The big man turned and put fingers to his lips to hush his companions.

The other warriors stifled their laughter and stumbled off onto the roof, grinning. As a group, they went to stand overlooking the Dancers. Wind buffeted their red capes around their legs. Two of the warriors were women. As their hoods flapped, Catkin saw their white face powder. They'd applied it thickly, in honor of White Shell Woman. One of the women looked familiar, tall and slender, but Catkin couldn't place where she'd seen her.

The big warrior elbowed one of his friends in the ribs and laughed.

On the roof of the kiva to their left, Corn Mother, Matron of Frosted Meadow Village, pointed a stern finger, and gave them all evil looks.

Cowed, the warriors shushed each other again and climbed down into the plaza. They lined the wall in front of Cloudblower's chamber.

Catkin had seen Hophorn crawl into the chamber a finger of time ago, but she looked down anyway, making certain none of the warriors had staggered through the door curtain on top of her. They stood with their fingers over their eyes, whispering to each other, but they seemed to have calmed down.

Catkin checked the positions of the other six guards standing on the high crumbling walls of Talon Town, then returned to her own position at the southeastern corner.

Catkin folded her arms beneath her white-feathered cape and focused on the potsherds that paved the wide road below. In the torchlight, they glittered and twinkled.

The two guards on the mounds to her right, faced south, gazing out across the starlit canyon bottom. They wore the painted yellow capes of Starburst Village warriors.

Catkin expelled a breath, and it frosted in the air before her. Her nerves, which had stretched tighter and tighter over the past quarter moon, hummed at the snapping point tonight. Something out there in the darkness watched her with feral eyes. She could feel that gaze upon her, unwavering, like a cat's as it stealthily closed in on prey.

A commotion broke out behind her, and Catkin saw the red-caped Frosted Meadow warriors climbing off the ladder onto the roof. They shoved and nudged each other, stumbled around, and choked back laughter. Two of the warriors supported another warrior between them, as if he'd passed out in the plaza. The incapacitated man's cape was much too long for him; it trailed the roof as they dragged him, grinning, toward the ladder down to the road.

Catkin called, "If you can't behave appropriately during the sacred Dances, I suggest you return to the Hillside plaza fire."

As if eager to obey, the big "grizzly bear" warrior tiptoed toward the ladder, but he couldn't quite keep his balance. When he tilted too far in one direction, his friends shoved him back up and snickered.

Catkin's heart lurched into her throat when the big man almost toppled over the edge, but his friends snatched the hem of his cape and tugged him backward in a flurry of waving arms and cries.

Catkin scowled at them.

The big warrior sheepishly climbed down the ladder. The two warriors dragging the other went next. They jostled the unconscious man until he roused, then shoved him onto the ladder. He climbed down unsteadily. The others filed behind him, and they staggered in a weaving, colliding herd back toward Hillside Village.

Jackrabbit met them as they rounded the south-eastern corner of the town, and hastily stepped back to let them pass. He wore a blue-and-green painted buffalohide cape, and his shoulder-length black hair shone as if freshly washed. He gazed up at Catkin and his pug nose crinkled. He said, "I saw them earlier. I didn't wish to be flattened."

"A prudent decision," she called.

Jackrabbit trotted to the ladder and climbed up. Just as he made it to the roof, the flute went silent, and the drums began, pounding out the heartbeat of Our Mother Earth, and introducing the Buffalo Dancers. They shuffled from the kiva with their curving black horns shining, shaking their shaggy heads. Long brown beards draped their red-painted chests. Buffalo brought the blessing winter snows that gave birth to spring grasses, and fed all creatures, small and large. They also possessed magical powers. They could live under lakes and run to the skyworlds by leaping from one cloud to the next. They were cousins to the Thunderbirds. They both made deep rumbling roars, and both brought water from the sky. Healing teas were always drunk from a buffalo horn cup, if possible.

Cloudblower led the Dancers around the plaza on a sinuous path, uttering a deep-throated call, the rumble a buffalo makes when she's searching for another animal in the herd.

The people in the crowd "rumbled" back to Buffalo Above, saying "Here we are, mother. We're right here. Give us your blessings."

Jackrabbit walked to Catkin and whispered, "Are you going to stay for the Dances?"

She shook her head. "I've been here since dawn. I

think I will return to my chamber and rest for a time. But I'll be back for the grand midnight Dance."

"Rest well. I will see you then."

Catkin started to walk away, then turned. "Jackrabbit, the Sunwatcher is in her chamber, but she may come back outside later. Please watch for her and let her know you are close."

He nodded, "I will. Is she still frightened?"

"Terrified. She came out for the first Dance, and saw the katsinas arrive, but went back into Cloudblower's chamber soon after."

"I will watch for her, Catkin. Don't fret."

She nodded and headed for the ladder.

Weary to the bone, her limbs felt like dead weights. She watched her feet as she walked toward the Hillside plaza fire. Six of the Frosted Meadow warriors clustered around the large jars of fermented juniper berry juice on the south side of the fire, dipping up cups, laughing too loudly.

The big bearlike warrior said, *"Is that what he told you when he borrowed your extra cape? He told me it was his sister, that he wanted us to help him play a joke on her. Some joke, she could barely walk!"*

His friends roared with laughter and stumbled around the fire.

Catkin passed them without a word. She was no longer on guard, and they were disturbing no one out here. Let them be happy.

As she neared the ladder that leaned against the side of Hillside Village, she stopped and frowned at the ground.

Though the snow had been churned up by

hundreds of sandals and hide boots, these tracks were fresh. And made by bare feet.

Catkin knelt and studied the toe and heel prints, A woman probably. Maybe a youth. She'd been staggering.

Catkin's gazed followed the tracks back toward the fire. Another person, wearing hide boots, had stepped on several of the barefoot tracks.

Catkin rose and walked alongside the tracks, tracing them across the front of Hillside Village, and onto the dirt trail that led to Kettle Town. Several of the gaps in the town's tumbled walls gleamed redly. Perhaps the two warriors had decided to return to their chambers for the evening?

Movement caught her gaze. Her eyes lifted to the cliff stairs. Two people climbed up. The red hood of the person on top had fallen back, revealing long black hair. The windblown flames and torchlight made it impossible to see the people clearly, one instant they were there, the next gone, swallowed by the darkness.

Catkin cocked her head, wondering. It was probably nothing, warriors climbing to get a better view of the Dances from the rim, but barefoot?

Her boot struck something buried in the snow.

Catkin took a last look at the figures, and knelt. She dug around in the snow until she felt a leather strap. As she pulled it out, it swung in her hand.

A necklace with a jet pendant carved into the shape of a serpent coiled inside a broken eggshell. The single coral eye glared at Catkin.

Her lungs started to heave. *She could barely walk...* "Blessed gods. No. I—I can't believe..."

The images of the Frosted Meadow warriors

flashed. Dragging a man with a cape much too long. She felt sick, shaky.

Catkin slipped the necklace over her head, drew her war club, and ran for the round tower at the base of the stairs.

15

The Buffalo Dancers trotted back for the kiva, breathing hard, their long beards shimmering with beads of sweat. Browser reverently lowered his gaze as they passed.

Cloudblower brought up the rear. She started to follow the other Dancers into the ceremonial chamber, but seemed to think better of it, and stopped beside Browser.

"How long did Hophorn watch?"

"Not long, Elder. Less than a finger of time."

Cloudblower sighed, "At least she saw the katsinas arrive. I'm grateful for that."

"I think she is, too, Elder. I'll look in on her as soon as I am able."

"Thank you, War Chief."

The next Dance would not start for half a hand of time.

The crowd rose and stretched. Conversations broke out.

On the kiva roof above him, Browser heard the clan

elders talking. Flame Carrier called, "War Chief? We are coming down."

"Yes, Matron."

Cloudblower clasped him on the shoulder, then ducked into the antechamber to attend to her kiva duties.

The elders walked from the kiva roof onto the roof of the long south-facing wall and toward the ladder. Their brilliant capes flashed. Flame Carrier chuckled at something Stone Ghost said.

Browser saw Jackrabbit crouching on the southeastern corner of the town. He searched for Catkin. He had assumed that once Jackrabbit had taken her position she would remain for the Dances, though warriors who'd stood guard since dawn certainly had the right to rest for a few hands of time before the midnight Dances.

Browser strode to the ladder and waited for the elders to climb down. He extended a hand to those who needed help stepping off.

Flame Carrier, Wading Bird, and Springbank came first, followed by Stone Ghost. His uncle grinned up at him and walked around to stand behind Browser, waiting while Browser helped the others down.

Most of the elders headed straight for the blankets covered with food—except for one man from Starburst Town.. Dressed in a yellow-painted deerhide cape, he stood at the foot of the ladder, staring at Stone Ghost. About forty summers, he had thick gray hair that hung to his shoulders, and a pale oval face. His dark eyes blazed.

Browser turned to Stone Ghost. His uncle stood quietly watching the people in the plaza.

Browser looked back at the Starburst elder. "May I help you, Elder?"

The man stepped forward as if walking through a snake's den, his steps light, cautious. He grabbed Stone Ghost's wrist in a hard grip, and demanded to know, "Where did you get this?"

Stone Ghost blinked. "What?"

"This anklet you're wearing!" He wrenched Stone Ghost's arm and hurled the old man to the ground. "Answer me!"

Browser leaped forward and shoved the Starburst elder away. "There is an explanation, Elder," he said. "Uncle?"

Stone Ghost frowned up in surprise, then as if sudden understanding washed over him, he removed the jet anklet and handed it to the man. "Did it belong to someone you cared about?"

The Starburst elder studied the exquisitely carved jet beads, and swallowed repeatedly, clearly having trouble controlling his emotions. His gaze slowly lifted to Stone Ghost. "Answer me. *Where* did you get this?"

"From a corpse."

The elder squeezed his eyes closed in pain. "Oh, no, no."

Stone Ghost softly asked, "When did she disappear?"

The elder bowed his head. "Seven days ago. Our son had just died. She wanted to be alone, and she..."

An odd ringing filled Browser's ears. His fingers lowered "and tightened around his war club as if it could save him from the horror stirring in his heart. Disbelief vied with certainty. He felt as if he were floating, disconnected from the earth and sky, hovering in some terrible void between. Had his souls separated from his body? How could he stand here so calmly? Why wasn't he dashing across the plaza, shouting her name, running to find her?

The gray-haired elder held the anklet to his breast like a beloved child. "Where did you find her?"

"Here." Stone Ghost pointed to the southeastern corner of Talon Town. "She was in a room up there. The murderer had wrapped her in yellow cloth."

"That's what she—she was wearing. When she left. A yellow cape." Tears blurred his eyes. "I want you to take me to her. Now! I have to see her with my own eyes!"

Browser couldn't move. He could not even force his eyes to look down at his uncle. He stared unblinking at Cloudblower's door curtain. It swayed in the wind, as if someone had just entered or...

Stone Ghost took Browser's arm and tugged. "Nephew? Listen to me for a few moments. There are things we must discuss."

Browser flung off Stone Ghost's hand and ran.

The people in the plaza whirled to watch him. Conversations halted for an instant, then a din of whispers erupted.

Browser ducked into Cloudblower's chamber. The breeze fanned the coals in the warming bowl, and a reddish gleam fluttered over the interior. The masks on the walls watched him in mute silence. The bedding hides lay rolled and tucked in the corners. The chamber was empty.

"No!" Browser cried. He lunged through the doorway and dashed for the ladder to the roof.

Jackrabbit met him at the top, red-faced with fear. "What's wrong, War Chief!"

"Where is Hophorn? Where did she go?"

Jackrabbit shook his head in confusion. "I do not know, War Chief. I—"

Browser grabbed the youth by the shoulders and shook him hard. "You have been standing guard since Catkin left! You must have seen her!"

"I didn't! I swear! I haven't seen the Sunwatcher all night! I don't know where Peavine's daughter is either! War Chief, many people have been coming and going, crowding the roof. It is impossible to—"

"Peavine's daughter?" Browser said. "What are you talking about?"

Jackrabbit lifted his arms in a helpless gesture. "A hand of time ago, Peavine was terrorizing the village, searching people's chambers without their permission, screaming that her daughter was missing. Perhaps she is with Hophorn?"

Browser glared into Jackrabbit's worried young eyes. "Hallowed gods," he whispered and stepped back.

"War Chief, what is it?"

In a bizarrely quiet voice, he said, "Find Catkin. Tell her I have gone in search of Hophorn and, perhaps, Yucca Blossom. Tell her to organize a search party and follow me."

"Yes, War Chief." Jackrabbit bowed obediently and ran for the ladder down.

Browser looked over the edge of the roof, down into the plaza where Stone Ghost stood. The old man's wispy white hair blew about his wrinkled face. Their gazes locked.

Browser called, "I'm going after her."

"No, Nephew! *Wait!*"

The words died in Stone Ghost's throat as Browser sprinted for the ladder and disappeared over the edge. "Blessed Ancestors," he whispered, "give him the strength to endure what he finds."

Voices rose across the plaza. Shouts rang out as people huddled together, whispering, shaking their heads. Children, sensing danger, grabbed onto their mothers, and peeked, wide-eyed, from behind the shelter of long colorful skirts. Flame Carrier examined the anklet that Rising Fawn held out. The other elders crowded around, hissing questions.

Rising Fawn grabbed Stone Ghost's wrist and twisted it. "I said *now!* I want to see my wife!"

Cloudblower stepped from the kiva's antechamber. Her white face powder had been freshly applied and glimmered with a ghostly radiance in the torchlight. She frowned at Rising Fawn. "I heard the commotion. What's wrong?"

Stone Ghost replied, "Yucca Blossom and Hophorn are both missing."

Cloudblower stared at him numbly, her mouth open, as if she hadn't heard what he'd said. Then she ran for her chamber, threw the curtain back, and ducked inside. A sharp cry split the night.

The crowd surged across the plaza like a tidal wave and massed outside her door.

Stone Ghost tugged against Rising Fawn's rock-hard grip. "I pledge that I will take you to your wife later, but at this moment, I must—"

"Healer?" Flame Carrier called to Cloudblower, "What's happening? Where is the War Chief? Why are you in there?"

Cloudblower ducked out of her chamber and shouldered through the sea of bodies, shouting, "Let me pass! Get out of my way! *I must speak with Stone Ghost!*"

She stopped in front of him with tears streaming down her face. "Elder, please. You must help me."

He disentangled his wrist from Rising Fawn's fingers. "I will help you. Tell me."

"Oh, Elder, no one knows. I'm sorry. I—I thought I could Heal her. I kept begging her to let me help, but she..." Sobs shook Cloudblower. "Elder, I tried so hard."

"I know you did, Cloudblower," he said gently, and took her by the arm. "Let us find a quiet place to speak."

"Not until I have more answers!" Rising Fawn shouted. He lunged for Stone Ghost's arm. "Who killed my wife? Was it you?"

"Please, I have no time for this now, I must—"

Rising Fawn grabbed Stone Ghost's cape and shook him until his head flopped on his shoulders like a rag doll's. Turkey feathers jerked loose and fluttered through the torchlight.

Flame Carrier yelled, "Water Snake? Skink? Hold that man!"

~

Catkin climbed the icy stairs with her war club in her fist. Light flooded the cliff. A man could be standing on the rim, watching her, and she would never see him.

She slid her knee over the next step and pulled herself up. A strange musty scent clung to the trail, fear sweat, and urine.

As she neared the rim, blood rushed so loudly in her

ears, she could barely hear the sounds of the people shouting in Talon Town below. She searched the darkness, trying to find form in it, an arm, a head, a flash of clothing.

She saw only blowing snow and flickering stars.

Catkin leaped from the last step onto the rim with her club in both hands, and spun around, panting, ready.

Wind Baby had blown large swaths of the rim clean, leaving an irregular black-and-white patchwork of pummeled snow, starlit rock, and a vast expanse of night sky.

Catkin 'stared into the darkness, forcing her eyes to adjust quickly. Familiar sandstone rises and distinctive lumps began to appear. Blades of grass thrust up through the snow-covered rock at her feet.

He-Who-Flies should be standing here. Where was he?

She held a hand up to block the glare from below and carefully searched the rim. At dusk, she'd seen three guards standing up here. Now, she saw none.

She stepped onto the beaten trail that led westward along the rim.

In the canyon below, the Dances had begun again. Drums beat, keeping time to sacred Songs. She could not look for fear of being night-blinded, but she knew that the twelve Antelope Dancers, led by Antelope Above, had just emerged from the kiva. Decorated alike, a white line would outline their chins, stretching from ear to ear. Their lower legs and arms would be painted white. Each would be wearing a fox skin over his back, a white kirtle, feathers in his hair, and beaded anklets. Antelope Above would carry a bowl of sacred water to be poured on the prayer stick, as the First People had done to bring trees to life.

The trail led down into a snow-filled depression, perhaps ten hands deep. An eerie sensation came over her. She stopped at the top and glanced over her shoulder.

Nothing moved, but she felt as if a monster walked behind her, his steps matching hers, his breathing timed to hers. A chameleon of light and dark, his colors shifting as he silently pursued her.

She gripped her war club in both hands. To fight down the panic, she painstakingly identified each clump of brush and rounded boulder, each shadow in the snow...

Catkin's eyes narrowed.

An oblong splotch darkened the bottom of the depression.

Catkin edged toward it with her club up.

She heard shell bells rattling in the wind.

Her breathing went shallow. She took another step.

Below her, long hair fluttered, and softly spread across the snow.

Catkin ran down the incline.

A woman. She lay on her stomach, her face half-obscured by her hair. The shell bells decorated the collar of her white cape. Her open mouth and staring eyes formed three pitch-black holes in her white face powder.

Catkin gripped the woman's wrist, testing for a pulse. Wind whimpered through the depression, and a haze of snow momentarily blinded Catkin. She let the dead woman's wrist drop and gripped her club, concentrating on the sounds of the night. Voices rose from

Talon Town. She could hear every word the Dancers Sang.

But she heard no feet crunching snow, no breathing, no clothing flapping in the wind.

Catkin grabbed the dead woman's sleeve and rolled her to her back.

"Peavine."

A wet mat of hair darkened the left side of her head. Catkin could smell the blood. She pulled the white cape away from Peavine's feet. Bare. Toenails shone in the starlight.

"Was it you I tracked, Peavine?"

Catkin touched the jet pendant she'd found in the snow and searched her memory. She did not recall seeing Hophorn wearing this pendant earlier in the evening. Had Hophorn given it to Peavine? Or perhaps loaned it to her for the ceremonial? Hophorn would give away everything she owned if someone asked her.

Catkin studied the trail. Tiny tornadoes of snow bobbed and careened across the rim.

Catkin rose to her feet.

The lilt of a flute rode the wind, and she could hear the Antelope Dancers calling to the rain god, *"Hututu! Hututu!"* Rattles shook, and feet stamped the ground.

Catkin started up the opposite side of the depression. Just before the crest, she slipped and scrambled to get her footing.

Soft laughter...

Catkin spun.

He seemed to rise up out of the snow in the bottom of the depression. The wolf fur on his mask blew in the wind. He gazed at her through dark empty 'eye sockets.

"You are early," he whispered, and Catkin recog-

nized that deep masculine voice. She'd heard him here on the rim last summer and in Talon Town two nights ago. *"I did not expect you until tomorrow."*

Heart thundering, she backed up. "Who are you?"

He laughed again, and tipped his chin, as if signaling someone behind Catkin. *"Yes, Shadow,"* he whispered, *"yours."*

"What—"

The blow took Catkin from behind, staggering her. She stumbled around, wildly swinging her club.

The next blow blasted through her skull with the force of a lightning bolt...

16

The Dances stopped. Wind Baby thrust icy fingers through the holes in Stone Ghost's turkey-feather cape and poked at his ribs. Stone Ghost folded his arms to block the assault and leaned against the wall. They'd found an empty, roofless chamber in the rear of Talon Town. Three-by-three body lengths, a gaping hole marred the south wall, leading out into the plaza, and a thick layer of wind-blown dirt, old juniper needles, and the debris from the fallen roof covered the floor.

Cloudblower sat in the far corner, to Stone Ghost's left, her face in her hands, rocking back and forth. The red paintings of the katsinas on her buffalohide cape swayed.

"I did this," she whispered.

"No, Healer. You did everything you could to help her."

"Gods, how did this happen?"

Torchlight fluttered over the walls, filling the chamber like fiery wings. "Murderers are not born,

Cloudblower. They are molded as children. It requires vicious, repeated, intolerable pain to chase away a child's souls and create a nest where a monster can be born inside them."

Cloudblower looked up through tormented eyes. "But she is a good, caring person, Elder. I thought she was just confused, heartsick."

"Confused?"

Cloudblower shook her fists. "Yes! Once, she came to me covered with blood, and told me she had done it while she was asleep. Then, a few months later, she insisted she hadn't done it at all. She claimed that her father had appeared out of nowhere, killed the girl, and forced her to drag the body away to a—a place she called the 'sanctuary.' I did not know what to believe! But I loved her, Elder. You must understand. I loved her, and I wanted to believe her."

"You didn't believe her father existed?"

Cloudblower ran a hand over her long graying-black braid. "No."

Stone Ghost pushed away from the wall and paced the chamber. "She may genuinely believe she didn't kill anyone. The monster soul is very curious. In my experience, it comes at a time when frightened children give up hope, when they know they cannot endure the pain alone. It is as if their own souls fission, and give birth to someone stronger, a protector who can shield them from the pain."

Cloudblower exhaled and her breath drifted across the chamber in a white cloud. "But Elder, if that is so, why wouldn't she remember what happened to her? She did not. I swear to you! I could tell by the look in her eyes. She believed she was telling me the truth!"

People had gathered outside the chamber, whispering. Snow squealed beneath shuffling feet.

Stone Ghost kept his voice low. "Tormented children rarely recall what happened to them, Healer. Only the monsters remember. And hate. And wait."

Cloudblower shook her head. "But Elder, if she was hurt so much as a child, why would she hurt others? Surely she would realize—"

"She may. But I doubt that *he* does."

Cloudblower remained silent, listening.

Stone Ghost walked toward her. "I have seen it many times, Healer. When they are old enough to inflict pain, the monster souls re-enact what happened to them, as if by hurting others, they can exorcise the memories of their own childish terror and weakness. I have often wondered if it isn't also an attempt to kill the terrified child who still huddles inside them."

Cloudblower murmured. "What do you mean?"

"By driving the child's soul out of the body entirely, the monster soul never again has to hear it crying or begging for help. Monster souls often resent the children they protected. After all, the monsters were the strong ones. They took the pain, and survived, while the child's soul huddled in terror with its back turned, unable even to watch."

Cloudblower rocked back and forth, her expression tormented. Tears had streaked the white powder on her triangular face, revealing the brown skin beneath. "I do not really understand this, Elder."

"Doesn't matter." Stone Ghost held up a hand. "The question is, where would she go? Where would she feel safe? We must find her, before she can kill again."

Cloudblower wiped the tears from her cheeks, smearing the powder, and straightened. "She called the place where she dragged the bodies the 'sanctuary.' Perhaps—"

"Did she say where this sanctuary was?"

"No. No, she didn't, but she told me once that it was on the road to the Land of the Dead."

"So. West, perhaps, where Father Sun slips into the underworlds at night? Or she may have meant somewhere along the Great North Road, to the sacred lake where the eyes of the dead sparkle."

"Perhaps." Cloudblower steepled her fingers over her mouth for several moments, as if mustering courage. Finally she said, "Elder. There is something else I must tell you."

Stone Ghost spread his feet He was tired and desperately worried about Browser and Catkin. Neither one of them understood what they would be facing. They would see the face of a loved one. Stone Ghost feared it might distract them until too late. "What is it, Healer?"

"It's about the club. The warrior who was killed two nights ago? He gave his club to Hophorn just before he left on his last war walk. They had"—she paused to swallow hard, as if it anguished her to reveal this secret—"last summer he was badly scarred in a battle, and his wife said she could not look at him. He moved into Talon Town for several moons. During that time, he and Hophorn became lovers. It ravaged her heart when he went back to Silk Moth, but they continued to care for each other. They became good friends. Hophorn told him, just before he left on the war walk, that she was frightened. He was worried about her. He gave her his club and made himself a new one. That is why—"

"Yes, I understand," Stone Ghost said, and nodded. "That explains many things. Thank you for telling me."

Stone Ghost walked to the gaping hole and gazed out at the plaza. A milling crowd of people waited for them. Flame Carrier stood in the front, her old eyes fixed on Stone Ghost.

"Elder?" Cloudblower called.

"Yes?" He turned.

She rose to her feet with her fists clenched at her sides. "Please? I know it will not be easy. Too many people have been hurt, but I beg you to bring her back alive. I can help her now. I'm sure of it. *Please.* Let me try?"

"I am willing, Healer," he answered, "but I am not so sure about the families of her victims."

Stone Ghost stepped into the plaza, and people rushed toward him.

∾

C atkin woke, but did not move. A man whispered a short distance to her right.

It was his *voice.*

She lay on her back, her head throbbing sickeningly. Ropes bound her hands and feet. Wind Baby had quieted. Not even a breeze disturbed the morning.

Snowflakes landed softly on Catkin's hot face.

Father Sun must have risen, but only dim gray light penetrated the clouds.

Catkin inched her head toward the man's voice and froze, unable to look away.

Less than six hands distant, a body lay, the arms and legs sprawled. The flesh had been stripped from the bones. Only the head remained intact.

Hophorn's long black hair haloed her pretty face. Her lips had parted, and snow melted on her wide dead eyes, leaving them shiny as if brimming with tears.

The murderer knelt at Hophorn's feet, using a red chert knife to scrape her lower leg bone. Tall, his blood-spattered white cape swung around him as he moved. The gray fur of his mask gleamed with a silver hue. An exquisite mask, expertly carved, long leather ears pricked alertly on top of his head. The white muzzle sparkled with sharp teeth. A black line, the breath road, ran from his nostrils, over the top of his head, and—though she couldn't see it, she knew—down his back to the base of his spine. As he scraped flesh from the bone, he whispered to himself.

Catkin subtly tested her ropes.

He stopped whispering. And turned. An odd black gleam shone through his eye sockets.

"I thought you were awake."

He rose from his grisly task and walked to stand over her. The pungent scent of fresh blood wafted from his swaying cape. Softly, he said, "Cloudblower told you, didn't she? She told you about me?"

Catkin shook her head. "I—I don't know."

"Yesterday morning on the rim. I heard part of it. She told you what Ash Girl's father did to her when she was a child, didn't she?"

The discussion about the woman?

"She—she might have. She told me about a woman who'd been hurt."

"Hurt?" he snorted in derision. "He used to shove

war clubs inside her when she two. Two!" He knelt and lowered his mask very close to Catkin's face, hissing, "Without me, he would have killed her."

Catkin choked back her nausea, and said, "Who are you?"

He sank down to the snow, his knees spread wide like an adolescent boy puffed up with himself. He toyed with the knife in his hands. "She was three. Maybe four when I came."

Catkin closed one eye, and the pain in her head dimmed a little. "What's your name?"

"Yellow Dove. I took care of her."

Catkin squinted. She'd never heard of him. He must not be from anywhere near Hillside Village. He seemed to be watching her intently, as if eager to talk.

Catkin forced a swallow down her dry throat. "What did her father do when you came?"

"He didn't even know I was there." With lightning quickness, he threw his knife and stuck it in the snow less a finger's width from Catkin's elbow. She flinched. He laughed, pulled the knife out, then he flipped it in his hands. His voice grew husky. "He'd taken her out into the forest, away from the village, because he didn't want people to hear her scream. When he started to hurt her, she fell asleep. Like always. That's when I came." He leaned forward, and Catkin could see a glimmer of black human eyes in the wolf's mask.

"Did you fight with him?"

"I made sure he couldn't hurt her anymore. I made her go away."

Catkin's vision blurred. The world spun around her in a haze of white, and gray. She closed her eyes. "Go where? Away from her village? Where did she go?"

Catkin eased onto her side, facing him, and opened her eyes.

He made a soft disgusted sound and got up. He started to walk away, then turned back. "He's the one who killed her, you know. She was going to have his baby and he knew it."

Nausea welled in Catkin's throat. She choked it back, and whispered, "Her father killed her?"

"Of course, he did. At the end, he kept asking her if she knew Death's name. But she'd never known. I knew. I could have told him. He used to threaten her with Shadow Woman as a child. He'd say, 'You'd better not tell your mother what we did today, or I'll tell Shadow Woman, and she'll chew your heart out of your body. He'd repeat the name over and over, *Shadow Woman, Shadow Woman,* as if it meant something that Ash Girl should understand."

Catkin said, "Who was Shadow Woman?"

"She helped him to kill Ash Girl. They both killed her. They wanted to kill her baby, too, but I wouldn't let them." He lowered a hand to his belly as though a child rested inside.

"Ash Girl's baby? You mean—her son?"

"I don't know what it was. But she hadn't had her bleeding in three moons. She was pregnant with her father's child, believe me,"

Catkin could feel herself on the verge of blacking out. A gray haze fluttered at the edges of her vision, and she was only hearing every few words he said. She had to keep him talking. The longer he talked the longer she lived. She laid her head in the snow. "How did her father kill her?"

"She thought he was a Spirit Helper. She begged

him to make the voices in her head go away. The old fool told her he could do it. He said he knew where voices lived." He aimed the knife at the snowy ground. "He used these women and girls to find out. When he hit them in the head, and they lost their abilities to speak, he knew." He turned suddenly and spat into the snow. "The voices in her head. She meant *me!* She wanted him to kill me! Can you believe that? After all I'd done for her. I'm the one who took the beatings! I'm the one who had to look into his eyes when he groaned on top of her!"

He turned to peer at Catkin through the black holes in the mask. "Oh, he could kill voices, all right. It worked with Ash Girl. But not the way he'd expected. He's kept me tied up in a cave for the past seven days, trying to figure out who I am, and how to get his daughter back." His deep voice went high, pitiful. "He wanted to hurt her more! I couldn't let him. I remember the way it was. I wouldn't let him do it!"

Gods, help me. His souls are loose. He's completely mad.

The pain in her head blinded her for several heartbeats. When the world came back into focus, she saw strange snow-frosted shapes around her: *Frozen fingers reaching for the sky. Twisted faces.*

The women and girls...

She sucked deep breaths into her lungs.

The Wolf katsina rose and returned to loom over Hophorn. "She knew," he said in a resentful voice. "She knew all about me. The War Chief used to whisper to her when they coupled. He thought his wife was talking in her sleep, using strange voices. He didn't know who I was, but he—"

"The War Chief?" Catkin said, barely audible. "Do you mean Browser?"

"Of course, I do. Oh, yes, he used to go to you for talk, but he went to her for what his wife wouldn't give him. And you were such a pathetic fool, you didn't know."

As Catkin's pulse rate increased, the pain seemed to jet through her veins. Browser and Hophorn? Lovers? In the past, yes, but...

The Wolf katsina grabbed Hophorn by the feet and dragged her to a shallow hole hacked into the ground. He threw her in face-first, then kicked at the snow until he found what he'd been searching for. He lifted a sandstone slab over his head and hurled it down on top of Hophorn. The splitting skull made a dull, watery crack.

"Why did you do—do that?" Catkin demanded to know. "She was a g-good woman. She wasn't a witch!"

"I don't want her soul coming after me. She's going to think I did this. I didn't, but she'll think so."

"Why would she think you killed her?"

"She can't tell the difference between me and Ash Girl's father. He's tricky. He disguises himself. Not even Ash Girl knew it was her father when he first came to her here in Straight Path Canyon. Oh, he called her 'daughter' and acted like he loved her, but she didn't know who he was until just before he killed her."

He knelt and started to shove dirt over Hophorn.

Catkin said. "Wait. Please."

He stared at her for a disconcerting time, before whispering, "Why?"

Catkin used her bound hands to pull the pendant over her head. "She lost this at the bottom of the cliff staircase. Please, give it back to her. She would want it."

Catkin held it out. The jet pendant swung, flashing in the gray light.

He walked over, and ripped it from Catkin's hand, then tipped his head to examine it through the eye sockets in his mask. "This is a Power object?"

"She thought it was. I don't know."

He slipped it over his own head and stroked the pendant. "She won't need it. I might. He's coming back, you know."

"Who is?"

"Her father. He's coming back. I'll bet that girl is dead by now. Which means he'll be here any moment."

Sick fear washed through her. "Girl? Yucca Blossom? He killed her?"

The Wolf katsina seemed to take it as an accusation. He swung around and shouted, "Of course, he killed her! You didn't think I did it, did you? I didn't kill any of them! I may have stripped the flesh from the bodies, and sealed the pots, but I've never murdered anyone!"

"I—I didn't mean it as an ac-accusation," Catkin panted, and tested her ropes. "Forgive me."

He did not answer. He shoved dirt over Hophorn until he'd filled in the shallow grave, then he stood and brushed off his hands. "He's coming for you, you know?"

"Me?"

"He thinks you have his Turquoise Wolf."

"But I—I don't."

He laughed, a low hideous sound. "He has done so many evil things in his life, he knows he will never find his way to the Land of the Dead without it. He'll be drawn down the Trail of Sorrows, and Spider Woman will burn him up in her pinyon pine fire." He paused.

"He dug in the ruins of Talon Town for ten sun cycles before he found that Wolf. He *wants* it."

"How did he lose it?"

"He didn't lose it. That woman"—he pointed to Hophorn—"tore it from around his throat when he jerked her club from her hand. She paid for it. He used her own club to strike her down, then tossed it into the fire and piled wood on top of it. The burial party was coming. He didn't have time to search for the Wolf."

Snow began to fall heavily, whirling around them in huge flakes. Catkin kept her eyes on the place he'd been, but he faded in and out of the storm.

"I am going to make sure he never finds that Wolf," he said softly.

Catkin caught movement and saw his red knife flash as he walked toward her.

~

Browser lay on his belly next to the toppled house, less than ten body lengths from Catkin. He had been listening for a finger of time and was shaking badly; he couldn't steady his aim. His arrow kept slipping free of the bow string. He fumbled to secure it again, and drew back, focusing on the man's chest.

How could this beast, this man-beast, know things about his wife that Browser had not? Could the things he'd said about Ash Girl and her father be true?

Why had no one in the Green Mesa villages ever spoken of his crimes? Had her mother kept the truth hidden so well that no one suspected?

The arrow shook loose from his bow again, and Browser rushed to get it back in place.

He'd thought when he left Talon Town that Ash Girl might be alive, perhaps being held captive. The hope had almost torn him apart. But this katsina had just said she was dead, that her father had killed her.

A new and desperate grief tightened his heart.

His bow wavered, and Browser clenched his teeth and hardened his muscles to keep it steady.

The Wolf katsina knelt beside Catkin. "If I kill you, and then kill Browser, Two Hearts will never find the Wolf." His voice had the menacing hiss of a rattlesnake about to strike.

"No," Catkin said, and squared her shoulders. "Nor will you." She seemed to be fighting back nausea. She swallowed, and her head trembled. Blood clotted the rear of her skull, and hung in long frozen stringers from her braid, and the back of her white-feathered cape. "Don't you wish to find your way to the Land of the Dead?"

He hesitated. "Do you know where the Wolf is?"

"Of course. I can take you there. It's hidden in a safe place. We didn't want to carry it around with us."

The Katsina remained motionless, staring at her, wondering whether to believe her or not.

Browser held his breath. Aimed. Let fly.

The arrow sailed through the falling snow, striking the right side of the Katsina's chest.

The man gasped, dropped his knife, and lurched to his feet, shrieking, *"Who did this?"* He stumbled around in a circle, frantically grabbing at the blood-slick shaft. *"You can't kill me! Who will protect her if I die?"*

Browser nocked another arrow and ran.

When the Katsina saw him emerge from the thick

blanket of snow, he let out a blood-chilling scream and turned to run.

Browser shot him in the back, and the man fell face-first into the snow. His legs kicked, as if he were trying to crawl away.

Browser knelt beside Catkin, pulled the red chert knife from the snow, and cut her bounds. "Are you all right?"

"Yes," she said hoarsely.

Browser gently touched her cheek, then rose to his feet, and ran for the Katsina. The man was still breathing, his back rising and falling. But both arrows had struck the lungs, he wouldn't breathe much longer.

Browser slung his bow, kicked the Katsina onto his back, and glared down into the dark eye sockets. *"Who are you?"* he shouted.

As he gripped the wolf fur and tore the mask from the man's head, the world died around Browser. He couldn't move or speak. The mask dangled in his numb fingers. "My...wife."

Ash Girl lifted her hands and, like a small child, rubbed her eyes with her bloody fists, as though awakening from a long nap. When she saw Browser standing over her, she smiled, then her body convulsed. Blood gushed from her wounded lungs and poured down her chin.

"Oh. Gods. What have I done?" A hoarse scream tore from his throat.

Browser threw himself to the ground and pulled her to his chest, his muscular arms shaking. "Ash Girl, Ash Girl"—he buried his face in her long hair—"I'm sorry. Gods, forgive me!"

Ash Girl's head trembled. She looked up at him

through eyes drowsy with death. Her voice was that of a child, high and frightened, "R-Red Buck..." she called him by his boy's name. "Go. H-Hurry...coming. He... he's..."

Slowly, as if it took time for her muscles to realize what was happening, her head fell back, and she went limp in his arms. Browser watched the soul drain from her dark eyes.

"I don't understand," he choked out angrily. "What happened?"

He lowered her to the ground and looked at the hot blood on his sleeves and hands. A hollow sense of terror expanded his chest.

"Catkin? I heard a man's voice. Whose voice was that?"

She walked toward him unsteadily, her eyes squinted in pain. Blood-clotted hair framed her face.

Ash Girl's left hand jerked, and Browser grabbed for his war club, afraid that whatever it was that lived inside her was trying to rise, to get to him, or Catkin. The bloody hand rose into the air, and reached for Browser, the fingers spread wide, straining. Then the arm fell to the snow.

Browser's eyes went huge. He backed up. "What was that—that creature? *Who* was it? Catkin? Did you hear that voice?"

Catkin placed a hand on his broad shoulder and fought to keep her stomach from heaving. "The only thing I know for certain, War Chief, is that I am alive because you killed it."

A chill went through Browser. He shivered and pulled away from her. Ash Girl stared up at him through still shining eyes. A serene expression slackened her bloody face.

"I just killed my wife. Dear gods." His legs felt like granite as he turned. He made it to Hophorn's grave before his knees gave way and he collapsed to the ground.

Browser curled on his side in the snow. Ash Girl had been in a hurry when she'd shoved dirt over Hophorn. She'd missed a few locks of Hophorn's long hair. They fringed the edges of the grave like delicate brushstrokes.

Browser's shoulders heaved. His body shook. But no tears came to wash away the sight.

17

As Catkin walked away from the burial, crimson light poured through the wispy clouds, turning the snow pink. One hundred hands away, Browser stood with his back to her, his hand braced on a large sandstone slab that leaned against the canyon wall. Twice his height, ten people could sit on the slab's flat surface.

Catkin made it as far as the small abandoned house and eased down onto the toppled western wall to watch him. The pain in her head grew unbearable if she opened her eyes all the way.

Eagles played over the cliff to her right. The female circled the male, shrieked, and tapped him with her wings. The male shrieked back. Snow striped the ledges of the cliff.

Browser was gazing upward, toward the eagles, but he did not seem to see them. He stood so still and quiet he did not even seem to be breathing.

Stone Ghost's search party had met them on the road back to Talon Town. He'd immediately sent a runner for the Hillside elders and insisted that Catkin and Browser accompany him back to the burial site to explain what had happened.

They'd waited for the elders for four hands of time.

A group of twenty guards had escorted the elders, including Jackrabbit and Skink, who now stood to Catkin's left, on the western end of the grave, murmuring, watching the elders.

Springbank, Wading Bird, and Cloudblower stood to the south. Flame Carrier and Stone Ghost stood on the north side of the grave. They wore white, the color of cleansing and renewal. Their elderly faces shone in the red light streaming across the canyon. Cloudblower sobbed silently. She had faithfully led the sacred Dances until dawn, then been called here for this ghastly duty. She looked exhausted. Black smudges marred the skin beneath her eyes.

Jackrabbit and Skink had worked for a full hand of time to scrape out the shallow hole where Ash Girl rested. No one had washed her body or dressed her in fine clothing. After hearing Catkin's story, they'd been afraid to touch her for fear that the evil would leech into them. Jackrabbit and Skink had used juniper poles to drag her to the grave and roll her over the edge. She lay sprawled in the pit.

Browser had not watched.

He'd been standing with his back to the ceremony since it began. His short black hair blew in the wind. He still wore the buckskin cape soaked with Ash Girl's blood.

Catkin let her head fall forward and tried just to breathe. She hurt for Browser. She could not imagine how he must be feeling. The malignant soul he'd killed had not been Ash Girl, but it had lived in Ash Girl's body. He must be wondering why he'd never seen it before. Or, perhaps, wondering if he had. The fiery black eyes that glared at Catkin through the mask were born in nightmares. If Browser had seen them, he would remember.

Flame Carrier said, "Cloudblower, you have the soul sticks."

"Yes, Matron."

Cloudblower wiped her cheeks, removed a handful of feathered prayer sticks from her belt, and walked around the grave, sticking them into the ground at the cardinal directions. The sticks would form a defensive line against the evil, keeping it in the grave. The yellow goldfinch feathers bobbed and twirled in the breeze. Cloudblower returned to her position and bowed her head.

"Jackrabbit? Skink? Bring the stone."

The two young warriors lifted the large sandstone slab and carried it to the head of the grave. They heaved it in unison, and it fell on Ash Girl's head.

Browser flinched, and Catkin saw him shaking. He braced his feet to steady himself.

Flame Carrier waved a frail old hand. "Fill the hole. Let us be done with this."

Jackrabbit and Skink shoved dirt over Ash Girl. Everyone else walked away.

There would be no sacred songs or speeches; no one would cut his hair in mourning or praise her life.

Catkin folded her arms and hugged herself. The stone, and the prayer sticks, would keep all of her souls locked in her bones forever, even the soul that had loved Browser and Grass Moon. Flame Carrier said they could take no chances the wicked soul might escape and secret itself in another body. Everyone agreed, even Catkin. But it seemed wrong somehow. Shouldn't Ash Girl's soul be free to go to the Land of the Dead? Why did they have to condemn her as well as the wicked boy?

Catkin looked back at the grave. Jackrabbit and Skink stood to the side, whispering. The fresh mound of earth looked dark against the snow. The elders had gathered over Hophorn's grave to Sing her to the afterlife. Flame Carrier's gravelly old voice rang out above the others. She had loved Hophorn a great deal. Cloud-blower knelt at the side of the grave, rocking back and forth, sobbing the Death Song.

Stone Ghost broke from the group and hobbled toward Catkin. His tattered turkey-feather cape caught the light.

The feathers that remained winked. It looked as if he hadn't combed his thin white hair in days. A spiky halo surrounded his wrinkled face.

He stopped beside Catkin and studied the cliff. The fires of sunset turned the sandstone into a glittering wall of gold and white.

"Do you think he's out there watching us?" Catkin asked.

Stone Ghost's eyes narrowed. "I don't know. Maybe."

He sat down beside Catkin on the low rock wall and braced his hands on his knees. "It is curious that the witch, Two Hearts, disappeared less than a sun cycle before Ash Girl's birth. It's possible that he found a village where no one recognized him and took a wife."

Catkin's heart started to pound. "He must be cunning."

"Oh, he had a reputation for being exceedingly clever. He was being hunted at the time. I remember that very clearly. Several villages had joined together to search for him. The number of women he was killing had soared. First it was one or two a sun cycle, then it was two or three a moon, as if he couldn't get enough of the blood. It's possible that he cloaked himself in Green Mesa Village for a few summers." Stone Ghost bowed his head. "I do not even wish to think of it, but I may be partly responsible for this terrible act."

"What?" Catkin said. "How could that be?"

"Twenty summers ago, when my sister was killed in Green Mesa Village, I went a little mad. I began a desperate search for the killer." He blinked at the snowy ground. "I now fear that I may have accused the wrong man. Perhaps if I had searched longer and more carefully, I would have discovered Two Hearts and stopped him twenty sun cycles ago. Instead..." The lines around his mouth pulled tight.

"But the murders ended didn't they?"

"Yes. Still, I'm not certain the man I accused deserved to die."

Catkin scooped a handful of snow from the rock and held it to the base of her head. It eased the hurt enough that she could get a full breath into her lungs. "It's so hard to believe, Elder."

"What is?"

"That Two Hearts cloaked himself among the Green Mesa clans and turned on his own child."

Stone Ghost smoothed his fingers over the stones in

the low wall, petting them as if to ease some hurt. "His souls are sick, Catkin. He must be dying inside."

She glared. "You *pity* him?"

"People who commit horrible acts are deeply wounded, Catkin. Often, they endured intense pain as children, and they grew up struggling to hide their suffering. The child was helpless to stop the agony, so the adult craves control. Hurting others is a demonstration of the killer's power. Especially the power over his own suffering."

Catkin lowered her hand to the deerbone stiletto she had borrowed from Jackrabbit. "I would gladly end his misery for him, Elder, if I knew where he was."

Stone Ghost's bushy brows drew together over his hooked nose. "If Two Hearts really was her father, he's a tormented man. After he left the Green Mesa Villages, he came to Talon Town, and apparently began a panicked search to save himself, digging up graves, searching room after room, until he found a Turquoise Wolf."

"You believe that story?"

Stone Ghost nodded. "It would not surprise me. Two Hearts is getting older. As the sun cycles pass, people think more and more about death. Two Hearts has good reason to worry. Spider Woman must be eagerly awaiting his arrival."

"I hope she's keeping her fire stoked up to a furious blaze."

Stone Ghost patted her knee and gazed at Catkin with luminous eyes. "How are you feeling?"

"I waver between wanting to throw up and wanting to sleep."

"Well, it won't be long now. I asked Jackrabbit and

Skink to cut poles for a ladder. They're going to carry you home. That way you can throw up, then fall asleep."

Catkin managed a smile that didn't hurt. "Thank you, Elder."

Stone Ghost glanced back at Hophorn's grave. "Flame Carrier says you will all be leaving here soon."

Catkin frowned. "Really? Where will we go?"

"I don't think she knows. The tunnel to the underworld did not open, as prophesied. She thinks you repaired the wrong kiva. She's going to keep searching."

Catkin blinked thoughtfully at the ground.

Stone Ghost said, "Will you go with her?"

She lifted a shoulder, and her gaze went to Browser. "I don't know, Elder."

A soft worried expression creased Stone Ghost's face. "What did he do when he found out it was his wife beneath that mask?"

"He fell to his knees and held her until she died. He kept telling her he was sorry."

The lines around Stone Ghost's eyes deepened. "He could not have acted differently, but he won't realize that for moons. You'll have to help him."

The love Catkin felt for Browser swelled painfully in her breast, and her head throbbed. She scooped another handful of snow and slowly ate it. "If he will let me, Elder, I'll help him in any way I can."

Catkin turned to squint at the rim, wondering. Jackrabbit told her that Water Snake was still out with a search party, combing the canyon for Yucca Blossom. But it had been snowing off and on since she'd disappeared. There would be no tracks. There would, Catkin suspected, be no trace at all. The killer was shrewd, and he'd been at it a long time. She doubted he would make a mistake now that...

Stone Ghost clasped her hand tightly. "I must speak with my nephew."

Catkin nodded. "I think he's been waiting for you. Hoping someone can give him a logical explanation."

"In cases like this, we're dealing with the logic of nightmares, Catkin. Nothing makes sense in an ordinary way." He got to his feet. "But I'll try."

The pink light of evening streamed through the clouds and dappled the canyon around him as Stone Ghost plodded across the snow toward Browser.

~

B rowser heard his uncle's steps crunching through the snow. He straightened, but didn't turn. Long ago, someone had carved a perfect spiral on the left side of the stone slab. It had four rings, one for each of the underworlds the people had traveled through to get here to this place of sunlight. The Sun Katsina, and Wolf Katsina, stood above the spiral, guarding the pathway to the underworlds. A zigzagging lightning bolt shot across the rock beneath the spiral, warning of the dangers that would be faced by those who dared to walk that legendary trail.

Browser reached inside his cape and touched the lump sewn into the seam of his buckskin cape. The Turquoise Wolf felt warm. After Stone Ghost told him that only someone with the sense of a blood-sucking fly would carry such a Power object on him, Browser figured there was no safer place for it.

Stone Ghost stopped on Browser's left and softly said,

"Are you well, my nephew?"

Browser looked down into the old man's luminous eyes. The breeze fluttered white hair around his wrinkled face.

"Do you..." Browser's voice came out hoarse, strained, "Uncle, do you know what it was? Inside her. That—that man?" Browser's shoulder muscles tensed and bulged through his cape. "The voice. The—the mannerisms. I can't believe that my..."

He couldn't say the rest. He couldn't even think about Ash Girl at the same time that he did that *thing*.

Stone Ghost folded his arms beneath his ratty cape and watched the eagles playing over the cliff for a several moments.

"Monster souls are rare, Nephew. I have met three in the past fifty sun cycles of solving murders. Each of those has had a profoundly different voice from the main soul. They are not easy to understand. They are often bizarre animalistic creatures that live in the deepest darkest corners of human beings. I remember one monster soul I met, oh, fifteen summers ago now. Her name was Silver Song. She lived inside a young man's body, but she was an old woman. She had come to live inside the boy one afternoon when his father had beaten him unconscious. The young boy had excellent vision, but the monstrous old woman couldn't see close up. She spoke in a high scratchy voice; the boy had a deep melodic voice. The boy could remember none of the terrifying murders committed by the old woman, but she reveled in every detail."

Browser looked down at the dried blood on his

hands. He had washed them in the snow, but red still crusted his fingernails. In a barely audible voice, he asked, "Is it witchery, Uncle?"

Stone Ghost spread his arms. "Not in the way we usually think of witchcraft, Nephew. I don't think monster souls come about from curses, or Power amulets, not even wicked potions, but I have often wondered if monster souls are not lost ghosts."

Browser's spine tingled. "You mean the forsaken ghosts that roam the earth?"

"Yes. They are desperate souls. I imagine they would take any chance to live in a body again, to speak with people, to feel the warmth of blood surging through their veins. Most healthy people are strong enough to keep them out. But wounded children?" He shook his head wearily. "They are defenseless."

Browser clenched his hands into hard fists. "Uncle, the woman that my son loved could not possibly have known about the malevolent boy inside her. She would have killed it if she had known, even if she'd had to rip out her own heart to do it."

Stone Ghost said, "She knew, Nephew."

Browser searched his face. "How can you say—"

"From the things Catkin told me. Ash Girl begged her father to kill the voices inside her. She heard the monstrous Yellow Dove whispering to her. Probably often."

Browser shifted to brace his hand on the stone slab again. "I think, maybe, I heard him, too, Uncle."

Stone Ghost peered up at him. "The boy talked when Ash Girl was asleep, didn't he?"

Browser kicked a small stone that lay at the base of

the slab. "Yes. I just thought it was...strange. I didn't understand—"

"I knew she had heard the boy at least once while she slept. She heard his voice, awoke lying beside you, and assumed it was you talking in your sleep. She ran to Cloudblower in terror. But it wasn't you, Browser. I'm fairly certain it was Yellow Dove she heard."

Browser's hand slowly fell to his side. *"Fairly* certain?"

"What I mean is that some people have more than one monster soul inside them. She may have heard Yellow Dove. But it might have been another monster soul that we know nothing about."

Browser mouthed the words, *another monster,* and closed his eyes, blocking out the world until he could get hold of his raging emotions. He longed to scream and slam his fists into something.

He breathed, "At least it's over. Thank the gods, it's over."

Stone Ghost didn't respond, and Browser opened his eyes to stare down into his uncle's serious face.

Stone Ghost paused for a long while, before saying, "I fear that none of the Katsinas' People understand what has happened. You see, the tunnel to the underworlds of the human soul did open. It opened last night. It's been yawning black and bottomless before us all day."

Browser swallowed hard. "You mean...it isn't over?"

Stone Ghost held Browser's gaze.

"You still have his Turquoise Wolf, Nephew. He'll be back for it. I *promise you.*"

∼

Dusty was thinking about his father when he heard the Bronco return. Over the years, he had come to know each sputter and metallic clink the Ford made.

He sighed and stretched out on the large sandstone slab that canted at an angle north of the site. It would hold five people stretched out side-by-side. He watched the last remnants of sunset burn across the sky. The cliff over his head glittered with a cinnamon hue. To his right, a spiral petroglyph etched the stone, along with two square-bodied kachina-like figures, and a zigzagging line.

Cool night air swirled around him, the desert coming alive after the long hot day. Field mice scampered through the dry grass around the boulder.

As nutty as your father...

The words were like stilettos in his heart.

In the beginning, it had been Dale who kept the lid on the nasty secret. Word was that Samuel had suffered a sudden "accident." Then, as the years passed, people simply assumed he'd died of a heart attack, or cirrhosis of the liver, or any of the other insidious things archaeologists fell prey to because of their rather peculiar lifestyles.

Finally, as in all things, Samuel Stewart simply faded away. Unlike a Lister, a Kidder, or a Fewkes, Samuel Stewart hadn't lived long enough to amass a large body of published works. His name still appeared in bibliographies of various theses and dissertations, and occasionally in an archaeological field report, but for the most part, he was forgotten.

Sometimes at the Pecos conference, or the Society

for American Archaeology meetings, one of the old-timers would mention his father in a passing reference, but that was the extent of it.

He stared up at the sky. As the last light faded from the western horizon, an infinity of tiny lights frosted the heavens.

An owl hooted on the rim high above him, and the muted chirrings of the insects filled the greasewood. The day's heat still radiated from the rock, warming his tired muscles.

Though they'd covered her back up, the sightless eyes of the last skeleton stared at him, bridging the gulf of time, whispering to him. Mrs. Walking Hawk had Sung over each of the burials, and sprinkled them with cornmeal, but Dusty wondered: Had their souls been freed? Had they found their way to the trail of the dead, and that terrible fork where, according to some myths, they would be judged? Which way had each gone? To her long-lost family and friends? Or down that other torturous route where the evil were forced to atone for their deeds?

"May the kachinas guide you," he said into the night, hoping that their journeys, no matter what they deserved, might be easier.

He heard the soft sound of boots in sand, but stared up at the Big Dipper; it had just sparkled to life on a blanket of slate blue.

"Am I disturbing you?" she called.

"Yes."

She threaded her way through the greasewood, a darker blot in a landscape of shadowed rocks and brush. A plastic grocery sack hung from her left elbow. She wore a clean pale blue T-shirt, but dust coated her jeans and hiking boots.

"Sylvia said she thought you were over here."

"Did she? I'm going to make her catalog potsherds for the rest of her life."

Maureen stopped at the base of the boulder and looked up at him. He lay near the top, ten feet away. A frown lined her tanned forehead. He heard her exhale, then she said, "Mind if I come up?"

"Yes, but you'll come up anyway." Dusty leaned forward, braced his left arm on the rock, and extended his right. "So, here. Take my hand. There's a ledge at about your waist."

Her fingers were warm in his, her grip strong. Heaving, he pulled her up, and she climbed over the edge onto the flat stone.

"Welcome to my palace." He stretched out again, his hands behind his head.

Her Levi's scraped the rough stone as she sat down and drew the sack into her lap.

"I brought you a peace offering." She pulled a bottle of Guinness from the sack, along with an opener, flipped the cap off, and handed it to him.

He took it. "Thanks. Your offering is accepted with pleasure and appreciation."

"It was a real test of will."

"How so?"

"I was feeling miserable. About what I said to you. I always crave a drink when I'm unhappy."

"Being around a bunch of archaeologists with their lubricated elbows must be difficult."

"A battle every day. Some, like today, are worse. But I'm tough. I can stand it."

The glass clinked on the stone, as he set the bottle to one side and shifted to look at her. "You okay?"

Maureen reached into the plastic sack again and pulled out a bottle of sparkling water. She unscrewed the cap and took a long drink before answering, "I'm really sorry for the things I said. I still don't understand how religious fundamentalism can be allowed to stifle scientific inquiry, but I wish I'd expressed my views to you in private." She let out a breath, as if bolstering her courage. "I especially want to apologize for what I said about you and your father, I—"

"Apology accepted." He ran his fingers down the warm sides of the Guinness bottle. "I don't want to talk about it, okay?"

"Okay."

The silence stretched.

"This is a funny job, Maureen. I spend my time trying to serve three different masters with three mutually exclusive agendas. Archaeology demands science. The native peoples want to take care of their ancestors. The client, NOAA in this case, wants their project permitted as quickly and cheaply as possible."

She drew one knee up and propped her bottle on it. "How do you keep them all happy?"

"I don't. I do the best I can for all three, but inevitably one or two of them will accuse me of favoritism, or shoddy work, or anything else to let me know they're displeased with the decisions I made." He lifted the Guinness and took a long drink of the rich dark beer. "The only thing I want you to know is that I *always* take care of the archaeology."

She nodded. "I believe that."

Dusty studied the elegant curve of her jaw, and the

delicate lines around her mouth. "Incidentally, while you were away, Maggie decided to deny the NOAA permit. We can all pack up and go home tomorrow. We've already back-filled every excavation-unit—"

"My God, what about the skulls! The bones!" she shouted and started to rise.

Dusty grabbed her arm, and gently tugged until she sat back down. "They're still in your tent. Mrs. Walking Hawk said she wanted you to study them, and when you're finished, she wants them ceremonially reburied to make sure the souls are able to go to the Land of the Dead."

Maureen grabbed a handful of the blue shirt over her heart. "Thank God for small miracles."

"It *is* a miracle," Dusty said. "I want you to appreciate it. She didn't have to allow any further study."

Her dark eyes glimmered. "Dusty, tell me something. Can a Christian fundamentalist, a deep believer in Creationism, come out here and shut down an excavation because you're uncovering ten-thousand-year-old burials? They believe the world is only six thousand years old. Your scientific discovery would be an affront to their religion, wouldn't it? Couldn't they shut down your excavation, just as Indian beliefs did today?"

He frowned at his bottle. "If we treated all religious beliefs equally, I guess se. Thank God we haven't had to face that one, yet."

"But you will someday. Don't you see that? If you give free reign to one variety of religious fundamentalism, albeit native fundamentalism—"

Dusty held up a hand. "Let it go, Doctor. Please? It's over. The decision's been made." His hand dropped to the rock. "And there's something else I want to talk to you about."

She sat for several seconds with her mouth open, as if wanting to press the issue, then finally sighed. "What is it?"

He toyed with his bottle. "I want you to know how much I've appreciated having you on site. You taught me things no one ever has. This burial site would still be a mystery if you hadn't come to New Mexico." He glanced up. "I guess what I really want to say is, thanks."

Maureen seemed taken aback. She pulled her gaze from his and squinted into the darkness. The shining path of the Milky Way splashed the sky, and bats flitted around the cliff face, diving and squeaking to each other.

"You taught me a lot, too, Dusty," Maureen said. "Thanks for taking the time."

He lifted a shoulder. "Digging is my life. I enjoyed showing you some of it. Dale says I'm driven to be perfect in the field because I'm a failure as a normal human being. A social misfit."

"Well," she said with a tilt of her head. "Physical anthropology is my life. When I'm not working, I'm home alone. In the summer, I sit on the porch and watch the lake. In the winter, I sit at the window and watch the lake."

He craned his neck to look at her. "What? No string of men knocking on your door? You're an intelligent, attractive woman. I thought men would be falling all over themselves to take you out to Tim Horton's."

She laughed, the sound musical. "Sorry, I have to

buy my own each morning before I dodge the potholes in the QEW."

"QEW?"

"The highway that takes me to Hamilton. That's where my university is."

Soft strains of conversation rose from the camp. Sylvia had just kindled the nightly fire. A wavering orange gleam sheathed the tents. Sylvia crouched in front of Hail's and Maggie's chairs, apparently blowing on the fire. Clouds of sparks periodically flooded into the night sky.

Dusty rubbed his fingers over the gritty surface of the rock. "Do you still miss him?"

"Who?"

"John."

As if he'd opened some private door, her voice turned guarded. "Why would you ask me that?"

"Isn't that why you stare out the window at the lake? You're living with John in your head? With what was. What might have been." He paused. "I used to do that after my father died. Except I was staring out at the desert."

She took another drink of sparkling water and wiped her mouth with the back of her hand. "For a while, I hated him for leaving me alone. As if by dying he'd betrayed me."

"I don't think he planned on having a heart attack that night, Maureen."

"Oh, I know. His death was just so unexpected. He was as healthy as a horse. Cooking supper one minute, dead the next. The doctors said it was a genetic defect, like that Russian figure skater, a flaw in the heart. Some odd form of arrhythmia." She lowered her head. "I miss him all the time."

Dusty saw the pain flash across her face and wondered about John—about how much it must have hurt him to be torn away from a woman like this one. No wonder he had followed her halfway across the continent.

If somebody loved me as much as she loved him, I'd probably fight death, too.

In the distance, Dale's camper creaked, and he stepped out and walked toward the blazing campfire. His gray hair had an amber gleam.

Maureen continued, "John's death left a big empty hole inside me, Stewart. I'm only half of a person. I spend a lot of time talking to my people about death."

"Your people? The Iroquois?"

She propped her elbows on her knees. No. The dead I spend my days with are in the lab. I think physical anthropologists have a different perspective on the dead than most people. I'm not afraid of them. They're my friends. We talk a lot about John, about dying. About how easy it would be to let go, then I could find John, and be whole again."

Dusty sat up and stared hard into her wide eyes. "If you ever get to the point where you're seriously contemplating 'letting go,' I'm a plane flight away. I'll send you a ticket. You can come down and spend a few days observing what suicide does to those who live through it." He thumped his chest with a fist.

She cocked her head, giving him that careful scrutiny he had come to appreciate. "Be careful, Stewart. That's the sort of thing a friend would say. Feeling dizzy? Slip of the tongue?"

"I've been feeling dizzy since I met you, Maureen. I thought it was the heat."

She laughed.

Dusty ran his fingers over the gritty surface of the rock. "Have you ever considered that maybe you need some time away? It can't be easy working and living in the same places where you built your life with John. Don't you see him everywhere?"

"Yes, I do." The lines around her eyes tightened. "I've considered taking a sabbatical. The university owes me one. For years I've covered everyone else's classes while they took time off for research, but I've never really had a reason to—"

"Well, you do now." He held a hand out to the site. In camp he saw Hail Walking Hawk rise from her chair and walk out toward the filled-in burials. "There are a lot of women down there who'd really like you to find out who they were, and why they died. You might say 'no' to me, but how can you say 'no' to them?"

Maureen used the bottom of her bottle to make small circles on the sandstone A grating sound filled the night. "I'll think about it. That's all I can promise."

He propped himself up on one elbow and inhaled the scent of the pinyon pine fire. The breeze had turned cool, soothing. It fluttered loose strands of hair around Maureen's face.

"That's enough, Maureen."

~

H ail took three steps and stopped to catch her breath. She could see the pile of dirt and fallen stone that marked the ancient pueblo to the east of the burials. The greasewood growing up through the middle shimmered pale blue in the evening light. She clenched the elk antler knob on her walking stick and fought the nausea that threatened to send her back to her sleeping bag. It had been a bad day. She'd been chewing pain pills like candy, but they'd barely dented the agony.

On the western horizon a single cloud hung, its charcoal center outlined with a brilliant pink halo. The night smelled sweetly of wood smoke and freshly turned earth. She forced her feet forward.

When she reached the pueblo she propped her walking stick and eased down onto the cornerstones. The rocks felt warm beneath her yellow-flowered white dress.

On the big rock to Hail's right Dusty and Washais talked, their voices rising and falling with the wind. They sounded happy.

Magpie still worked in front of their tent, packing things as Hail had ordered, but her eyes were fixed on Hail. She lifted a bony hand to her niece to tell her she was all right, and Magpie waved back, but it was a tense gesture. Sweat matted Magpie's short black hair to her round face, making her dark eyes seem as large as a wounded doe's.

Hail smiled sadly. She knew what it was to watch a loved one fail before your eyes. You felt helpless and broken. But that was the way Utsiti had created the universe. People's times came and went. That was all.

Just like these poor women.

The freshly filled graves resembled dark freckles on the land. She'd sprinkled corn pollen on the Haze child and sung his spirit to the Land of the Dead. As he'd climbed out of the grave and flown away, his joy had almost burst Hail's heart.

But...

She frowned.

The evil was growing, as though once loosed the witch's soul was pulling Power from the glistening stars and gusts of wind. She could feel him slipping around her on ghostly feet, watching and whispering in a language she did not understand. He'd been Powerful. Much more powerful than Hail, especially in her condition. His presence had left a stain on the very air she breathed, on the grains of sand, and the twinkling sky. What sort of creature had such Power? Only the Shiwanna, known as Kachinas by other tribes, could breathe their souls into the world and have them stay for a thousand years. Perhaps he had not been human at all. Maybe he—

"Aunt?"

Hail squinted her white-filmed eyes at Magpie. Her niece walked toward her with her arms folded over her chest. Her white T-shirt blazed against the background of dark cliffs.

"You just couldn't stay away, eh?"

Magpie tilted her head, embarrassed. "I came to tell you that I've finished packing. We can leave whenever you want to." She sat down on the toppled wall beside Hail and gave her a worried look. "Are you ready?"

Hail pointed with a crooked finger. "Our red tent is still up."

"Sylvia said she would take it down tomorrow and keep it for me. I want to take you home, Aunt. Please?"

She'd watched Hail eat pain pills all day, even poured them out for her when Hail's hands shook too badly to open the bottle. With each pill Magpie's face had lost a little more color, her eyes had gone a little wider.

"I guess I'm ready. There's nothing more I can do here. The evil is too great for me."

"Too great for anyone, I imagine. That's why it's still here." Magpie took Hail's hand and held it tightly. Her skin felt cool. "Let's go, Aunt Hail."

Hail sucked in a deep breath of the fragrant night air and let it out slowly, savoring the feel of her lungs moving, and her heart beating.

"I'm ready, child."

Magpie helped Hail to her feet, and they walked back through the silver veil of starlight holding each other as if for the last time.

Just before they reached the campfire Hail heard a deep male voice. She stopped dead in her tracks, and her eyes lifted to the canyon rim. Ghostly laughter echoed, vicious, frightening. The hair at her nape stood on end.

"Aunt?" Magpie said in sudden terror. "What's wrong?"

Hail's eyes narrowed. Junipers swayed in the wind on the rim. "Nothing, child," she whispered. "He just knows he's won.

"...Again."

Epilogue

As night settles upon the land, the snow trailing beneath the clouds turns into a gray starlit veil. I watch it blow across the canyon. Its movements are sinuous, graceful.

The snowflakes cool my hot skin. The day has been long and arduous. My hands are shaking. As the flakes melt, and mix with the blood on my face, red tears roll down my cheeks, and drop silently onto my white deer-hide cape.

"Please!" the girl calls from behind me. "Don't hurt me again!"

She breaks into sobs.

I inhale the fragrances of snow and damp stone.

From my essence and light, I have created six gods. This girl is not one of them, but she will do until I find the rest. I know where three of those gods sleep... including the one lying beneath the fresh mound of earth below. They put a stone on her head. I watched them do it. Her souls are locked in the earth now. The wrenching *sounds of her little girl cries are gone, wiped clean from my souls. She'll never be able to hurt me again.*

I'm free. I have been forgiven.

For now.

"Two Hearts? I'm sorry for whatever I did! Please, I beg you! Let me go!"

Shadow's footsteps on the bare sandstone are quick and impatient. Breath hisses in and out of her nostrils. At moments like this, just before the end, she has a pungent feral scent, like an animal in heat. It stokes the fire in my veins.

I hear her voice in the soft patting of snowflakes on the rim, whispering, "Now, now, now."

My hands shake more violently.

I turn, and my eyes fasten on the girl's young body staked out naked in the falling snow. Blood flows from a hundred small, carefully placed incisions. Shadow stanched each with a glowing stick, but the blisters ooze. She is so beautiful. Long black hair haloes her face.

"Two Hearts!"

"Yes, my daughter, I'm coming."

My steps are those of a wolf, graceful, silent...

Bibliography

Acatos, Sylvio. *Pueblos: Prehistoric Indian Cultures of the Southwest.* Translation of 1989 edition of *Die Pueblos.* New York: Facts on File, 1990.

Adams, E. Charles. *The Origin and Development of the Pueblo Katsina Cult.* Tucson: University of Arizona Press, 1991.

Adler, Michael A. *The Prehistoric Pueblo World a.d. 1150-1350.* Tucson: University of Arizona Press, 1996.

Allen, Paula Gunn. *Spider Woman's Granddaughters.* New York: Ballantine Books, 1989.

Arnberger, Leslie P. *Flowers of the Southwest Mountains.* Tucson, Arizona: Southwest Parks and Monuments Association, 1982.

Aufderheide, Arthur C. *The Cambridge Encyclopedia of Human Paleopathology.* Cambridge: Cambridge University Press, 1998.

Baars, Donald L. *Navajo Country: A Geological and Natural History of the Four Corners Region.* Albuquerque: University of New Mexico Press, 1995.

Becket, Patrick H., ed. *Mogollon V.* Report of Fifth Mogollon Conference. Las Cruces, New Mexico: COAS Publishing and Research, 1991.

Boissiere, Robert. *The Return of Pahana: A Hopi Myth.* Santa Fe, New Mexico: Bear & Company Publishing, 1990.

Bowers, Janice Emily. *Shrubs and Trees of the Southwest Deserts.* Tucson, Arizona: Southwest Parks and Monuments Association, 1993.

Brody, J. J. *The Anasazi.* New York: Rizzoli International Publications, 1990.

Brothwell, Don, and A. T. Sandison. *Diseases in Antiquity.* Springfield, Ill.: Charles C. Thomas Publisher, 1967.

Bunzel, Ruth L. *Zuni Katcinas.* Reprint of Forty-seventh Annual Report of the Bureau of American Ethnography, 1929-1930. Glorietta, New Mexico: Rio Grande Press, 1984.

Colton, Harold S. *Black Sand: Prehistory in Northern Arizona.* Albuquerque: University of New Mexico Press, 1960.

Cordell, Linda S. "Predicting Site Abandonment at Wetherill Mesa." *The Kiva* 40(3): 189-202, 1975.

—. *Prehistory of the Southwest.* New York: Academic Press, 1984.

—. *Ancient Pueblo Peoples.* Smithsonian Exploring the Ancient World Series. Montreal: St. Remy Press; and Washington, D.C.: Smithsonian Institution, 1994.

Cordell, Linda S., and George J. Gumerman, eds. *Dynamics of Southwest Prehistory.* Washington, D.C.: Smithsonian Institution Press, 1989.

Crown, Patricia, and W. James Judge, eds. *Chaco and Hohokam: Prehistoric Regional Systems in the American Southwest.* Santa Fe, New Mexico: School of American Research Press, 1991.

Cummings, Linda Scott. "Anasazi Subsistence Activity Areas Reflected in the Pollen Records." Paper presented to the Society for American Archaeology Meetings. New Orleans, 1986.

—. "Anasazi Diet: Variety in the Hoy House and Lion House Coprolite Record and Nutritional Analysis," in *Paleonutrition: The Diet and Health of Prehistoric Americans.* Southern-Illinois University at Carbondale, Occasional Paper No. 22, Sobolik, ed., 1994.

Dodge, Natt N. *Flowers of the Southwest Deserts.* Tucson, Arizona: Southwest Parks and Monument Association, 1985.

Dooling, D. M., and Paul Jordan-Smith, eds. *I Become Part of It: Sacred Dimensions in Native American Life.* San Francisco: A Parabola Book, Harper; New York: Harper Collins Publishers, 1989.

Douglas, John E. "Autonomy and Regional Systems in the Late Prehistoric Southern Southwest." *American Antiquity* 60:240-257, 1995.

Downum, Christian E. *Between Desert and River: Hohokam Settlement and Land Use in the Los Robles Community.* Anthropological Papers of the University of Arizona. Tucson: University of Arizona Press, 1993.

Dunmire, William W., and Gail Tierney. *Wild Plants of the Pueblo Province: Exploring Ancient and Enduring Uses.* Santa Fe: Museum of New Mexico Press, 1995.

Ellis, Florence Hawley. "Patterns of Aggression and the War Cult in Southwestern Pueblos." *Southwestern Journal of Anthropology* 7:177-201, 1951.

Elmore, Francis H. *Shrubs and Trees of the Southwest Uplands.* Tucson, Arizona: Southwest Parks and Monuments Association, 1976.

Ericson, Jonathan E., and Timothy G. Baugh, eds. *The American Southwest and Mesoamerica: Systems of Prehistoric Exchange.* New York: Plenum Press, 1991.

Fagan, Brian M. *Ancient North America.* New York: Thames and Hudson, 1991.

Farmer, Malcom F. "A Suggested Typology of Defensive Systems of the Southwest." *Southwestern Journal of Archaeology* 13:249-266, 1957.

Fewkes, J. Walter, and J. J. Brody, eds. *The Mimbres: Art and Archaeology.* Albuquerque, New Mexico: Avanyu Publishing, 1989.

Fish, Suzanne, K., Paul Fish, and John H. Madsen, eds. *The Marana Community in the Hohokam World.* Anthropological Papers of the University of Arizona, No. 56. Tucson: University of Arizona Press, 1992.

Frank, Larry, and Francis H. Harlow. *Historic Pottery of the Pueblo Indians: 1600-1880.* West Chester, Pennsylvania: Schiffler Publishing, 1990.

Frazier, Kendrick. *People of Chaco: A Canyon and Its Culture.* New York: W.W. Norton & Co., 1986.

Gabriel, Kathryn. *Roads to Center Place: A Cultural Atlas of Chaco Canyon and the Anasazi.* Boulder, Colorado: Johnson Books, 1991.

Gumerman, George J., ed. *The Anasazi in a Changing Environment.* New York: School of American Research, Cambridge University Press, 1988.

—. *Exploring the Hohokam: Prehistoric Peoples of the American Southwest.* Albuquerque: Amerind Foundation; University of New Mexico Press, 1991.

—. *Themes in Southwest Prehistory.* Santa Fe, New Mexico: School of American Research Press, 1994.

Haas, Jonathan. "Warfare and the Evolution of Tribal Polities in the Prehistoric Southwest," in *The Anthropology of War,* Jonathan Haas, ed. Cambridge, U.K.: Cambridge University Press, 1990.

Haas, Jonathan, and Winifred Creamer. "A History of Pueblo Warfare." Paper Presented at the 60th Annual Meeting for the Society of American Archaeology. Minneapolis, 1995.

—. *Stress and Warfare Among the Kayenta Anasazi of the Thirteenth Century A.D.* Chicago: Field Museum of Natural History, 1993.

Haury, Emil. *Mogollon Culture in the Forestdale Valley, East-Central Arizona.* Tucson: University of' Arizona Press, 1985.

Hayes, Alden C, David M. Burgge, and W. James Judge. *Archaeoloical Surveys of Chaco Canyon, New Mex'ico.* Reprint of National Park Service Report. Albuquerque: University of New Mexico Press, 1981. Hultkrantz, Ake. *Native Religions: The Power of Visions and Fertility.* New York: Harper & Row, 1987.

Jacobs, Sue-Ellen. "Continuity and Change in Gender Roles at San Juan Pueblo," in *Women and Power in Native North America*. Norman, Oklahoma: University of Oklahoma Press, 1995.

Jernigan, E. Wesley. *Jewelry of the Prehistoric Southwest*. Albuquerque: School of American Research; University of New Mexico Press, 1978.

Jett, Stephen C. "Pueblo Indian Migrations: An Evaluation of the Possible Physical and Cultural Determinants." *American Antiquity* 29:281-300, 1964.

Komarek, Susan. *Flora of the San Juans: A Field Guide to the Mountain Plants of Southwestern. Colorado*. Durango, Colorado: Kivaki Press, 1994.

Lange, Frederick, Nancy Mahaney, Joe Ben Wheat, Mark L. Chenault, and John Carter. *Yellow Jacket: A Four Corners Anasazi Ceremonial Center*. Boulder, Colorado: Johnson Books, 1988.

LeBlanc, Steven A. *Prehistoric Warfare in the American Southwest*. University of Utah Press, Salt Lake City, 1999.

Lekson, Stephen H. *Mimbres Archaeology of the Upper Gila, New Mexico*. Anthropological papers of the University of Arizona, No. 53. Tucson: University of Arizona Press, 1990.

Lekson, Stephen, Thomas C. Windes, John R. Stein, and W. James Judge. "The Chaco Canyon Community" *Scientific American* 259(1): 100-109, 1988.

Lewis, Dorothy Otnow. *Guilty by Reason of Insanity. A Psychiatrist Explores the Minds of Killers*. New York: The Ballantine Publishing Group, 1998.

Lipe, W. D., and Michelle Hegemon, eds. *The Architecture of Social Integration in Prehistoric Pueblos*. Occasional Papers of the Crow Canyon Archaeological Center No. 1. Cortez, Colorado: Crow Canyon Archaeological Center, 1989.

Lister, Florence C. *In the Shadow of the Rocks: Archaeology of the Chimney Rock District in Southern Colorado*. Niwot, Colorado: University Press of Colorado, 1993.

Lister, Robert H., and Florence C. Lister. *Chaco Canyon*. Albuquerque: University of New Mexico Press, 1981.

Lomatuway'ma, Michael, Lorena Lomatuway'ma, and Sidney Namingha, Jr. *Hopi Ruin Legends*. Edited by Ekkehart Malotki. Lincoln: Published for Northern Arizona University by University of Nebraska Press, L993.

Malotki, Ekkehart. *Gullible Coyote: Una'ihu: A Bilingual Collection of Hopi Coyote Stories*. Tucson: University of Arizona Press, 1985.

Malotki, Ekkehart, and Michael Lomatuway'ma. *Maasaw: Profile of a Hopi God.* American Tribal Religions, Vol. XI; Lincoln: University of Nebraska Press, 1987.

Malville, J. McKimm, and Claudia Putman. *Prehistoric Astronomy in the Southwest.* Boulder, Colorado: Johnson Books, 1987.

Mann, Coramae Richey. *When Women Kill.* New York: State University of New York Press, 1996.

Martin, Debra L. "Lives Unlived: The Political Economy of Violence Against Anasazi Women." Paper presented to the Society for American Archaeology 60th Annual Meetings. Minneapolis, 1995.

Martin, Debra L., Alan H. Goodman, George Armelagos, and Ann L. Magennis. *Black Mesa Anasazi Health: Reconstructing Life from Patterns of Death and Disease.* Occasional Paper No. 14. C.arbondale, Illinois: Southern Illinois University, 1991.

Mayes, Vernon O., and Barbara Bayless Lacy. *Nanise: A Navajo Herbal.* Tsaile, Arizona: Navajo Community College Press, 1989.

McGuire, Randall H., and Michael Schiffer, eds. *Hohokam and Patayan: Prehistory of Southwestern Arizona.* New York: Academic Press, 1982.

McNitt, Frank. *Richard Wetherill Anasazi.* Albuquerque: University of New Mexico Press, 1996.

Minnis, Paul E., and Charles L. Redman, eds. *Perspectives on Southwestern Prehistory.* Boulder, Colorado: Westview Press, 1990.

Mullet, G. M. *Spider Woman Stories: Legends of the Hopi Indians.* Tucson, Arizona: University of Arizona Press, 1979.

Nabahan, Gary Paul. *Enduring Seeds: Native American Agriculture and Wild Plant Conservation.* San Francisco: North Point Press, 1989.

Noble, David Grant. *Ancient Ruins of the Southwest: An Archaeological Guide.* Flagstaff, Arizona: Northland Publishing, 1991.

Ortjz, Alfonzo, ed., *Handbook of North American Indians.* Washington, D.C.: Smithsonian Institution, 1983.

Palkovich, Ann M. *The Arroyo Hondo Skeletal and Mortuary Remains.* Arroyo Hondo Archaeological Series, Vol. 3. Santa Fe, New Mexico: School of American Research Press, 1980.

Parson, Elsie Clews. *Tewa Tales,* reprint of 1924 edition. Tucson: University of Arizona Press, 1994.

Pepper, George H. *Pueblo Bonito,* reprint of 1920 edition. Albuquerque: University of New Mexico Press, 1996.

Pike, Donald G., and David Muench. *Anasazi: Ancient People of the Rock*. New York: Crown Publishers, 1974.

Reid, J. Jefferson, and David E. Doyel, eds. *Emil Haury's Prehistory of the American Southwest*. Tucson: University of Arizona Press, 1992.

Riley, Carroll L. *Rio del Norte: People of the Upper Rio Grande from the Earliest Times to the Pueblo Revolt*. Salt Lake City, Utah: University of Utah Press, 1995.

Rocek, Thomas R. "Sedentarization and Agricultural Dependence: Perspectives from the Pithouse-to-Pueblo Transition in the American Southwest." *American Antiquity* 60:218-239, 1995.

Schaafsma, Polly. *Indian Rock Art of the Southwest*. Albuquerque: School of American Research; University of New Mexico Press, 1980.

Sebastian, Lynne. *The Chaco Anasazi: Sociopolitical Evolution in the Prehistoric Southwest*. Cambridge, U.K.: Cambridge University Press, 1992.

Simmons, MaTc. *Witchcraft in the Southwest*. Bison Books, reprint of 1974 edition. Lincoln: University of Nebraska Press, 1980.

Slifer, Dennis, and James Duffield. *Kokopelli: Flute Player Images in Rock Art*. Santa Fe, New Mexico: Ancient City Press, 1994.

Smith, Watson, with Raymond H. Thompson, ed. *When Is a Kiva: And Other Questions About Southwestern Archaeology*. Tucson: University of Arizona Press, 1990.

Sobolik, Kristin D. *Paleonutrition: The Diet and Health of Prehistoric Americans*. Occasional Paper No. 22. Carbondale: Center for Archaeological Investigations, Southern Illinois University, 1994.

Sullivan, Alan P. "Pinyon Nuts and Other Wild Resources in Western Anasazi Subsistence Economies." *Research in Economic Anthropology* Supplement 6:195-239, 1992.

Tedlock, Barbara. *The Beautiful and the Dangerous: Encounters with the Zuni Indians*. New York: Viking Press, 1992.

Trombold, Charles D., ed. *Ancient Road Networks and Settlement Hierarchies in the New World*. Cambridge, U.K.: Cambridge University Press, 1991.

Turner, Christy G. and Jaqueline A. Turner. *Man Corn: Canabalism and Violence in the Prehistoric American Southwest*. Salt Lake City, Utah: University of Utah Press, 1999.

Tyler, Hamilton A. *Pueblo Gods and Myths*. Norman, Oklahoma: University of Oklahoma Press, 1964.

Underhill, Ruth. *Life in the Pueblos,* reprint of 1964 Bureau of Indian Affairs Report. Santa Fe, New Mexico: Ancient City Press, 1991.

Upham, Steadman, Kent G. Lightfoot, and Roberta A. Jewett, eds. *The Sociopolitical Structure of Prehistoric Southwestern Societies.* San Francisco: West-view Press, 1989.

Vivian, Gordon, and Tom W. Mathews. *Kin Kletso: A Pueblo III Community in Chaco Canyon, New Mexico,* Vol. 6. Globe, Arizona: Southwest Parks and Monuments Association, 1973.

Vivian, Gordon, and Paul Reiter. *The Great Kivas of Chaco Canyon and Their Relationships.* School of American Research Monograph no. 22, Santa Fe, New Mexico: 1965.

Vivian, R. Gwinn. *The Chacoan Prehistory of the San Juan Basin.* New York: Academic Press, 1990.

Waters, Frank. *Book of the Hopi.* New York: The Viking Press, 1963.

Wetterstrom, Wilma. *Food, Diet, and Population at Prehistoric Arroyo Hondo Pueblo, New Mexico.* Arroyo Hondo Archaeological Series, Vol. 6. Santa Fe, New Mexico: School of American Research Press, 1986.

White, Tim D. *Prehistoric Cannibalism at Mancos 5MTUMR-2346.* Princeton, New Jersey: Princeton University Press, 1992.

Williamson, Ray A. *Living the Sky: The Cosmos of the American Indian.* Norman, Oklahoma: University of Oklahoma Press, 1984.

Wills, W.H., and Robert D. Leonard, eds. *The Ancient Southwestern Community.* Albuquerque: University of New Mexico Press, 1994.

Woodbury, Richard B. "A Reconsideration of Pueblo Warfare in the Southwestern United States." *Actas del XXXIII Congreso Internacional de Americanistas,* 11:124-133. San Jose, Costa Rica, 1959.

—. "Climatic Changes and Prehistoric Agriculture in the Southwestern United States." *New York Academy of Sciences Annals,* Vol. 95, Article 1. New York, 1961.

Wright, Barton. *Katchinas: The Barry Goldwater Collection at the Heard Museum.* Phoenix, Arizona: Heard Museum, 1975.

A look at Book Three:
The Summoning God

From *New York Times* bestselling authors W. Michael Gear and Kathleen O'Neal Gear comes part three in their gripping Anasazi mystery series.

After uncovering an ancient mass grave in New Mexico, Archaeologists Dusty Stewart and Maureen Cole think things can't get any worse—until they begin excavating the charred remains of a ceremonial chamber and discover it's filled with the brutalized bones of children.

Maureen, having analyzed similar mass graves in Iraq, takes it in stride. But Dusty's nightmares become so severe that he feels as though an evil presence has stepped across a narrow bridge of time and now walks the site beside them, invisible, but always present and haunting. With every uncovered artifact seemingly whispering in the voices of dead children, Dusty and Maureen begin to wonder if the overwhelming feeling of being followed will ever go away.

In the year A.D. 1263, War Chief Browser enters the very same ceremonial chamber—but this time, it's filled with freshly dead bodies. Knowing there's a killer moving unseen through the ruins of a dying civilization, Browser recruits the skills of an old shaman to help him uncover the truth about the enigmatic murderer who's terrorizing their people.

Will Dusty and Maureen ever be able to escape an ancient haunting and unearth truths based on archaeological findings alone?

AVAILABLE NOVEMBER 2023

About W. Michael Gear

W. Michael Gear is a *New York Times, USA Today,* and international bestselling author of sixty novels. With close to eighteen million copies of his books in print worldwide, his work has been translated into twenty-nine languages.

Gear has been inducted into the Western Writers Hall of Fame and the Colorado Authors' Hall of Fame —as well as won the Owen Wister Award, the Golden Spur Award, and the International Book Award for both Science Fiction and Action Suspense Fiction. He is also the recipient of the Frank Waters Award for lifetime contributions to Western writing.

Gear's work, inspired by anthropology and archaeology, is multilayered and has been called compelling, insidiously realistic, and masterful. Currently, he lives in northwestern Wyoming with his award-winning wife and co-author, Kathleen O'Neal Gear, and a charming sheltie named, Jake.

About Kathleen O'Neal Gear

Kathleen O'Neal Gear is a *New York Times* bestselling author of fifty-seven books and a national award-winning archaeologist. The U.S. Department of the Interior has awarded her two Special Achievement awards for outstanding management of America's cultural resources.

In 2015 the United States Congress honored her with a Certificate of Special Congressional Recognition, and the California State Legislature passed Joint Member Resolution #117 saying, "The contributions of Kathleen O'Neal Gear to the fields of history, archaeology, and writing have been invaluable..."

In 2021 she received the Owen Wister Award for lifetime contributions to western literature, and in 2023 received the Frank Waters Award for "a body of work representing excellence in writing and storytelling that embodies the spirit of the American West."

Made in the USA
Middletown, DE
21 May 2024